A Butterfly
in Flame

Books by Nicholas Kilmer

O Sacred Head
Man with a Squirrel
Harmony in Flesh and Black
Dirty Linen
Lazarus Arise
Madonna of the Apes
A Butterfly in Flame

A Butterfly
in Flame

Nicholas Kilmer

Poisoned Pen Press

Copyright © 2010 by Nicholas Kilmer

First Edition 2010

10 9 8 7 6 5 4 3 2 1

Library of Congress Catalog Card Number: 2010923866

ISBN: 9781590587911 Hardcover
9781590587935 Trade Paperback

Poisoned Pen Press
6962 E. First Ave., Ste. 103
Scottsdale, AZ 85251
www.poisonedpenpress.com
info@poisonedpenpress.com

Printed in the United States of America

for Reg Norris

Acknowledgments

Thanks to Bob Gulick and Fred Hill, of counsel. Thanks specially to Anne Hillis for several readings as inventive as they were implacable. If I have failed to take advantage of any of her many helpful suggestions, it is only because I learned early in life to disregard the wisdom of this valued older sister. NK

Chapter One

"Fred, here's the situation," Clay said. "As of two days ago, one of the instructors went missing. His disappearance would not be an issue, except for the fact…"

"One of his students is missing also," Parker Stillton added.

The three men in the Clayton Reed's front parlor were seated, holding cut-glass sherry glasses. Parker Stillton was familiar, a man rendered bulky by good fortune. The other…

"Forgive me," Clay said. "Because the occasion hints at the Homeric, I have begun *in medias res*. May I present Fred Taylor? Parker Stillton I believe you know," Clay continued as the familiar one inclined his head. "Mr. Abraham Baum." Clay gestured to the other man who, as he stood to hold up his right hand, corrected, "Abe." His hand was large, red, hairy, friendly, moist.

"Fred," Fred confirmed. "Fill me in."

Abe Baum sat again, lowering himself with a careful discomfort calibrated to acknowledge the delicacy of the Queen Anne chair Clay had put him in. When he picked up the sherry glass again from the side table where he'd placed it in order to execute this maneuver, he and the glass looked as if they had come from opposite planets. Both of Clay's visitors were dressed, like Clay, for Boston: gray suit, white shirt, and tie. Stillton and Baum were patently bedecked by Brooks Brothers. Clayton's version of exactly the same outfit came from a place where you are out of luck unless they know you.

Fred had thrown on his second-hand Keezer's sport coat as he climbed the stairs, responding to the emergency signal from the buzzer at his desk. He'd burned his necktie years ago.

Clay lifted his glass to the level of his elaborate tangle of white wind-swept hair. "Sherry?" he invited. So Fred's inclusion was, or was to appear, social.

Fred shook his head and sat.

"Background," Parker Stillton said. "Of course. You know Stillton Academy, Stillton Academy of Art, I should say, to give the college its full title."

Fred said, "Give me the high points."

"Not the full orchestral version," Abe Baum growled.

Parker Stillton's cough reminded the world of his importance. He spread his hands to indicate impending brevity. "You will have noted the coincidence, which I won't belabor. Stillton Academy of Art is in Stillton, Massachusetts, an erstwhile fishing town on the North Shore which, since it was located on a narrow promontory, has escaped the random and obscene development that has metastasized from Rockport, for example; or Newburyport or Gloucester.

"A distant collateral ancestor of mine left New England and made a small fortune in Wyoming, I don't know how. I don't care how. It was Wyoming. Even so, mindful of the fact that he and the town of his origin both owed their names to the same vital source—Stilltons were among the earliest European settlers—he thought of the town when it came his time to die. Being childless, he left as much of his small fortune as he could manage to the charitable organization he directed should be established by his bequest. Like most such late-nineteenth-century exercises, the project was more generous than carefully thought out."

Abe put in, "That doesn't concern us. What Josephus Stillton contemplated was a quiet place of retreat where the widows and daughters of deceased fishermen might find refuge while they were given instruction in useful domestic trades."

"I've driven past Stillton, Massachusetts," Fred said. "Heading north. But I've never driven down that promontory. What is it, five miles? Ten? Twenty? I never bothered."

"Which is why the town has survived. So far," Abe Baum said. He shifted uncomfortably in his chair, thumbing the empty glass.

"That's the origin myth," Parker Stillton resumed, turning his head so as to follow Fred while he rose to put the decanter within reach. "Of course, no bequest is foolproof. The world turns, and as it turns, it exposes loopholes. The refuge became a school; the school became an academy; the academy became an art school, went co-ed, is now an almost-credible four-year college and is, as we speak, seeking accreditation by the NEASC."

He paused portentously.

Fred resisted providing the rewarding comment, "Well, I never," limiting himself to inquiring, "NEASC? I'm guessing the N and the E stand for New England. After that, you've got me."

"Association of Schools and Colleges," Abe Baum interrupted. "Professional organization. Which is why we cannot take our concern to law enforcement, notoriously indiscreet. It's vital for Stillton Academy that they pass the accreditation reviews. Vital."

"So that it can award degrees," Parker added.

"At the moment, the best Stillton Academy can award is a certificate," Baum said. "Take that and your portfolio to the admissions office of any graduate school, you hear them laughing before you open the office door. Hell, try to transfer Stillton's credits to an undergraduate art program like Cooper Union— they'll laugh as hard. Never mind the significant achievements of such an alumnus as, for example, Basil Houel. 'I don't care how well you can draw', the committee will say. 'Start over!'"

Chapter Two

"Houel can draw, but he shouldn't," Clay said. "Salvador Dali shared the disease."

"This has been very interesting," Fred told the group, rising. "You mentioned a missing instructor. A missing student."

"You need background," Clay objected.

"Even more than I need background, I need beer," Fred said. "If I may, Clay? Abe, will you join me?"

"I wouldn't mind," Baum said. "No offense to the sherry. The instructor is male. The student female. The female is the problem. In my experience, the female always is the...strike that," Abe said.

"Background first," Clay insisted.

Fred nipped into the kitchen and returned with two bottles of Clayton's Amstel, opened, with a mug for Abe.

"Stillton Academy is simply not viable as it is," Abe announced. "The endowment is next to depleted. Without accreditation, it will certainly die."

Parker Stillton, helping himself to sherry, went on, "If all it has to sell is worthless certificates of time served and courses completed, why should anyone buy those?"

"It might help if I knew where I fit in," Fred said.

"There must not be a hint of scandal," Clay said. "At this point, the slightest breath of scandal would at least postpone the accreditation examination. On top of everything else, if it's postponed, it might as well be cancelled. Should this happen..."

Clay paused. Fred had the choice of allowing the pregnant

pause to extend into the coming week, or of supplying the prompt Clay's pause entreated.

"Should this happen," Fred helped.

"The board disposes of the remaining assets," Parker Stillton said ominously.

Abe said, "Everything becomes public. Everything becomes open. Everything becomes subject to the cold, hard gaze of Charity."

"Assets?" Fred said. "What are there? Easels? Desks?"

"A stampede could bring disaster," Clay said.

"And perhaps sensing that all was not well in this little Eden, one of the instructors found better work at a McDonald's?" Fred asked. The beer was cold and thin and vaguely urinous. He took another sip. "You are connected in some way to Stillton Academy?" he asked, letting the question extend to both the visitors.

"I advise them," Abe Beam granted. "I am an attorney. Not contracted to them. A friend. I do give them advice. When asked. And Parker is a colleague."

"An attorney also, as you know," Clay reminded Fred.

"I have been invited to join the board of trustees," Parker said. "The invitation is being taken under advisement. That fact should not leave this room."

"From what I know so far, it sounds like being invited to pilot the *Titanic*," Fred said, "after the iceberg hove in sight."

"The situation is parlous," Parker Stillton said.

Neither he nor Abe Baum showed the slightest interest in the surroundings. The paintings on the walls, just in this room, were enough to occupy anyone with an eye for many hours. Dominating the room—it would have dominated any room—was Turner's *Danae*. Clayton had finally, and recently, given his discovery a name. Since it was his discovery, he could call it whatever he wished. It filled the wall above the fireplace, which was never used. What vandal would subject paintings to smoke? Six feet by four, in a gold frame just barely enough to conceal its edges, it represented a writhing coil of gold and flesh and crimson that embodied, as Clay put it, "the most carnal expressions of the male spiritual force and the female human power."

"Or he could save himself the trouble and just call it 'a girl humping a god,'" Molly had remarked. "With maybe some money changing hands."

And the Turner was just a start.

"It gets worse," Parker Stillton went on. "The board fired the director last October. Some minor peccadillo. The endowment, as I told you, has dwindled drastically. The present board demurs at the idea of hiring a fund-raiser, and in any case, how do you mount a capital campaign without the likely prospect of accreditation? The buildings are in bad shape, calling for at least three new roofs. The tuition is already low but even so, many students depend on state or federal grants or loans to pay them, and those grants or loans, in turn, depend on the prospect of accreditation. At the same time, of course, the academy's basic survival depends on those tuitions. Maintenance is chiefly at the whim of students on work-study programs…"

"How many students?" Fred asked.

"Over a hundred. Not much over a hundred," Baum said. "I'm not that close to the operation."

"Hundred and seven," Parker Stillton said. "That's live bodies, not tuitions. Not full-time equivalents. Lots of students are part time. As of last week, when I talked with their steering committee. The same steering committee that set their course in the direction of the aforementioned iceberg."

"Well," Fred said. He looked toward Clayton. Where was this heading? A conversation this long, between consenting adults all of whom spoke the same language, should by now have revealed the direction in which at least one of its participants wished it to go.

"Plus there is significant faculty unrest," Baum said, "if you can call anything generated by that motley gang significant."

"Tenure and all that?" Fred asked. "I have to tell you, my own experience of college life was minimal."

"Fred's a Harvard Man," Clay inserted.

"For long enough to learn where Elsie's was, and the Fogg Museum. I got done with college faster than most. In the years since, though, I've noticed that an unhappy faculty and tenure issues can go together."

"Tenure's not an issue at Stillton," Abe assured him. "Once accreditation comes, it could become so. Maybe. Maybe not. But up to now, the board and the directors—right through the one who was canned last October—have kept the faculty to one-year contracts. And there aren't that many anyway. Lots are part-time."

"Such as they are, then," Fred said, "they are underpaid and overworked and *looking* for work. How do I fit in? You mentioned assets a few paragraphs back. And it's an art school. Do I assume, Clay—after all, here you are!—that among the assets…"

Clay interrupted sharply, holding up a hand and shaking his head slightly. "The female is the main concern. She is eighteen. A first year student. Daughter of the academy's only significant donor. The instructor missed his classes last Saturday. And the girl hasn't been seen since, either."

"She must be found," Abe said.

"It's a pretty old story," Fred said. "Once we fight our way past all the scenery you spread around getting up to this action, it's one old story. A girl gets caught in a romance with an older guy. He's married? Still an old story. Gossip, sure, there will be—but where's your scandal?"

"There's no sign of either of them," Baum said.

"That may be their plan."

"What we fear is a double suicide," Parker Stillton said. "And the fear is well based."

Abe pulled a folded paper from his jacket pocket, opened it flat, and handed it to Fred. "Read this," he said. "It's her handwriting. Melissa Tutunjian. Found on her desk by her room-mate. Read it."

A spidery round hand in peacock blue ink, the "i"s dotted with little hearts, on plain copy paper. Fred read aloud, "I died for beauty but was scarce / Adjusted in the tomb, / When one who died for truth was lain / In an adjoining room."

"Poetry is always a bad sign," Clay said. "We want you to find out what happened."

Chapter Three

"Find the girl, that's key. Keeping it really quiet," Abe said. "Under the radar. Unless our worse fears are realized. But I can't emphasize enough, we want you to find the girl."

"If out worst fears are realized, ideally, we consult again before you act," Parker added. "Should you discover their bodies in some compromising circumstance, you will have a legal obligation to report them—but it may be that some shading…"

"This isn't what I do," Fred said.

Clay interposed, "There may be extenuating circumstances. As a favor to me, Fred, I would appreciate your suspending your natural objections long enough to hear our thinking. Time's a consideration. You and I can discuss your reservations later."

"Taking this little ditty as your clue, you've jumped to a conclusion," Fred said. "Two people missing, a man, a girl. This scrap of paper," he waved the bit of verse, "left for someone to find. 'I died for beauty' is supposed to be the girl, I guess? Check. The beautiful student. At least beautiful once she goes missing. Therefore 'One who died for truth' is the seasoned and admired older man. The teacher. It's too easy. Just because you find it, that doesn't make it a clue, or even evidence. What does he teach, the missing instructor?"

"English, which we all know," Abe said. "That's the beauty of it. If his subject was Graphic Design or 3-D you might be in trouble. But everyone knows English anyway. Also Art History, which you can do."

"What?"

Clay eased in softly, "We'll talk later, Fred. The idea is for you, as a temporary replacement, to take over Mr. Flower's classes. Morgan Flower. The missing instructor."

Fred's dramatic failure to respond was not feigned.

"That gives you a reason to be there," Parker Stillton said. "Helps keep you under the radar."

"They have no standards at all at Stillton Academy?" Fred protested. "I don't care how hard they're scratching to stay alive. They'd never hire me. I don't even have a bachelor's degree. Hell, they shouldn't let me teach for free."

"It puts you there and we need you there," Parker said.

"*I* need you there," Clay added. His elegant fingers tapped against the chair arm.

"What's wrong with these people? They don't have the power to slam the doors when they see me coming?" Fred said. "No faculty vigilance committee? No dean who's awake?"

"We're wasting time," Abe said. "It's taken care of. All we need is for you to say Yes. I advise the president of the board. She's also the acting director of the academy, after the unpleasantness of last October. Especially after the resolution of that unpleasantness, anyone employed by the academy who wants to *stay* employed, does what she wants. There are other complications I don't have time for. I have to get to Lowell, talk to Melissa's father. They call her Missy. Keep him on the ranch."

"You'll want this paper," Fred said, holding out Melissa's holograph.

"No point upsetting him. Not yet," Abe said, waving the paper away. "You keep it. For now, we assume they are fine. Just missing."

Parker growled, "As far as anyone knows, the two are holding hands in Atlantic City or Capri."

"We'd really appreciate it," Abe said. "If you can agree. First class is tomorrow at eight-thirty. English One. This being his suggestion, Mr. Reed has generously offered to continue your compensation as usual, and any incidentals…"

"Not an issue," Clay said.

"What the hell," Fred said. "It can't be worse than jumping into a jungle at night by parachute. I'll give it a week. What's tomorrow, Tuesday? By Wednesday of next week, either Morgan's back in the saddle, or you find a guy with chalk marks all over him to do the job those kids deserve."

"I appreciate this," Abe said. "I know Stillton Academy will appreciate it. We'll go, then."

"Does the town of Stillton have a hotel?" Fred asked. "Just curious."

"You stay in Morgan Flower's rooms," Abe said, standing and taking an envelope from a side pocket. It bulged and rattled with what must be keys. "The place belongs to the academy, so it's no problem for you to be there. You might pick up some insights."

Parker stood also, asking Abe Baum, "You want me with you while you talk with Missy's father?"

"We'll discuss it. Two people might spook him. Here are directions, Mr. Taylor, and your schedule." He handed Fred the envelope. "My number's inside. Check in with the acting director, Elizabeth Harmony. Her number's there also. She wants to meet with you tomorrow morning. Eight O'clock, she said. In her office. For coffee."

"Let us know if we can be helpful," Parker said. "When you learn something."

"You say Morgan Flower's place belongs to the academy," Fred said. He'd opened the envelope, pocketed the keys, and was glancing through the notes and schedules. "They own all this property? Or do they rent?"

"Stillton Academy owns property in the town," Abe said, making for the door.

"So," Fred said, "this failing college could be sitting on a gold mine of prime waterfront property."

"Point noted," Parker Stillton confirmed, "Not relevant." He reached to shake Fred's hand, and Clayton's, and followed Abe Baum into the entrance hall. The hall was hung, this month, with Japanese and Persian exercises in calligraphy, the walls that pomegranate color you see in British films of country houses.

The floors were lavishly rugged with Orientals. "It's as if he's Catherine the Great condemned to come back as somebody's maiden aunt," Molly had said once after a prolonged glass of sherry at Christmas time.

Fred let Clay do the honors at the front door, which opened onto the ivied wilds of Beacon Hill. He had a fresh beer in hand when Clayton reentered the parlor. "There is some plan at work here?" he demanded. "Aside from your customary eleemosynary activity, which in this case you wish me to carry out?"

"Charity is not beyond me," Clay snorted. "But my charities are my business. I would not ask you to participate. Nor would I tell you of them. Charity, like sex and religion, should be kept close to the vest."

Fred said, "Explain."

"I refer to the *New Testament* parable of the Publican and the Pharisee," Clay said.

"Explain the Stillton Academy diversion."

"There are wheels within wheels," Clay proclaimed.

"*Ezekiel* won't help either," Fred said.

Clay writhed a moment until he resolved the agony of indecision by pouring himself another glass of sherry. "Almonds?" he asked.

"Clarity. Before I head north. Unless I change my mind," Fred said.

Clay sat with his sherry and stared across it with suspicion. He said, "For years I have wished to find a subterfuge by which to get an inside look at Stillton Academy."

"You didn't relish standing in front of English One yourself?" Fred asked.

Clayton gave the remark the peremptory wave it merited, sipped sherry, and continued, "Therefore when Parker telephoned last evening and laid out the situation as you have now heard it, I was intrigued by the coincidence of his need and my desire, and I began to think."

He leaned forward and fixed a beady eye on Fred. "I want your eyes. I want your candid and independent evaluation of the present state of Stillton Academy of Art. Its persons and practices, its vulnerabilities. You, Fred, are blessedly unconfined and uncontaminated by academic prejudice. Do what you can, by all means, to resolve Mr. Baum's quandary. But above all, keep your eyes open and report to me."

"I'm looking for what, exactly?" Fred asked.

"I will not tip the balance," Clay said. "You know me and you know I have my reasons. Find some way to see everything. Keep your eyes open and report."

Chapter Four

Fifty miles north of Boston, the turnoff that would lead to Stillton beckoned Fred to the right, and east. He was driving his generic old brown car, though Molly had offered the use of her Honda during her absence. Fortunately, he had stuck to his own vehicle. Almost immediately it became apparent that his choice was a good one. The road degenerated into a track that resembled what would result if the Taliban and the local Historical Commission conspired to supervise public works.

For weeks there'd been nothing of interest. Not two hours ago, before Clay's summons, Fred had tossed the Bonhams catalogue for a coming London sale onto the floor, complaining, "Tedious, tired, tepid, timid, trendy—but mostly, Holy Mackerel!—who cares? Even that Sargent portrait of the Duchess of Twaddle—she's like all his other women. Butter wouldn't melt if she sat on it."

So there was not much stirring in the Boston office.

Since it was spring break, Molly and her kids had gone to visit her mother in Florida. Molly knew better than to extend the invitation to her live-in lover. So her house in Arlington was empty, and there was nothing stirring there either.

Whatever motive Clay had at work in that Chinese box of a mind, at least it had gotten Fred out into the world, and moving. Though it was irritating in a familiar way not to perceive what was really on Clay's mind. Closely as they might be obliged to work together, Clayton Reed's native paranoia normally kept him at the edge of catatonia. He called this condition caution. "Suppose we were playing bridge," Fred tried once, hoping for an elucidating metaphor. "Wouldn't you want to send your partner—me, for example—a signal of what was in your hand?"

"I do not wish them to know what I am thinking," Clay replied, making it clear that even after some years of operating cheek by jowl, as far as Clay was concerned Fred would always be included in the concept *them*.

For all Fred knew, when he raced up the spiral staircase in response to Clay's summons, the pair of stuffed suits had come with the intention to knock Clay on the head with something harder. But no. Perhaps second best, they had at least brought with them an excuse for Fred to busy himself with something active.

A chill, wet evening was descending fast. It was not raining, exactly, but the air was saturated with moisture. In less than ten minutes of slow going the promontory narrowed to the extent that the darkening ocean was visible on both sides. Wind-stunted pines hung on at the roadside; and small, bare trunks of trees that might, when they developed leaves, turn out to be oaks or maples.

Ten minutes further on—the driving was slowed by the condition of the road—the ground rose and widened into a simple, rounded, graceful hill, "evocative of femality," Fred said as he jounced along. The promontory, and the hill also, were presumably glacial moraines, like their much larger sisters further south, Long Island and Cape Cod. The town of Stillton occupied the hill.

"What is this, a joke?" Fred marveled. "It can't be real." Stillton was like a movie set for a story, perhaps set in the innocent 1950s, in which some dreadful things are going to happen to quaintly unsuspecting salt-of-the-earth New Englanders. With maybe one foreigner—perhaps of undefined Jewishness—whom everyone suspects until he or, perhaps, she, turns out to be the one who saves the day.

"Not even a McDonald's?" Fred expostulated. He'd counted on a mess of hamburgers, along with something crisply greasy. Beer he had with him. Most of the town's buildings were cottages, two stories, sided with clapboard or gray weathered shingles. The small Main Street offered two places to buy groceries, two cafés, a gas station, "J & J Service," and the Stillton Inn. Its faded "Vacancy" sign did not project optimism. The sign swung dismally although there was no wind. Perhaps the people who had designed this movie set had wired it to swing. Maybe it could creak as well, when things got tense.

At the far side of the town's commercial district, after the "Co-Ed Hair Salon," Main Street ended abruptly at a cross street, Academy Lane, on the far side of which the academy's main buildings—apparently three in all—occupied the frontage overlooking the shingle beach and the long gray ocean. It was an unimpressive spread. Two long buildings, one of which was identified as Stillton Hall, were of a single story in white clapboard, and a third, more cottage-like, had, in the shade of its porch, a sign saying *Admissions*.

If joke it was, the town was, in its simple way, a lovely joke. An overall sense of shabby seediness gave it an air of honesty, as if the only reason for its buildings was protection from the weather, rather than ostentation. At either end of the town, circling the hill that ended the promontory, small cottages, not the monstrosities Newport calls cottages, but the kind Hansel and Gretel lived in, had small bare yards sloping to the beaches, where lobster traps were piled, or buoys, hunks of Styrofoam. Overturned dinghies waited out of reach of high tide. The smell was salt and gradual marine decay; the sky raucous with birds.

Fred parked his car near Stillton Hall and strolled. The place had everything: just enough people of assorted ages were in the streets. Not many. The weather was unpleasant and you would only be out in it if you had good reason. Around the academy buildings, the visible people tended to be of student age, but in motion, not just hanging around. As he moved away from the academy's buildings, and toward the edge of town, the right number of pickup trucks was waiting for the last trumpet in side yards. A causeway—this was too much!—led to a little white lighthouse whose photo-electric mechanisms, as Fred stared at it, caused its light to begin its revolving flash, accompanied by a reassuringly mournful hoot of foghorn. At rickety small pilings, and the town dock, below the academy buildings, both honest fishing boats and pleasure craft bobbed side by side.

It was too good to trust. "It's too much," Fred grumbled. "All it lacks is the 'lone seagull.'" There were so many seagulls, and they were so insistent, it was impossible to believe that any one of them had ever known a moment's peace, or solitude. Except in evocative literary pleas for sympathy, a lone seagull is a rare bird indeed. "Bring this set to Paramount, they'd laugh at you. They'd tell you—and it's true—'Nobody'd buy this.'"

Except—and the obvious truth of the observation followed him, and filled him with misgivings—anyone *would* buy all of this. Why hadn't they? Something was terribly wrong here. It was unnatural. The entire town of Stillton, Massachusetts, should long since have been bought by developers and ruined. There should be motels, boardwalks, and liquor stores. McMansions or their 1920s ancestors, the "cottages" of the idle rich, should bulge along the beach, stealing the view from honest folk, each with its private dock and floating heated swimming pool. Unnatural? It was almost creepy. Like Williamsburg, Sturbridge Village, or the so-called Plimouth Plantation south of Boston where mournful actors, unable to find work, dragged around in costumes pretending to be pilgrims. In the case of these three amusement parks, though, it was clear that cultural tourism compelled and controlled the subterfuge. In the case of Stillton, Massachusetts, it was not evident to the naked eye what forces kept the town in the eighteenth—or was it the seventeenth?—century.

Stillton was just a charming New England, old-fashioned unspoiled fishing village not much more than an hour's commute to Boston. It made no sense. There wasn't even a parking meter anywhere. No signs to tell you that you either could or could not park.

The address of Morgan Flower's habitation was on Shore Road, which ran parallel to Main Street and two blocks north. As Fred, in his car again, explored the town with increasing disorientation, he did note the existence of a one-horse firehouse, next to an abandoned police station, both on Dock Street.

Morgan Flower's rooms were on the second floor of a cottage that should overlook the beach, the lighthouse, and all those lone seagulls. It started raining as Fred put one of the two keys into the front door's lock. Someone lived on the first floor—the name was there on a door from the small corridor he entered: *Meg Harrison*. The door at the top of the stairs had a similar label reading *Morgan Flower*. Fred knocked. He waited three minutes and knocked again, waiting three more minutes before opening the door with the second key. He had the overnight bag he kept on Mountjoy Street in case of the unexpected, as well as a paper sack of provisions—fortunately, given the dearth of available fast food.

Two days hadn't given Morgan Flower's place enough time to smell vacant or neglected. It was modest indeed, although the building itself, if priced as part of a desirable resort community, this close to Boston, should bring six figures. Fred dropped the overnight bag and looked around. The entrance led through a tiny galley kitchen, neat enough, though there were dirty dishes in the sink. Fred shoved Morgan's supplies to one side and put the sack of provisions on the counter next to the sink.

"Morgan?"

The female voice came from behind him, continuing, as he turned, "You're not Morgan."

Chapter Five

She hesitated, turned to run.

"Molly tells me I look dangerous," Fred said.

The woman turned back. She was tall, slender—well, skinny, actually—with lank black hair roped into a pony tail, jeans. Something on top made by indigenous persons who were not indigenous to Stillton, Massachusetts. Her feet were bare, and knobby, as if they, also, were not indigenous to Stillton, Massachusetts. "I'll go," she said. She hesitated. "I don't know Molly."

Fred told her, "You're Meg. Just guessing."

"How did you get Morgan's keys?" she demanded. Her suspicious fright was well barricaded behind the mask of authority. This was her turf until Fred could prove otherwise.

"This'll take a minute, and I'm just getting settled," Fred said.

"I heard you knock."

"What we could do—I see Morgan has a couple of chairs overlooking the view," Fred countered. "Let's talk." Fred strolled into the living area that opened from the kitchen. Couple of ratty stuffed chairs, a table with mugs and plates and a basket of fruit past its prime. A rudimentary couch whose fund of stories you might not want to know. Closed doors would mean bedroom, closet, bath. Things on the wall he'd look at later. No desk? "You take the chair nearest the exit," Fred suggested, sitting in the other.

"It's not a joke," she scolded. "A woman…"

"Not joking," Fred said. "I'd offer you tea, but I don't know…"

"Tea downstairs," she said. So. This and the absence of denial seemed to confirm her identity. "I'll get it." She loped out.

Fred stayed put, letting his gaze take in the walls. A calendar showing the wrong month of the wrong year exhibited a photo of half-naked human females taking the sun on a tropical beach. Poster of a show of Vallotton: little girl walking with a basket through an ominous woods; calendar with the right month of the present year, topped by a generic waterfall and a motto that couldn't be read from where he was, but could be presumed to encourage the principled stewardship of nature's expiring bounty; big poster of a Harley, more suitable to the bedroom of a high school student.

The woman came in again, holding an outsized blue china mug.

"It *is* Meg, isn't it?" Fred asked.

She nodded and sat in the other chair, of yellowing, ancient plaid Herculon. That chair would be out on the sidewalk as soon as Morgan Flower spied his ship on the horizon.

"Fred," Fred said. "I'm taking Morgan's classes."

"Jesus!" Meg's mouth tightened and she shook her head. The room was chilly. Even so, her tea failed to emit steam.

"The authorities, whatever you call them," Fred said. "That's how I come to have keys. They're not Morgan's. The powers that be. What's her name?" He took out the envelope and, from the information provided, picked out the name "Elizabeth Harmony."

Meg's mouth tightened again. The room grew chillier. "Not that I give a shit," she said. "But where do you come from?"

"I'm a bookmark. Told them I'd fill in for a week. That gives Morgan a chance to come back from his bender or, if he's found something better to do, it gives them time to do it right."

"Them?" Meg sneered.

"The powers that be. Them. You. The search committee. Whatever," Fred said.

Meg took a sip from the blue mug.

"Faculty housing?" Fred asked, making an inclusive gesture. Meg shrugged. "In lieu of decent wages. Not that we have no choice. We can rent something else somewhere else, but the salary doesn't change. Take it or leave it. No offense. It's kind of a sore point with most of us. What are they paying you? For the week you're working?"

"The use of Morgan's rooms," Fred said. "I see what you mean. Otherwise, it's a favor for a friend of a friend of a friend. And, to be frank, it's a good time for a change of scene. Nobody who's looking for me is going to look for me here."

"Believe me, nobody is going to look for *anybody* here. Whose nephew are you, is that it?"

"We seem to be starting wrong," Fred said. "Let's try this way. You're on the faculty at Stillton, yes?"

"They claim they want accreditation," Meg persisted. "Bull shit! There are procedures to follow, even here. Like you advertise the position and interview candidates and all that. Equal opportunity. It's like we are North Korea and claim to be a democracy for the simple reason that democracy's a good thing to claim to be, but we go on at the same time doing whatever the fuck we feel like, and just *say* if we're doing it, that proves it's what democracies do. If you don't like it, we shoot you as undemocratic. No, they shove you down our throats without even waving you at senior faculty first."

"Or we could try it this way," Fred said. "You and I find we are neighbors. Just happen to live next door to each other. Not having any particular reason to fight—unless I play loud music and throw bottles out the windows and blood leaks through your ceiling after an especially good party—we pass the time of day. Then, after a week, I'm gone."

"Drawing and painting," Meg said. "I run the life room." She took another sip from the blue mug.

"I have beer," Fred said. "If you'll visit a spell, I'll have one. I could open another for you, to add to your tea."

"Caught me. I've gotten so used to setting a good example," Meg said, "It's almost second nature. We know we've become adults when the natural sneakiness of the child becomes full-fledged hypocrisy. I'll take a beer, thanks. In a glass. I hate it out of china. Thing is, you can't see through…"

Fred did the honors, finding that he was obliged to wash one of the dirty glasses in the sink in order to honor his guest's demand. Meg went on talking. "Fine. Since we are accidental neighbors, I'll assume you are ignorant. Insurance broker. Stillton Academy: it might be the only almost genuine 19th century French academy of art left in this country, maybe in the world. There's nothing left like it in France, anyway, not for the last fifty years. I teach first- and second-year drawing, painting for second- and third-year students. And as I said, I run the life room. Also I teach figure modeling. That's clay. It works out for me. Clay is my medium."

"The life room," Fred said, presenting her with the damp glass and a tall can of Ballantine ale. He carried another can with him to his chair. "That's where students work from the model."

"The live model. Always nude," Meg said, "until the second half of the third year, when we let the painters start working with drapery as well. I said we were 19th century, but not even we work from cadavers. Not since about seventy-five years back."

Chapter Six

"Too expensive?" Fred guessed.

"Extraneous people in authority started wondering who they were," Meg said. "It's a teeny place, our students come from nowhere and most of them go nowhere. I make exactly enough money to break even if I go to New York four times a year, as long as I stay with friends. The administration treats us like shit and they don't either know or care what we are doing. The work is long and hard and I love it. You'll be in Stillton B."

She took a swig. "Ale isn't beer."

Fred said, "I saw it. Stillton Hall. On the way over."

"Nobody knows we're here," Meg said. "Especially since, recently, even the most free-wheeling grad schools got legalistic. That's accreditation for you. It has its downside. Until then we got the occasional kid into a good grad school just on the strength of an excellent portfolio. Basil Houel is one. Not that you'd care. Not that you'd know his work."

"Rusty empty tin cans in urban landscapes," Fred said. "Discarded cartons from juice, milk. Scraps of bubble wrap. Packaging with weeds growing through it. I remember a dismembered Barbie...sometimes there's a human shadow; an occasional bare foot strolling past. Small, tight, colors tending toward lurid..."

"Nobody knows Basil's work," Meg said, letting her mouth hang open.

"Stillton B," Fred prompted.

"I'm there in Stillton B three days a week, Monday, Wednesday, and Friday. Tuesdays, tomorrow, I'm Stillton A. Figure Modeling," Meg said. "Sometimes Thursdays too. Studio classes run six hours. Breaks for the model or a smoke, and lunch, run the day longer. Your lib arts classes meet on Tuesday and Thursday."

"Jeekers!" Fred said. "Six hours?"

"Not lib arts," Meg assured him. "You'll be OK if you can keep them guessing an hour and a half. I can't believe you know Basil's work. I wish—but hell, what difference does it make? You're here for a week. Wear old clothes. They paint in that room too."

"Who else does lib arts, as you call it?" Fred asked.

"You're it. Morgan, that is. He's the lib arts department. And even the one faculty member in anything outside studio arts, that's you, is new last year. For balance. They make us. To prove we mean it. For accreditation. NEASC. You know what that is?"

Fred nodded. "As much as I want to."

The fog horn's regular hooting made an unwanted third party in the conversation. Rain rattled against the windows steadily now. Morgan Flower had neither blinds nor curtains on the windows overlooking the view of lighthouse and dark water whose slow, small swells lit up in regular shafts as the light of the lighthouse swept across them.

Meg said, "If you run what you want to call even a barber college these days, supposing you want all the licenses and permissions, which means you want accreditation, you have to show that the students are exposed to an educational standard that includes balance as well as specialization. Enough science, history, literature, as well as enough specialized attention to whiskers and split ends, so they can function as literate general human barbers when they achieve their degrees.

"Before we brought Morgan in we shipped the students out to take the minimum required extraneous credits in nearby colleges though even the nearest college is forty minutes away. But the schedules weren't compatible and besides, someone figured out that it was cheaper to hire one more miserable instructor full time than pay for the bus, the driver, the insurance, and the scheduling headache. So. We hired a lib arts department. That's Morgan. Therefore you are the substitute lib arts department. What do you know?"

The foghorn hooted. A lone gull responded. With all the others.

"Where *is* Morgan," Fred asked.

Meg shrugged. "His car is out front is all I know. They didn't give you keys to that, I guess? That's still regarded as his property? How do you spell Basil's last name?"

"It's pronounced 'Howell,'" Fred said. "But it's spelled H-O-U-E-L. A French name, I'm guessing."

"I still can't get over…"

"I like pictures," Fred said. "I don't like Houel's pictures but I've noticed them, and thought about them. They seem mean. You know the guy?"

Meg poured the remainder of the ale into her glass and stood. "I'll bring this back. See you tomorrow," she said. "I'll be in Stillton A. Life Modeling. Clay. Clay makes such a mess it's all we do in there. Thanks for this." She raised the glass and left, descending the stairs without closing Fred's door.

If that was a habit of hers, it indicated a degree of familiarity with the place or its previous occupant. Fred closed the door and began the tour of inspection he had been about to start when Meg walked in. If Morgan Flower taught liberal arts—English and Art History at least—where were his books? Oh, here. The closet was full of them. Crammed shelves lined the back and side walls and boxes of books were piled in the remaining space, as high as Fred's shoulders. A fast glance proved the collection to be remaindered art books—mostly Impressionists and Italian Renaissance war horses—and the texts assigned in low level college introductory lit classes a couple of generations back: *Portrait of the Artist as a Young Man; A Room of One's Own.*

A second closet held a parka, sport coats, pants on hangers. The third door opened into Morgan Flower's Spartan bedroom. Spartan? Almost monastic. The single bed was made: metal frame, no headboard or footboard. The last blue chenille bed-spread in the known world lay across it. The hooked rug in the room's center must come with the place. A wooden desk held a tablet of lined yellow paper, legal size; a notebook and seven books. Next to the desk a ratty, two-drawer file cabinet might bear looking into later. The bureau held underwear, shirts, socks and—the top drawer—an assortment of foreign money that, put together, might trade for three hundred dollars at the most.

No passport.

No phone anywhere in the place. Presuming that he had one, he depended on a cell phone, iPhone, or so-called smartphone. Therefore no helpful answering machine with stowed messages.

Shoes under the bed: loafers, sneakers, boots for the winter.

The search was quick, since there was nothing much to search. Bathroom off the bedroom yielded a slightly running toilet—Fred looked into the tank and adjusted the ball cock—a tub with one of those infuriating contraptions rigged above it to allow the landlord to claim the existence of a shower—sink, and towels that looked to have come from the same yard sale as the Herculon-upholstered chair. The bathroom window when he raised the blind looked directly into the bathroom of the next cottage over, ten feet away, across a dark side yard.

He couldn't smell the man or get a feel for him. The shelf of condiments in the bathroom didn't show such obvious lacunae as to demonstrate the absence of their owner. There was no sign either that he had departed or that he was expected home. In the whole apartment, in fact, so far, there was nothing a man would mind leaving, and nothing much to come back to.

"The fridge, then," Fred said, making his way back to the galley kitchen through which he had entered. Ice, ice cream, most of a bottle of vodka, two fat frozen pork chops and a square of lima beans in the upper compartment. In the lower, milk, half a lemon—the man had no TV set? Remarkable. Maybe they were forbidden in Stillton? No, that was the drone of TV evening news coming up through the floor from Meg Harrison's apartment. Come to think of it, there was no stereo equipment either. No computer? Did the guy live his life by cell phone, iPod, and BlackBerry?—and—still in the fridge—most of a loaf of whole wheat bread of an unpretentious brand; peanut butter, grape jelly, a withering bowl of spaghetti in browning sauce, beer, and more wine than you'd think was necessary until you began to speculate what life must be like in Stillton, Massachusetts.

Chapter Seven

Fred washed and dried the dishes and figured out what might be an acceptable approximation of putting them away. He took his perishables from the sack and put them into the fridge: four cans of ale, bread, cheddar, bananas, carrots, apples, sliced ham. If he got hungry either he'd go out and find something, or slap a sandwich together here. The cans of beans and tea bags he left on the counter, and he was moved in.

The bag of trash, under the counter beside the cleanser and the wooden box of onions and sprouted potatoes, he could go through later. No. Might as well get it done. Egg shells and an empty egg carton. The bone from a beefsteak. No coffee grounds? No, a collection of cardboard cups from the Stillton Café holding a residue of whitened liquid that smelled of coffee and vanilla and, even worse, hazelnut. A foam package had held some kind of meal. Empty cans were in an orange recycle container in the broom cupboard (one broom; one red plastic dustpan), along with catalogs from Land's End and L. L. Bean. No magazines or newspapers. Of course not. If Morgan Flower wanted news, he'd get it from his BlackBerry or iPhone.

"Brave new world," Fred muttered. If these people's machines disappeared along with them, you'd never know who they had been. On the other hand, find the machines, crack the codes, divine the obvious passwords, and you're in. The individual laid bare.

Would Stillton Academy provide faculty offices to search through? Not likely.

Fred carried his ale back to the bedroom. The liquid's level was lowering only slowly. He'd wanted it as a diversion more than as a beverage. The desk was placed perpendicular to one of two windows that overlooked the same view as the living room. Rain stroked the glass. The other window, Fred noted, gave access to a wooden porch and fire escape. The window was not latched. Fred sat on the desk chair. It was a penance: stiff, hard, the wrong size and the wrong shape for any human born of woman. Start with the books. Tomorrow he'd be standing in front of classes, and he didn't have a clue.

If you could take seven books with you to the desert island, would it be these? An *American Heritage Dictionary,* college edition, the red paperback. Well, why not? The skinny Laurel Poetry Series *Emily Dickinson*—"Of course!" Fred said, and thumped his forehead with the heel of his hand. "It's little Emily."—Thomas Craven's *Famous Artists and their Models,* Gauguin's *Tahitian Diary*—"Good choice!"—*Moby Dick; The Stranger,* and Sir Kenneth Clark's *The Nude,* also in paper. "If that's his idea of teaching art history, it's kind of a cop out."

Fred picked up the Emily Dickinson and thumbed through the index to confirm. *I died for beauty,* on page 54, was checked in pencil. Missy Tutunjian's so-called message from beyond the grave was an assignment, as in, "OK, class. Choose one stanza of any Dickinson poem you wish, and leave it behind in such a way that folks think it's a suicide note."—or, rather, taken from an assignment. "I died for beauty, but was scarce / Adjusted in the tomb, / When one who died for truth was lain / In an adjoining room." He ran his eye down the two remaining stanzas. Beauty and truth—you could argue about it—seemed to be strangers, not lovers. They referred to themselves as brethren and kinsmen and there was no hint of carnal intimacy. Just two strangers chatting between graves until their names were mossed over.

Just to be sure, Fred checked Melissa's transcription against the poet's text. Some altered word might signal a dark intent.

No, aside from the little hearts, the transcription was accurate. He leafed through the book noting the couple of dozen additional check marks, most applied to the obvious candidates for assignment: *Because I could not stop for Death; Hope is the thing with feathers; I never saw a moor;* along with others you'd have to work at longer to figure out if they meant anything different if you read them backwards.

Fred opened the notebook. Class records. Good. He carried it with him into the living area and sat down to it in the chair he had adopted as his own. The book held records for the past two years. It would be useful at least to give him a hint of what the devil he was supposed to pretend to teach as well as to whom. For each of the three classes he was assigned for the present semester, the students' names were listed under the titles of the class, in a crabby handwriting Fred would have guessed was an old lady's. Next to each name was a record of attendance, as well as an occasional grade.

Melissa Tutunjian was where you would expect to find her, toward the bottom end of the current victims of *English One, Intro to Literature.* Her attendance record was commendable, her grades, until recently, tending to remain at the high C's level. She'd been doing better since the January thaw.

The other two courses were entitled *Lives and Loves of the Artists* and, for third year students, *Writing About Your Problems.*

"I see a far horizon," Fred remarked. "And nowhere upon it do I sense a hint of the remotest possibility of accreditation for Stillton Academy of Art. Unless there are truly no academic standards left in this land. Maybe you'd get away with the *Intro to Lit* class—who could take exception to Emily and Moby Dickinson? But the other two courses? Forget it. *Lives and Loves of the Artists?* For serious art students? It's an abomination. Whomever they hump has nothing to do with art. It's just how they direct their excess energy."

He'd dropped the record book to the floor and was staring out the window at the rain and the dark water and the missionary work of the lighthouse, busy in its task of spreading light that was immediately swallowed up. The light shining in darkness. Like all the rest of those who lived (or died) for beauty and/or truth, no? Get over it, Emily.

Fred rose and strode to the closet. What was the size and heft of the instructor in whose living space he found himself? A quick comparison of himself against a pair of the missing teacher's pants, and a brown sport coat that was mostly elbow patches, proved that Fred would need to drop four inches of height, and a good deal of girth, if he wanted to make a convincing match tomorrow. Better that he not try to look like the man he was replacing.

"Do they work from anything like a plan, or wing it?" Fred wondered. "Lecture from notes? Talking points? Don't I recall one moth-eaten old guy reading from a yellow legal pad? If I'm hoping for any kind of cover, what in blazes am I going to do for an hour and a half, three times over, just tomorrow? Are these people crazy?"

There must be something useful in the file cabinet.

Fred took one of the two chairs from the small table in the living area and carried it into the bedroom. The desk chair wasn't even good enough to burn. He shoved it aside and replaced it with something a human could tolerate. There should be financial records, class notes, the beginnings of hopeless manuscripts Flower would never finish, papers awaiting grades, old blue books with mid-terms or whatever they did here....

No. If Morgan Flower had a financial profile, it was rattling around in the ether. He'd gone paperless. Address? Where did Morgan's mama live, or the cousins, siblings, the whole Christmas card list? Nothing. All on the iPhone? If he lost that, Morgan wouldn't even know himself who he was.

There was a folder filled with lamentable student prose, all of it hand-written, whose subjects would fit within the broad umbrella *Writing About Your Problems.* The title *The time I was almost pregnant* caught Fred's eye. Judging from the dates on the papers, he'd meet this gang tomorrow. If he had time, maybe he'd skim through the collection tonight; get an introduction to his students. They deserved something for their money. Something better than Fred, anyway.

Jeekers! Did Morgan Flower let the kids read each other's work? Did he make them read it aloud? Would the other half of the almost-pregnancy be present in the room? That could be fun.

Then, in the next folder along, in the bottom drawer—what was this?

Chapter Eight

The penciled title on the Manila folder read *Stillton Sound—A Private Community.*

"Not that I saw," Fred said, letting the folder fall open on the desk. Inside were many sheets of the yellow lined paper Morgan Flower favored, from the tablet on the desk or from another like it. The handwriting, in pencil, with many erasures and emendations, was the same as that preserved in the class record book; a hand Fred would have guessed belonged to a constipated older woman.

The Inn and Spa at Stillton Sound, one page began. *Indulge in all the responsible luxury of life at Stillton Sound. The lovingly restored Residences feature multiple exposures, ocean views, windowed kitchens, wood-burning fireplaces, and impeccably re-engineered interiors—and all executed with such elegant understatement you will assure yourself that you are truly living in Thoreauvian simplicity. Meanwhile the pleasures of daily life are enhanced and enriched by the unique club privileges that are the hallmark of your membership in the Stillton Sound Community. The spa and heated indoor pool, overlooking the sound, provide for unique year-round* "blah, blah, blah," Fred grumbled, *while the elegant dining room, under the magic touch of acclaimed three-star chef [name to be supplied]…*

Fred flipped pages, allowing phrases to float up from the morass of Morgan Flower's imaginings. *Quaint small town;*

unspoiled; a spectacular unique commitment to the ultimate in green restoration; marina and lap pool; guaranteed privacy; contemporary traditional; traditional contemporary; just minutes to Logan Airport, Paris, Venice or Shanghai; impeccable perfection; superb...

There must be twenty pages of these exercises in the pastiche of fragments of filched puffery. Their superlatives were clearly designed to appeal to people who would prefer to live at considerable remove from those who are employed to clean their toilets. *Minutes from Logan Airport, Paris, Venice and Shanghai* had a nice ring if you were in the market for nice ring. "Is it not also true," Fred mused, "that we are just minutes from the War of 1812? Are we not mere minutes from the North Pole, traveling by dogsled?

During what must be long tedious winter nights in which he was obliged to entertain himself by plumbing the remarkably shallow depths of his creative romance, Flower had evidently concentrated not on his own love poems, nor on yet another definitive biography of Emily Dickinson, but on this palpable fantasy—worthy almost of being made into a video game—of inventing the idle cloud cuckoo-land *Stillton Sound—A Private Community*. Stillton Sound haunted his waking moments and tormented his sleep. On the last page in the folder, drawn with an obsessive attention to detail Fred had not seen since the battle pictures made by colleagues in the fourth grade, there was even an aerial view of the entire fiction, fully laid out and elaborated. *Stillton Sound—A Private Community* occupied all of the area presently filled by the town of Stillton. A gate was drawn across the peninsula that permitted access only to the elect. Gate? Why not a moat? It was as complete and absurd as a cross between Celesteville and Frank Lloyd Wright's Living City. As Fred puzzled out Morgan Flower's fevered imaginings, he realized that the focus of the creation, the *Inn and Spa at Stillton Sound*, so labeled on the map, was to be found where the main buildings of Stillton Academy of Art presently stood.

The Inn and Spa at Stillton Sound, indeed, might constitute the lovingly (and "greenly") "restored" buildings that presently stood overlooking the ocean in so non-profit a way. Here were guest cottages, three restaurants, two pools, the gym, a concert and movie and lecture hall, blocks and blocks of residences, the marina on the northern coast and, on the less exposed southern side, a bathing beach. An area marked "commercial" more or less where the present attempts at commerce were, included an X labeled "office."

"His big problem is gonna be golf," Fred said, putting the frenzied fable back in the file cabinet. "There's no room left on the point to swing a club. The peninsula, on one side or the other, of that two-lane road, might give you room enough to drive the ball—but no possibility for eighteen holes unless you do it in a straight line east-west. That's much too inventive for New England. Plus the odd slice costs windshields here and there. Even if you are rich enough to aspire to Thoreauvian simplicity, can you do without golf?

"Hell, if he plans to pump that much imaginary money into the operation, what's wrong with a floating golf course? Reel it in in the winter, roll it and store it or—this could be better—roof it and heat it. In the worst of the winter the kids can still go clamming in the sand traps.

"Holy Toledo."

The strength of Fred's response had lifted him from the chair and carried him out of the bedroom and into the living area again. What was this? He was pacing? The isolation of living and working in Stillton, Massachusetts, had already driven him to such a pass? Soon he'd be designing his own wave-lapped rest home and retirement village, complete with all the luxurious responsibility that could be desired. No, that was wrong. Responsible luxury was the *phrase juste*.

It was just after eight o'clock. The rain was steady, but Fred had a jacket in the car. He couldn't rest until he had a sense of where he was. More than these rooms. The bigger where. The geographical setting as a whole made him uneasy, since it had only one exit, unless you counted the water, in which case it was almost all exit.

◇◇◇

Streetlights were sparse, but present, and worked through the rain sufficiently to allow a general idea of the terrain. The flavor was genuinely working seaside, uncontaminated by either success or extraneous money. However the local fishing economy might fit into the big picture that included packing, freezing, warehousing, and sales, that could not be inferred from what was visible. Lights in the windows of the small clapboard or shingled houses showed either couples or small families at a table, or doing dishes, or watching television or, in some houses, a lighted blind upstairs might show where a child was being readied for bed.

The fog horn continued its work.

The sidewalks everywhere but on Main Street were dirt, lined with wet bushes that would turn out to be lilac or privet or the invasive barberry. To quote one of the phrases Morgan Flower had not hit upon for his rhapsodies, it was all *pleasantly impoverished.*

Closer to Stillton Academy's main buildings, the houses were more lively. The inhabitants were students, in larger groups, with music, loud talk. Some lighted windows showed rooms that were serving as studios, with paintings in progress on easels, or tables serving as desks, the walls around them festooned with mixed sketches and ideas, including many geometric essays in black and white.

He hadn't thought about it before. "The students live here?" Fred marveled. "Of course it's the back of beyond. How are they going to commute from anywhere, gas being what it is?"

More cars were parked in this part of town, many of them as seedy even as Fred's.

Fred's walk along portions of the outside circumference of the town had brought him to Stillton Hall, where he'd be teaching tomorrow. The building was dark. Its front door did not respond to his tug.

"Milan locks up at eight-thirty." The male voice spoke from behind him. Fred turned and discovered a couple. Inside their rain gear they looked young: a male and a female in a close unit.

Chapter Nine

Assume the absence of suspicion.

"That's why," Fred said. "Just curious."

The pair gathered its forces to move on.

"Don't know the town," Fred told them, approaching. He never bothered with a hat, and rain was coursing down through the stubble of hair he kept short, and down his face and neck. "I'd heard of Stillton Academy, took the turn, and here I am on a bad evening. Where should I go for a meal?"

"There's two places, you want to sit down," the female said. She wore what might be her big brother's black raincoat, if her big brother happened to be a police officer, and a blue hat that went with someone else's big brother's outfit.

"But one of them's closed," the male added. "Closes at eight. Bee's Beehive. What's open is the Stillton Café." He pointed down Main Street, away from the sea, the lighthouse, and all the rest of the view. His outer garb was the transparent plastic raincoat the drug store sells you in emergencies—ripped and splattered with paint. He was tall, lean, and dark-haired, and as recently as yesterday had been clean-shaven.

Fred told them, "Thanks," and followed the direction they suggested. When he turned to look back at where he had left them, they were turning the corner of Stillton Hall as if to go behind it. "Not much privacy in Stillton, Massachusetts," Fred observed, "Maybe there's shelter back there? A shed? A summer house or bandstand?"

Main Street offered, absolutely and absurdly, *nothing* for tourists. Again, the easiest explanation seemed to be a pervasive influence of the Taliban and the Stillton Historical Commission. No antique or thrift shop. No real estate office. No gift boutique or shop specializing in cheese and wines from far away. There was a bait-and-tackle shop near the docks, but Main Street was without its upscale equivalent, Le Chandlerie, where you could meet your scrimshaw needs.

Maggie's Provisions was closed, but through the generous front windows Fred could see that it was a place to buy an honest pickle, toilet paper, the *Boston Globe* or *Herald,* a lettuce or green pepper, frozen food, a ready-made baloney sandwich, beer or wine that didn't claim to come from anywhere. Etc. Art supplies? Where did those come from. Books? There wasn't even a used book store to aid in the recirculation of vacation reading.

The Stillton Café stood out by being open, under most of a blinking neon sign in blue and orange. It was across Main Street from Bee's Beehive, which was closed. The café was a single large storefront room with a counter along the back separating the tables from the small, very visible kitchen. There might be a dozen people in evidence, between clients, the man cooking, and waiters. No one was older than the mid-twenties. Fred took an empty table from which he could see the room, hung his wet jacket over a chair back, and used a couple of paper napkins to swab his head, face and neck.

"Use my towel," a young woman suggested, taking the white cloth from the sash of her apron. The label on her left breast said *Marci.* Fred used the towel, which left behind it on his skin a redolence of the concentrated essences of hamburgers and fries.

"Thanks, Marci." He handed back the towel, which was folded again and replaced at the ready, over the sash of the apron emblazoned with the motto *Stillton Café.* That was company issue, but the waitress hadn't been forced to wear a uniform. Fred demanded cheeseburgers and fries, with water from the tap and "coleslaw, if you have it."

"Of course," Marci assured him. "We don't make it, but we have it. He gets it in big tubs. No problem." She yelled past the counter in back, "Two Stilltons with cheddar." On her way to the counter to deal with the issues of Fred's water and off-the-rack coleslaw, she stopped to talk with two male students who were drinking beer intently while disregarding the silent basketball game on the TV above the counter.

The conversation was too discreet to be overheard, other than the name, repeated several times, "Hag Harrison." Everyone in the café, like everyone else Fred had seen on the peninsula, was one of the variant mongrel mixtures Americans call "white." It was disconcerting, this close to the city of Boston, to seem to have arrived so very far away.

Marci came back to his table with the water and a shallow dish of coleslaw, along with a plate with two slices of one-size-fits-all white bread and a suspiciously yellow pat of something greasy. "You don't want a beer?" Marci asked.

"Student at the Academy," Fred said.

"You are?" Marci asked. "Oh. You mean, am I? Sure. My first year."

"But you're not from here," Fred said.

She shook her head and laughed. "Colebrook, New Hampshire," she said. "About as far north as you can go before you fall off."

"Into Canada," Fred finished. "No beer, thanks."

Marci shrugged and wandered back toward the counter, pausing to tell the couple of students drinking beer, over her shoulder, "What I did, I'm holding a broom."

"Just like Daygah would have done," the rosier and plumper of the two men said. He and his companion laughed in the patronizing way that demonstrates the tenuous self-confidence that comes from barely superior age. "We all get over it eventually," he added.

"Not Lambert. He should have used the Meeker Method." The chuckles continued into conversation.

At another table it was two young women in consultation over a basket of fries into which each dipped now and then, in order to select a strand of potato to swirl in a puddle of ketchup and eat with deliberation, after using it to make a point in the air. Fred raised his glass to them, having caught their eyes, and was rebuffed. Both women wore jeans that had seen hard times, and shapeless sweaters. One had an orange kerchief over red hair. The other—her name might be Anna if he'd heard correctly—had black hair in a thick braid down her back.

Marci returned with a large plate fragrant with cheeseburgers and piled fries. "Not to hurry you, but if you'll be wanting dessert, can you tell me? We start cleaning the kitchen in ten minutes. There's chocolate cake and two slices of apple pie left that isn't bad."

Picking up the first of the pair of burgers, Fred shook his head and remarked, "I was half expecting to run into Morgan Flower."

The room grew still and paid attention.

"The weed?" Marci said, and bit her lip. "No disrespect," she added hastily.

"English One. And the rest of it," Fred said. "Emily Dickinson. *Moby Dick.*"

"Moby Dick?" The question came from one of the two women who were entertaining fries.

There was a clattering in the kitchen and the man who had been cooking, swishing his stained yellow apron as if herding chickens, came to the counter to call out, "Kitchen's closed."

Chapter Ten

"Relax," Marci called. "Eat, take your time." But the room had changed as if Fred's identity had suddenly been exposed as a poisonous fog.

"I'm in his class," Marci said. "We all are. One class or another. Except for part-timers. They make you."

"He wasn't here earlier?" Fred asked.

One of the beer-drinking men took a final pull and put his glass down with a sharp clack. "He eats sometimes," he said.

"Not tonight," one of the pair of young women with French fries said, punctuating her observation by inserting a red-tipped fry into her mouth.

Her partner added, "He missed that thing on Saturday he calls a seminar. I had to get up for it and he didn't show." She shrugged. "I went back to bed."

"After twenty minutes," Marci explained, "they can't mark you absent if they're the one late."

"Speaking of late, I guess it's too late for that pie," Fred said.

"Steve's got the mop out," Marci said.

The student diners were gathering themselves and their belongings, and putting on whatever rain gear they intended to interpose between themselves and the weather. "Since I'm kind of his guest speaker tomorrow," Fred said, picking up the last of his fries. He let it hang.

People were leaving the café in a more or less general way. Marci took a slip of paper from her pocket and put it beside

Fred's plate, frankly face up. "Since I guess you can't want anything else," she said.

Fred started counting money from a damp wallet. "You're first year, so you're *Intro to Lit*," Fred said, adding an ostentatious five dollar bill to the cost of the meal. "So I'll see you in class. I'll catch him in the morning before class, but that doesn't give me much lead time. If Morgan Flower was here to clue me in, what would he tell me to do or say? What's missing so far?"

Marci twisted his money with the bill, shoved it into an apron pocket, and said, "We figured he might not show. You want change?"

Fred shook his head. "Thanks for the use of the towel."

"You're going to get wet again," Marci told him, gesturing toward the street.

"It was good to be dry while I ate," Fred said. "See you tomorrow."

Marci's repeated shrug defied interpretation.

The rain hadn't let up, but it had taken on a different slant. Or was it that Fred was now walking in a different direction? In ten wet minutes he had reached the cottage occupied by Meg Harrison and by now, for all anyone knew, by Morgan Flower himself, back from an unexpected trip to China, and even now turning out the contents of Fred's bag, speculating about the identity of the absent intruder. Nothing had looked permanent about the instructor's absence.

"I might have telephoned Molly," Fred mused. "And I would now if Flower had a land line. It'll wait till tomorrow."

The apartment was still as vacant as it had been, with no further sign of its indignant tenant. Fred was so wet that he stripped, wrung his clothes out over the kitchen sink and hung them over the pipe from which the shower curtain was suspended. No source of clean towels being apparent, he made do with Morgan Flower's slightly rancid towel, taking it from its hook behind the bathroom door. When it had done its job, he spread it to dry over one of the chairs at the dining table. It would have a better chance there. The apartment's air was chilly. He pulled dry clothes from the overnight bag and put them on.

The students in the café had been talking about someone they called "Hag Harrison." That was presumably his downstairs neighbor. Morgan Flower was, not very inventively, "weed." Should he give the impending requirements of pretending to be a teacher any thought? Anyone could do English Lit he'd been assured. As far as that went, to start with, he might have to throw himself upon the mercy, if any, of his students. The course called *Writing About Your Problems* couldn't be prepared for. Should he take the five minutes it deserved to inform his students that to him the subject seemed lazy, cynical, and cavalier? A gut course from the instructor's point of view.

That left *Lives and Loves of the Artists*. So-called. There'd been a folder in the top drawer of the file cabinet that looked helpful, labeled "Course Syllabi." That hadn't been what Fred was looking for on his first examination. When he went back and pulled it out he found the Manila folder woefully thin. Nevertheless, he sat in the armchair of his choice before opening the folder to study.

It gave him all of a single yellow sheet, folded, on which were notes in Flower's now familiar hand: *Lives and Loves of the Artists*. Term One. 1. Da Vinci, 2. Michelangelo, 3. Titian, 4. Holbein, 5. Rubens, 6. Rembrandt, 7. Velasquez, 8. Goya, 9. Hogarth, 10. Blake, 11. Turner, 12. Audubon, 13. Daumier, 14. Review and final. Term two. 1. Manet, 2. Lautrec, 3. Van Gogh, 4. Cézanne, 5. Bellows, 6. Burchfield & Benton, 7. Wood & Curry, 8. Marsh & Gauguin, 9.—13. The Nude, 14. Review & final.

"A strange parade," Fred said, running his eye over it. "Can this joker really be giving equal weight to Rembrandt and John Steuart Curry? Gauguin and Reginald Marsh in the same week? Where's Balthus? Where's Matisse? Tintoretto? *Lives and Loves of the Artists?* What's Audubon doing in the lineup anyway, unless there's something I don't want to know about between him and some hen turkey?"

Judging from the evidence at hand, a term must be fourteen weeks. Figure they might be about seven weeks more or less into this second term, the grand disjointed progression might have reached Thomas Hart Benton and Charles Burchfield. If Fred had ever had a friendly word to say for either of these unnecessarily muscular and twisted American painters, he couldn't remember what it was. "In which case, maybe my job, as a ship passing in the night, is to unload scorn," he concluded.

The Timex said 9:45. He was fed, rain-washed and dry, not to mention clothed. He dithered a minute before he decided, put his wet shoes on again and went downstairs to tap at Meg Harrison's door, once he had assured himself that the sounds of her TV gave him a right to conclude she was awake.

She called out, "Who is it?"

"Fred. From upstairs."

"Give me a minute."

Fred gave her five.

She opened the door wearing a large loose blue garment somewhere between a smock and a caftan.

"Not borrowing sugar," Fred said. "Looking for guidance, really, if you have a minute. And, do you mind? Since I see you have a phone. Land line. May I use it? Collect, obviously. Molly's in Florida."

Meg nodded him in.

Chapter Eleven

The room he entered—through an untidy version of a kitchen like his own—was sparse, even barren. Other than the red telephone he had spotted from the doorway, there was nothing on the walls. You might guess that a nun lived here except, where was the crucifix? Wouldn't there be a calendar with pictures of Saint Theresa and the perennially blessed Mother Seton? And what did a nun want with the full-length mirror propped against what should be a closet door?

"Whatever you want, as long as I'm in bed by ten-thirty," Meg said. "Early day tomorrow." She had no sofa but three yard-sale armchairs. She sat in one of them and gestured toward the phone—a portable. Her layout was the same as Fred's. The doors to her bedroom and closets were closed and without ornament. The TV sounds, continuing, came from the bedroom.

"This happened so fast," Fred explained. "Molly won't have a clue how to find me."

Molly was brisk once Fred had gotten past her eager daughter Terry, who wished to describe each one of the shells she had found. Fred had dropped the code word "perfect"—a word not otherwise called for in his daily parlance—which Molly recognized as the signal that this particular phone call couldn't do much more than to assure her that Fred was alive and well. More information would follow when it could do so in a less public way.

Fred replaced the phone and said, "I have to say, Meg, I'm going to be flying blind tomorrow and that's about the total of what I know. Beyond the names of the classes and the names of the students in them, I am in the dark." While he spoke Meg was gesturing him toward another, and the worst, of the three armchairs. Her feet, still bare—her legs being crossed—exhibited a tension well suppressed in the rest of her demeanor.

Meg started slowly, "I can't say I pay attention to what he's doing, and the kids—the students—don't talk about Flower's classes. If they have to write something they grumble. Beyond that, I don't hear."

"This lineup of artists he assigns in, what is it, a second-year course? *Lives and Loves of the Artists.* Does the rest of the faculty have anything to say about who he puts in front of his students? I mean, Burchfield? When you can have Matisse? Or, I don't know, Copley?"

Meg looked at her watch. "People are going to ask, so I might as well. You said that you came as a favor for a friend of a friend of a friend. Never mind they're acting pretty fast for a guy who's been missing such a short time, unless they know something. Never mind. What I want to know is, who is this friend of a friend of a friend? Who is the friend of a friend? Who is the friend? And how come, if you have Morgan Flower's keys from Elizabeth Harmony, you had to look her name up on a piece of paper?"

She crossed her legs the other way and her knobbed feet twisted.

Fred said, "For example, if I found I was going to do the job for real, and I was designing a course about painters, I'd ask you and the other members of the faculty which painters you want your students looking at. Who do you care about? Burchfield? Who's going to learn anything useful from Burchfield?"

"Another time," Meg said. "You want to play employment interview? Theoretical? It's my turf. I start with the question—say I come in late, I never bothered reading your résumé or application letter, all that—I'm an artist anyway so I don't read—I ask, 'So, Fred, where have you been teaching until now? What courses? While we're at it, what's your last name?"

"Fair question. Taylor," Fred said, and let his mouth close in a deliberate way.

"The other questions?"

Fred rested mute. Meg twitched, and scratched the side of her face, and studied him. "If I get my friend to Google 'Fred Taylor,' there'll be eighteen or nineteen million possible matches," she said.

"Thought I might see some examples of your work," Fred remarked. "Since you live here."

"I don't shit in the nest," she said. "Or to say it cleaner, I don't bring work home. At home, if I want to think, I want to think about something else."

"Does Stillton Academy have a catalogue I could look at, get my bearings a little bit?"

Meg stood. "We're done. I don't bring my work home. Period. Looks like that includes you. It's been real."

"I guess I'll see the rest of the faculty here and there," Fred said.

"Faculty meeting tomorrow. Four- thirty," Meg said. "If it's true you're here for a week, I'd skip it. If it's true."

"Meaning that in your experience sometimes a temporary gesture slides imperceptibly into an unintended permanence?" Fred said.

"Meaning if I see you at that faculty meeting, I'll have a good idea how temporary you are." She paused, deliberating the next gambit. "If those are Morgan's keys you got in with, if he sent you as his ringer, how come his car's still on the street?"

Fred spread his arms in the universal gesture that means whatever that universal gesture hopes to mean at the time.

After she had closed him out, Fred heard, from the other side of the door, Meg's raised voice, "They're all such liars!"

"Time we considered sleeping arrangements," Fred decided, once back in Morgan Flower's apartment. He'd replayed the inconclusive conference with Meg Harrison while climbing the stairs, and registered the fact that what he knew best, now, was that she bristled with a suspicion that amounted almost to paranoia. If she decided that Fred was acting *for* Morgan Flower, or in collusion with him, Meg Harrison wanted no part of him.

Since Fred was an unknown quantity to her, that seemed a vehement response on first acquaintance.

"These academics," Fred said.

The few grains tossed into the coop make trouble among the chickens.

No lamp next to the bed. Did Morgan Flower not read before he slept? No. There was no bedside table with a dog-eared book. No radio. He didn't read, he didn't smoke. What did the man do, just lie down and turn off?

Do we give the man a shock, letting him stagger in late and find himself at the climactic scene in *Goldilocks*—there's *Intro to Lit* for you—with Fred in the role of the heroine? Fred turned down the blue chenille coverlet—checking for sperm?—to reveal the splotched pillow and then, progressively, but gingerly, the continuation of the interior of a bed whose owner's mother would have recoiled in dismay.

Not that he hadn't slept in worse. Still, Fred pulled the coverlet up again as it had been, and smoothed it gently into place. Not for the first time in his life, he stretched out on an inadequate couch and considered the vagaries of sleep.

Chapter Twelve

"Wait in my office, would you, Professor Taylor?" Elizabeth Harmony soothed. "Tom" —-to the student at the reception desk—"if Professor Taylor wants coffee, would you arrange it?"

Fred held out the cup he had brought with him—bad black coffee from the Stillton Café. "It's Fred," he said.

Elizabeth Harmony turned and moved off with swift purpose, as if bent on reprimanding a delinquent caddie. Tall and broad hipped, her white hair clipped into a Prince Valiant helmet, her perfunctory greeting had hardly rippled heavy features that revealed that she had gotten the better of many encounters with the Demon Rum.

Fred had found her in the small cottage marked *Administration*, engaged in a conversation with Tom, whose desk, on which were a telephone, a typewriter and a sign saying *Reception*, occupied a space that would otherwise be called the front hall. The sign on the door behind him, which was ajar, said *Director*.

"I'll hang out with Tom," Fred said to her striding back.

"My name's not Tom," the young man said. "Tom Meeker sits here sometimes. As far as she's concerned, we're all…"

The desk telephone rang. The man whose name was not Tom noted which light was blinking before he told the receiver, "Stillton Academy. Admissions." A pause while he noted some information from dictation—a name and address—before he continued, "The new catalogue is in preparation. What she'll need in the meantime is the brochure, and an application form.

Have her return the form, with the deposit, and the next thing is the admissions interview and portfolio review." A pause. "Yes, that will be with one of our studio faculty. The admissions director is presently…excuse me, may I put you on hold?"

He switched to another line, told it, "Stillton," listened and continued, "No, he's here. At least, there's another guy. So it's meeting…. I don't know. Professor Taylor. Search me." He switched back to the earlier line, failed to get a response and told it, "Shit!" before he hung up. "I probably cut them off," he said.

"'Meeker,' Fred said. "That rings a bell. Something I heard in the café. "I know, 'The Meeker Method.' What's that?"

The question got a grin, but no response. "I go by Fred," Fred said. "If I let them call me Professor, I have to get new shoes and everything. Can I see one of the brochures?"

Not-Tom fiddled with the *Reception* sign on his desk. It was one of the triangular bars which, after he had played with it, exposed a second side: *Admissions*.

"You'll have to wait," not-Tom said. "Let me put this in the pending file or I'll forget." The slip of paper on which he had recorded the name and address of the prospective student went into a folder, along with several others.

"No brochure?" Fred prompted.

"She's having a new one printed."

"I'll settle for an old one."

Not-Tom shook his head. "Recycled," he said. "It had the name of the old director. President Harmony didn't want…"

"*President* Harmony?"

"She says, if this is supposed to be a college, and if she's supposed to be…" his face went blank. Elizabeth Harmony's reappearance had been as quick as it was stealthy. She placed on not-Tom's desk a sign that read *ELIZABETH HARMONY, PRESIDENT* and instructed him, "Have Milan put this on my door, Tom, would you? As soon as he can. Have the other one taken down. It's confusing. Also, I'll have coffee. In the china cup, please. Cream and sugar beside it. On a tray. With a napkin. You are sure you won't…?" she asked Fred. He shook his head.

"Knock before you come in," she instructed, leading the way into an office that had almost nothing in it but a desk, three chairs, a memo pad, a telephone, a file cabinet. "I hate a cardboard cup," she continued, closing the door. "It sets such a poor..." Taking note of Fred's cup, she did not finish her thought aloud, but took a detour. "We'll give you a coaster," she promised doubtfully, as if speculating whether she would be obliged to instruct him in its proper use.

"Where were we?" she asked, as they sat down. "I appreciate your joining us at such short notice." She spoke as if she was used to having her whims made flesh. They sat, she gaining credibility as she took her position behind the desk.

"I haven't joined you," Fred pointed out. "Your attorney asked me to gather some information, Mrs. Harmony, in the guise..."

"President," she demurred. "Speak softly. The walls..."

"And there's a problem," Fred continued. "First a question. Everyone seems to assume that Morgan Flower is gone for good. Why?" He took a sip of his coffee and held onto the cup, disregarding the coaster she had placed on the edge of her desk. "The way I work, I like to be direct. Ask questions straight. The way this situation ties me up, me pretending to be..."

A knock on the door was followed by the entrance of the man she called Tom, carrying a tray on which objects in flower-sprigged china clinked furtively, although he was walking as evenly as he could manage.

"On the desk," President Harmony instructed.

She made the student stand in abeyance while she reviewed the tray's contents—coffee, two cups, sugar, creamer, cloth napkins, silver spoons. "Very well," she dismissed him. "Tom is a work-study student," she explained as he was making for the door. "Our tax money at work," she finished in a whisper as the door was closing. She got busy serving herself as Fred continued.

"... me pretending to be a member of the faculty. It means I'll be wasting a lot of time. With students and faculty I have to back in to the questions I need answers to. For example, what kind of car does Morgan Flower drive?"

"Good heavens, I don't know," Harmony said. "I should think a Mercedes, wouldn't you? Green. Yes, that would suit him."

"That was a for instance," Fred said. "My point is, with everyone else around here…"

"We can't take chances. Can't let any trouble start," Harmony interrupted. "In terms, you asked, why do we assume he is not coming back? What *I* assume, since you ask, I won't *have* him back. After what I think he's done. I have no interest in finding him at all. The man, I could care less. The thing is the girl. Find the girl, that is the essential thing."

"Moving on, my point is," Fred said, "with everyone else, I have to pull my punches and not show an interest in anything beyond what a substitute teacher wants to know. On the other hand, with you I can be straight. There's twenty minutes before my first class starts, next door. Let's use it. When did you last see Morgan Flower?"

"You are sure you won't have coffee?" she asked, raising her cup. "It's my own service from home, naturally. The college has nothing appropriate. I'm petrified they'll break it. They are so…"

"How large was Missy Tutunjian's father's gift? This past year. He is said to be a significant contributor."

"The treasurer would have that," President Harmony said. "The treasurer is a board member."

"How large is your board? Who is on the board? How selected? Aside from the suspicion, is there evidence that Morgan Flower and this student had a sexual relationship? Who knows? Who knew? What is the school policy about such relationships? How does Flower get along with his colleagues? Where is his personnel file? I want to see it. Missy Tutunjian's records. I want the name of her roommate, the address…"

The telephone rang. Harmony pressed a button, told it, "I am in conference," and pressed the button again.

Chapter Thirteen

"We don't need all this hoo-hah," Harmony interrupted. "What are you thinking? What we want and need is simple and straight-forward." She gazed at Fred severely across the top of her flowered china cup. "Find that girl. Deal with it. Deal with her. Find her and report back to me. She must be protected, before…"

"My questions continue," Fred said evenly. "There was a time when Flower did not work here. Then he did. How did that change come about? What's his prior history? I want the address of your predecessor, the director who was fired last fall. Also your director of admissions—you have one?"

"Not presently."

"I'll talk to the old one. Your receptionist…is all that business done by what you call work-study students?"

"We had a disagreement with the former receptionist," President Harmony said. "She had been here for many years, and the variety and intricacy of the position…old wood…you understand."

"No, but maybe I will when I talk with her. What else? I'll take a look at the books."

"The library? We have no…"

"The finances. What comes in, what goes out. I'll let you know."

"This is unheard of," Harmony protested. "Working for me you are in no position to make conditions."

Fred said, "Pushing on: you, as chairman of the board and acting director—president as you call it—what are the terms and conditions of your office? Are you paid? How much? What..."

"This is outrageous!"

"Yes," Fred said. "My first class is about to start. I don't want to be late. Bad way to start. I'll stop back at lunch, whenever that is, and get started with your answers. You'll think of other things, too, that will help."

He left the office before she could reply.

The students gathered in Stillton B looked up at Fred with a hostility tempered only by indifference. Stillton Hall proved to be a long, low frame building, one story high, under a peaked roof high enough to contain a garret. A hallway running along the entire front of the building would seem a waste of space, except that it gave a place, this damp morning, for students to congregate around the lockers assigned to them there.

Fred's arrival had been at close to eight-thirty, the supposed start of class. At that hour a variety of students was still milling about the corridor, conversing in small groups, talking on cell phones, pulling material out of lockers or, just generally, putting off the moment of entering either Fred's Stillton B, or Stillton A next to it, where Meg Harrison's figure modeling class was supposed to be meeting.

The big room itself, Stillton B, was oddly unprepared for any exercise that carried the title *Intro to Lit*. Redolent of turpentine, paint thinner and mediums, and marked with streaks of paint on exposed sinks and surfaces, its furniture was notable for what wasn't there—anything like a desk or chair. Sturdy metal easels were bunched together against one wall, to either side of the big sinks. A back wall, along the longest side, was all windows whose lower halves were masked with a material that would discourage and disappoint neighborhood boys. A third wall—more easels and some tall stools—had at its center closed sliding doors behind which, from the gabble and clatter of industry that issued from the far side, Meg Harrison's figure modeling class was in progress. At the center of Fred's classroom a heavy square platform, a foot high, was festooned with stools and drapes in varied colors. A plastic bowl of discouraged fruit sat on an orange cloth there, and beside that a pinned paper notice "Do not move. MH."

In a more or less random circular pattern around this platform, Fred's students began to sit on simple, squareish home-made looking contraptions like no other furniture in the known world. Each was basically a bench, not quite large enough for two people, and with the leg at one end extended upward to a height that made it seem a back rest, except that the students tended to be sitting astride and resting their arms across these uprights. There might be as many as twenty people, drifting in, getting settled, finishing their conversations, taking out pencils or charcoal with which to sketch on the tablets some carried—the only sign that anyone had come to class with paper, of any kind, for any purpose.

Fred stood in front of the model stand—that was what it must be, but with the model absent—and started, "I guess we've all kind of been thrown to the wolves. Imagine if we had to use the bathrooms Emily Dickinson was used to." A mild incredulity tinged the indifference that mitigated the general hostility. "Like anything else that started over a hundred years ago—plumbing, railroads—there's lots of room for improvement. Where's Missy Tutunjian?"

The students stared and mumbled to themselves or to each other until a young man in ripped jeans and a streaked sweatshirt challenged, "Who are you?"

"The guy noticing that nobody in this so-called lit class seems to be carrying a book," Fred said. "What do you do with Morgan Flower, sing? I don't care. I'm here. He's not. I expected to see Marci. You all know her. Moonlights at the Stillton Café."

"Marci Patenaude," two of the females agreed, but talking to each other in undertones. Everyone looked around the room the way that's learned in high school, to establish a fictive communal ignorance and putative innocence.

Fred said, "If it was my class, and it's not, I'd say the way you understand a book, a novel, like *Moby Dick,* is by the end, figure out who's left? Who's missing. If this was a book we'd count three people missing anyway, and ask how come? Missy, Marci, Morgan Flower. Who hates them? Are they in China? Dead? Sick? Kidnapped? Lazy? Asleep? Do they think it's Wednesday?

"But pushing on, since it's not my class—or we'd, if we really wanted to find out, talk to Missy Tutunjian's roommate or—but I don't have much time. Since Emily Dickinson's day we've made the toilets better, we've improved the railroads, let's see what we can do with Emily's poems.

"Here's the assignment. While you work on it I'll talk to you one at a time, see where we are. Here's the assignment. Take any poem by Emily Dickinson. Find your books, share them, whatever. Copy the poem. Write it again making it better by subtracting six words. Write it again, making it better by adding six words. Write it again, making it better by removing twelve words and substituting twelve different words. For extra credit write an extra stanza of your own and stick it in somewhere. Make it so much like one of Emily's that we can't tell—A stanza is one of those blocks of lines, usually four lines in Emily's poems—that we can't tell which is the fake. Right." He looked at his watch. "Get started.

"At the same time we'll begin getting acquainted."

He motioned to the woman who had flinched when he mentioned Missy Tutunjian's roommate.

Chapter Fourteen

The young woman rose, gave a brief, inquiring look at the girl next to her, and pulled from the back pocket of her jeans the copy of Emily Dickinson that she had been sitting on. She looked to Fred the question whether she should also gather up her canvas bag. Fred shook his head and gestured, then led the way, to the corner farthest from the sounds of the neighboring classroom, and cleared a space amongst the easels, next to the sink.

The student following him was tall and pink, with curly red hair both short and unkempt. She was pretty in a distracted way. As she approached, her colleagues were either finding their books among their belongings, or easing closer to people who had them or—a few of them—drifting toward the door that would lead them to their lockers or toward escape.

"Let's grab a couple of these things," Fred suggested, laying hold of one of the unfamiliar objects of furniture. "What do you call them?"

"Horses. I don't know why," she said. "The neck, maybe." She stroked the high side.

"Or it's translated from French," Fred suggested. "Easel is *chevalet* and a *cheval* is a horse. Come to think, easel means donkey in some language, maybe Dutch.

"I'm Fred."

The horses were positioned with their high ends close to each other. "Susan," she said, sitting astride her horse and crossing her arms on the high end. Her shirt was of a heavy green, almost military twill, and a black cotton vest with brass buttons bibbed the copious breasts.

Fred sat and crossed his arms. "When you draw, I guess the drawing board is supported on the neck of the horse?"

"One end. The other end goes here," Susan said. She pointed toward the dark line across her thighs where a continual rain of particles of charcoal must fall while she was working, drawing.

"What's the hardest thing you're doing? The hardest class this year?"

"So far nothing's been easy," Susan said. "First you think, heck, it's art, how hard can that be? Then it's six hours drawing one thing and getting it wrong a hundred ways, after you get started. Then they grade you. Can you believe it? A grade on a drawing? Can you believe I flunked a drawing of a cube first term? I couldn't believe it. A cube. Six sides but the most you can possibly see at one time is four of them and mostly it's three unless it sits on one point. I couldn't believe it. I flunked it."

"So that's the hardest thing?"

"No. Jesus, that was only the wakeup. No, the hardest thing is what she's making us do now."

"She, meaning Meg Harrison?"

"Right." Susan nodded. She fiddled with her Laurel Poetry Series *Emily Dickinson.*

"Yes?" Fred prompted.

"You mean, the assignment? We all have to do it. The second semester's life drawing, see. You come in, you draw from the model, Harrison sneaks around and tells you what's wrong. But the hard thing's the homework. We have two months. Each person has to draw a nude self-portrait, life size."

"It would be a problem just getting the paper," Fred said.

"There's nothing about it that isn't a problem," Susan said. "Where do you do it, how do you do it, can you find a mirror that big? Some of the people, especially the guys, are shy about, you know. And also, too…"

"Seems to me…is there any way you and Missy can help each other? Being roommates…"

"How do you know that?"

"Wild guess, but not really," Fred said, "Since I happened to notice you when I…did you say two months? One drawing, two months?"

"We started two weeks ago. It's like one of the guys keeps saying, you feel like such an idiot when you're only wearing a pencil."

"I can't see Emily Dickinson doing it, that's true," Fred said. "So you got started already?"

"Taking turns. We just have the one mirror, on the closet door. No way could we work at the same time. There's no room. Then the paper's so big, and the plywood it's on, just it's no picnic trying to see around it, or move it."

"So she's serious," Fred said.

"Sure. Who? Don't you want to talk to the next person?"

"Meg Harrison," Fred said. "I mean, she's serious?"

"Her and all the rest of the teachers," Susan said. "The studio teachers."

"You mean Flower…"

"How can you tell? English lit is bullshit. I mean, no offense…"

"Thanks. I'll remember, Susan. You'll want to get started. Give me your last name so I can mark you present."

The intensity of labor being exhibited in the room was a good deal more serious than anything Fred's initial impression had hinted at. These characters could work if they were engaged. Fred checked Susan Muller's name on the list he had copied from Morgan Flower's class record book, and called a name he chose at random, "Arthur Geekas." When that produced a candidate, he proceeded.

By nine-thirty, a reasonable picture of the place was forming. The students, though naïve, were serious and by no means cynical, as they might be if they found themselves in one of the elite schools. Generally speaking, they gave evidence of an eager optimism that made them seem unspoiled by the boundless trivia of urban semi-culture; as if they, too, despite whatever up-to-date gadgets they might carry, were stuck, like the town of Stillton, somewhere in the late nineteenth century. They had likes and dislikes among the faculty but none expressed doubt about the integrity of the program. Morgan Flower, though not admired, did not seem to be hated. If there was a thing going between him and his student, Missy Tutunjian, nobody would drop a hint of it—not surprising, anyway, on such brief acquaintance.

At nine-thirty a student Fred now knew as Randy raised his hand and said, "There's usually a break by now."

"Sure," Fred agreed. Maybe coffee existed somewhere. "Fifteen minutes?"

Fred joined the students strolling into the hall. "I'm taking orders," Randy said.

"I've got my bike. I'll be back in five minutes." He took Fred's order, and his money.

Fred wandered down the hall, giving his students some room. The double doors of Stillton A opened as he reached them. Meg Harrison, pushing through, yelled at Randy's retreating back, "Large. Cream and sugar." The studio behind her smelled of fresh earth.

"Come on in," she invited. "We don't break for another ten minutes."

Within the big studio students were standing, each at a private raised stand two feet square, on which a metal armature—the room held a forest of them—had been shaped to repeat the structural core of the woman who stood on the model stand at the room's center. She was twisted, with her arms clasped behind her head. She was no longer wearing the apron that said *Stillton Café*.

Chapter Fifteen

"That's my student," Fred said. "Marci belongs in my classroom."

A pinkness suffused the model. Without moving her head, she protested, "We didn't think you'd show."

"We'll talk when you break," Fred said. He turned to Meg Harrison. "That setup you have in the middle of my classroom. It doesn't bother Flower? I didn't move it, but I can tell you it's in the way."

"Most of them really need the money," Meg Harrison said.

"I don't haul students out of your class to do something for me," Fred continued.

The students, looking from the model to their work, applied small gobs of clay with their fingers, studied the result, then added or subtracted, or scraped at their figures with a variety of tools. Without exception, they listened for Meg's reply.

"If you don't give this girl some buttocks," she told the nearest student, taking a brisk slap at the relevant portion of the form, "no way in the world can she twist her shoulders. It's all connected. Feel it yourself. Twist the same way. Go up and look at Marci. Come back and feel it. Get some yeast in the dough."

The student wiped his hands on the towel at his waist and went to examine the model.

"Let's take it outside," Meg Harrison suggested, turning and leading the way into the corridor and outside. She called back over her shoulder, "Five minutes, Marci."

Outside, the students smoking in the damp chill of the morning drew aside to give them room—but not so much room as to miss anything that might develop. "The regular model called in sick yesterday," Meg said. "Marci is about the right size and shape to take her place. Who knew you were coming and, if you did, who knew you cared?"

Randy appeared, on his bike, with an elaborate construction that allowed him to carry a couple dozen cups of coffee. He studied the labels on their lids and began to distribute them.

"Meaning you assumed or knew Morgan Flower wouldn't show this morning," Fred said.

"Meaning if Morgan Flower showed, he either wouldn't know or wouldn't give a shit. So Marci had a chance to earn some cash. She needs it. And she's a good model. Thanks, Randy." She and Fred accepted their coffee, and Meg paid for hers. "So when you told me last night that you were taking Flower's classes, I gave her a call."

"And I'm not happy about it," Fred said. "As long as she's my student."

"I hear you. So mark her absent," Meg said.

Marci came outside, wrapped in a beaten-up red corduroy bathrobe, and wearing plastic thong slippers. Randy appeared and gave her the final cup. "I'll get the assignment from someone," Marci told Fred.

"Fine. Except I'm talking with each of the students also," Fred said. "While the rest work on the assignment."

"Talk now," Meg Harrison said. "I won't get in your way."

"We'll use the classroom. If Marci's late, you'll understand," Fred said.

Marci, following him, muttered, "Tug of war. My parents divorced. I know all about it." She sat side-saddle on the horse Fred designated and started, "Last night, when we happened to talk, I hadn't decided—thought I might call Harrison back again and say—but then—please don't mark me absent."

"I thought Flower didn't care."

"He doesn't. But he still marks you absent. If he notices."

Fred pulled the class list he had made out of his shirt pocket and placed a check mark by her name. "You are present," he assured her. "Or we couldn't be talking. You're holding a broom in yours?"

"My what? Oh, you saw? How? No. Last night. You heard me. Talking. The big drawing. The nude. Obviously, and that's so obvious. So I got a broom and I'm holding it like "present arms." It's harder than I thought. You have to try to remember what your arms and hands are doing. It was a mistake."

"So, then, is Missy Tutunjian doing a modeling gig for some other class?" Fred asked. "I called her name. She didn't answer."

Students were trickling back into the room and settling into their places again. Marci checked the band of white skin on her left wrist. Fred pushed on, "Do you know? I'm trying to learn who's who and who's here."

"There's some in the class, it seemed like, when Harrison made the assignment, the big self-portrait nude, seemed like they'd never been naked before. The guys especially, like in case we were going to come out with rulers, you know. It isn't hard, really, I mean, there's the psychology, but after that, and then, but, then, as I say, with some people it's like they've never been that way and they're, not even by themselves, and so, but, basically. Missy is one of those. If you were a prude when you started, by this time in the first year it's not easy to still be one, but Missy is. She even tried to make Harrison make an exception, couldn't she pay her roommate to model for her instead, but Harrison wouldn't. 'If there's something funny about you, fudge it,' Harrison said. 'That's what art means,' is all she'd say. And so she pretty much had to. Missy."

"Why do you think Emily Dickinson writes about death so much?" Fred asked.

"Besides, there's no other classes today that use models," Marci said. "Otherwise there's first year drawing. Figure modeling. Third year painting. Sometimes fourth-year. That's the works. Printmaking, they could but they don't, don't ask me why. I guess they're so taken up with the inks and the presses and the rest of that mess. It's a whole other world over there, but it looks like fun. It's what I might…"

"Gotcha," Fred said. "Emily. Death. She goes on and on about it. In fact she won't shut up. How come?"

"Maybe she thinks if she keeps telling herself, she'll finally believe it. Like Christmas, only worse. I have to go back in there. Really."

Fred nodded her release. A few students waved her good-bye in a friendly way. "Later, Marci," Randy said.

The group was already tight, just after the few months that had passed since classes started in September. A small town in a small town in a small town.

"Let's see how we're doing," Fred proposed to the class as the door opened and Abe Baum, in full business regalia, looked in and beckoned.

"I'm teaching," Fred said.

"You are trespassing," Baum countered.

Chapter Sixteen

"This is private property."

"Interesting development," Fred said, strolling toward the source of the interruption.

"Trespassing on private property. Get out or we throw you out," Baum said.

Fred turned to the class and spread his arms wide. "What would Emily Dickinson do?" he asked. "Keep working. You know what you're doing." He more or less shoved Abe Baum into the hallway and closed the door. Behind them the classroom listened.

"You have ten minutes," Baum said.

"Self-styled President Harmony finds her feathers ruffled?" Fred asked.

"Out!"

"What do you want?"

"You on your way to Boston."

"You want things quiet, you said. It may already be too late. This place is ready to blow, never mind the little problem you brought me in for. One call to Fox News, it's all over."

"Add the threat of blackmail to trespassing," Baum said. "You're suggesting..."

"I'm suggesting come off the cowboy act, which you don't have the balls for anyway, and let's walk over to President pro-tem Harmony's office and work out something. Because, my friend, you are not going to run me out of town."

Abe stroked his necktie. "You're making trouble," he said. "*Finding* trouble. There's more. I smell it everywhere," Fred said. "So far I'm reserving judgment. Come on. We sit down with Harmony, see where this goes next."

When Fred led Abe Baum into the office Harmony said, "Later," into the phone and hung up. "Well?" she demanded.

"I'll use the desk," Fred said, sitting on a corner of it and moving a vase of flowers aside to make room. "Take a chair, Abe. Here's what I propose."

"I make the proposals in this room, at this desk," Harmony started.

"You're making a move for accreditation," Fred pushed on. "Even before this mess you suspect, between a missing teacher, male, and his missing student, female, even without this you're in trouble. I've been here a few hours. If I can spot this, and I know blame all about whatever the accreditation honchos do, I know you've got problems.

"Item: You lost your old director or you fired him, or her, I don't know which. Item: the chairman of the board is filling in, and are you looking for a replacement? Item: you have no admissions director. No admissions means no school. Q. E. D. And during class time you don't even have a student at the receptionist's desk. Item:…"

Abe Baum broke in, "I'll call the officers to remove this man. Trespassing, public nuisance, hell, Liz, for all I know he's already started molesting students."

"And I can tell there's not much agreement between the academy's board and administration (such as it is) and the students and faculty," Fred persisted.

"The faculty has been stirred up," Liz Harmony announced. "That's one reason…"

"That's been dealt with. It's being dealt with," Abe Baum interposed.

President Harmony frowned and pursed her lips as if seeking an appropriate place to spit.

"What are they doing, threatening to stop shopping at the company store?" Fred asked. "It's not enough you keep your faculty barefoot and pregnant; you want them to love you too?"

"The faculty is nothing to you," Abe Baum growled.

"Wrong. I have the honor to have been appointed to the faculty of Stillton Academy of Art. To date it is the high point of my academic career, and I take the position seriously. Whatever is going on here, it's more than a missing teacher and a missing student. I said I had a proposal. You might as well listen, since I'm not going away."

"We are listening," Harmony said. Fred's looming presence on the corner of her desk had caused her to edge her chair back.

"The first thing is, look like you want me here," Fred said. "I've gotten you upset. Fine. Forget it. You gave me a job, I'm doing it. But my hands are tied. I can't move. As a mere member of the faculty, there's too much I can't get next to. If I'm going to find out where that student is, and Morgan Flower, supposing they are together—and I don't buy the double suicide by the way; it's too easy—here's what we do.

"There's a faculty meeting this afternoon. You introduce me as—I'm teaching, yes—but my real function is, I'm a trouble shooter, an independent eye, here in disguise. My real mission is to study this place inside and out and tell you if it makes sense to go ahead with accreditation or, if not, what you should do instead."

"You said yourself you don't know a thing about…" Harmony objected.

"I'll handle that. You whistled and I came to you. I'm here. I don't like it. You don't like it. Still, I'm not going. Not for a week.

"What you'll say is, I have your go-ahead to look anywhere, ask any questions, look at whatever I can find, and all with the blessing of the powers that be."

"It's unheard of," President Harmony said, not for the first time. "Abe, it was a crazy idea to bring in a stranger. I want him gone."

"It might not be as bad an idea as Fox News," Abe Baum reminded her. "It's quiet so far."

"What time does the faculty meet?" Fred said.

"Step outside. I'll confer with my client," Abe Baum said. "I'll call you. Don't leave the reception area."

"Hell, I can answer the phone," Fred said. "Good Morning. Stillton Academy of Art. Where is everyone?"

The previous receptionist had evidently been of ample girth, and inclined toward comfort. Fred sat in her padded swivel desk chair and considered the typewriter that should, by this day and age, have been a computer. The bottom desk drawer had files labeled *Admissions, Maintenance, Alumni, NEASC, Bills Pending, Personnel, Student Records, Class Syllabi...*"

"Who could care?" Fred asked. "Who in the name of God could want to know all this?" The file marked *Personnel* was empty. The phone rang. Fred picked up the receiver and told it, "Stillton Academy," and nothing happened. Lighted buttons on the console blinked in a meaningless way. He punched one and, though it ceased blinking, it produced no voice in his ear.

Abe Baum put his head through the door. "We'll talk," he said.

Chapter Seventeen

Liz Harmony demanded, "Close the door."

Fred stood inside it. "My class," he started.

"Stop playing games," Abe Baum cut him off. "We made a mistake. We see that. Getting you involved. Taking the advice of an associate we had understood…this was our mistake…that…"

The phone rang. President Harmony suppressed it with a button.

"How do you know which one to push?" Fred asked.

"…you were willing to volunteer your time. Busy man like yourself. *Pro bono*. But why should you?" Abe Baum drove on. "Why work for nothing? Stillton Academy means nothing to you. Why should it? We appreciate all you've done. The offer is ten thousand dollars, with our thanks."

"Mighty generous, considering the place is on its way down the toilet," Fred said. "For one week's teaching?"

"With the understanding that you pack your bags now and leave," Harmony added.

"I'll stay with my proposal," Fred said.

"Liz, let me handle this." Abe Baum gestured to close off the argument that was coming to Liz Harmony's lips. "Fifteen."

Fred leaned against the inside of the office door and put his hands in his pockets. "You're bidding against yourself. If I had time it would be fun to see how high you'd go. Don't misunderstand the situation here. I don't work *for* you. I don't work against you either. Simply because I am here, I have become part of the equation. Your offer is interesting but not attractive. I'll be at that faculty meeting. Talk it over. Either introduce me according to the outline I gave you, Ms. Harmony, or else—it might be easier—I'll introduce myself to my new colleagues and explain what's going on. Don't make other offers or suggestions. I get confused."

He strode out before his companions could interpose another theme. In any case, neither of them seemed to have anything to say.

Intro to Lit period had run out. The students had decamped, taking with them any efforts they might have made to carry out his assignment. Meg Harrison's students were smoking outdoors or wandering the hallway or taking advantage of an extended break. Fred walked into the studio. It was a friendly thing to be surrounded by so much concentrated effort.

"May I?" Fred asked Meg. "I'd love to see what your students are doing."

Meg's earlier hostility was, for the moment, put aside. "If you want."

Because each of the figures in progress was the same size, roughly two feet tall, each made of the same gray clay, and each representing the entire standing figure, it was possible to appreciate how differently the individual students saw, or real-ized, the same object.

"And because it's three-dimensional, it's no excuse they see her from different angles," Meg said. "Since they can damned well move around and see what happens from all the other angles." She was following him. Suspiciously? Never mind. Whatever.

A couple of barrels of damp clay stood in a corner by the sinks. Individual supplies of clay that the students had taken for their individual use were clumped on their modeling stands, keeping pliable under damp cloths, next to the works in progress.

"The first two weeks of the pose, they do the armature. The metal skeleton that supports the flesh. If the armature is off the proportions are wrong and you can kiss the rest good-bye. Everyone's going to have trouble with the arms. You'll see. Well, no, you won't, but more than half will likely fall off in the firing if we get that far."

Fred had stopped next to an effort to which not much clay had yet been applied. The metal rods represented the model's central, skeletal support. "Could make a person think Giacometti," he remarked. "Except it hasn't been elongated to the point where gravity seems to be an afterthought. So you have a kiln."

Meg gestured with a nod in the direction of the sea, back beyond the studio windows, toward a large dilapidated shed. "The big grinder to prepare the clay, also," she said. "Sure. The ones that are good enough get fired," she said. "Propane. I built the kiln myself. For my own stuff as well."

"I'd like to see it," Fred said. "Your work."

Meg responded, "I'll get Marci rounded up. Otherwise these kids take the excuse to fuck around."

Fred said, "That President Harmony. Does she care if Stillton Academy lives or dies?"

"Who's asking?" Meg said. "It depends who's asking."

Her students were trickling in again, approaching their own work or looking at others'. Marci appeared, putting down her coffee cup and shedding her robe onto the floor as she stepped up to her pose again. "I got the assignment," she told Fred. Meg started to adjust the placement of her feet and the degree of twist to her back.

"*Lives and Loves of the Artists,*" Fred told Meg. "Can you believe it? I'd better get in gear."

Word had gotten around. Aside from Marci and Missy Tutunjian, there had been seven students absent from *Intro to Lit,* as Fred had learned when he talked with them individually. But *Lives and Loves*—that's what the students called the course—was missing only one, as Fred learned when he read out the class list. "Not to find out if you're not here so I can hurt you," he said, "but since I don't know much about what's going on."

A number of the names were of Greek, or French, or Portuguese origin. Descendants of fishermen, most likely. If a person had either the time or the inclination, it would be interesting to know…

"How do you folks expect to make your living?" Fred asked. "Just a question that popped up in my mind. Rubens. If you asked him when he was twenty years old, let's say, how would he answer?"

The question achieved a blank stare of varied disinterest or intensity.

"Because I hope you know," Fred said, "most people who make art do not make a living at it. Take van Gogh. Without the rich brother…moving on…did these people promise you, when you were done, you'd be able to make a living as an artist?"

A male student broke the silence that Fred allowed to extend until it became obvious that he wasn't going to let his audience off the hook. "They didn't even promise we'd get a lover, as an artist," he said. "Anyone here knows you're on your own."

"Unless you're Design," a female added.

"Graphic Design," another explained. "Posters, packaging, book covers, illustration, CD covers, that."

"Commercial." The general agreement was not enthusiastic.

"OK. *Lives and Loves of the Artists*," Fred said. "That's somebody's idea of a course and I'm not anybody's idea of a teacher, so it evens out. Where I come from, I don't care who it is—Gauguin, Rembrandt, Audubon—when I look at what the artist made, what I want to know is, what does this guy want? Figure that out, the rest starts falling into place. Maybe. At least it's a start. Beyond enough to eat and a dry place to sleep, what does Michelangelo want? Maybe the work tells you. The guy is long dead. We can't ask him. Make it easier, forget artists for a minute, as an example—start from what you know—you've been with him two years—what does Morgan Flower want?"

Chapter Eighteen

"You're a friend of his?" It was the same male student who had broken the silence earlier.

Fred shook his head. "Sorry. I kind of jumped into the middle. My name is Fred. Since Morgan Flower's out, I'm filling in, but I don't know him. What I'm really doing is looking around, getting to know the place. I have nothing for Morgan Flower and nothing against him. He's a for instance. Like Rembrandt, where you look at the paintings as evidence and draw some conclusions—I'm guessing—is that what you do in this class?"

"Xerox copies," somebody said.

"Not even in color mostly," from another voice.

Fred went on, "I'm only saying, let's take a guy you actually know, look at the evidence you have, and figure the guy out backwards, starting with the main questions. So. Once again, what does Morgan Flower want?"

"Coffee."

"A folded tarp to sit on.

"The guy hates to get dirty."

And they were off.

The problem was, Fred's correspondents did not know a great deal, and they were most reticent about what he most wanted to hear: for example, the teacher's relations with his female students. The conversation turned, almost randomly, goofy, enthusiastic, poignant, and even—despite the hard world these students were heading into—even optimistic, as if the armor of artistic endeavor was bound to see them through.

Apparently Flower was not one of those teachers who made up for other deficiencies by filling out the time with irrelevant facts concerning his own life and loves. Nobody even knew where he'd been born.

By the time they were done it was lunch time. Fred dismissed the class without making the assignment that occurred to him: Write a list of the twenty movies Rubens would like most. The twenty he would hate most. Say why.

What Fred knew now about Morgan Flower was the make and color of his car, the fact that he had worn a necktie the first day he had appeared in class two years ago, and never again; that occasionally he mentioned the movie *The Wizard of Oz* when searching for examples for some point he was raising, that he brought a blue tarpaulin with him to sit on, after one bad experience with paint.

In short, nothing useful, and nothing that seemed remotely relevant. Education? Place of birth? Age? Marital status? Favorite color? Zero.

The students wandered off. There would be an hour before his final class started—the three-hour session to which Morgan Flower had given the name *Writing About Your Problems.* Fred had started toward home and a sandwich when Meg Harrison caught up with him. "Some of us get together at Bee's Beehive," she said. "If you care to join us."

"Thought I might get away for a bit," Fred confessed.

The weather was bracing, even invigorating, in a way that seemed hopelessly irrelevant to the matter at hand. The job he'd undertaken, or the project, or whatever it was, could not be done while he meandered around in tight circles in front of a passel of students, pretending to be something he wasn't. The teacher's life was constructed of acres of wasted time.

"But sure. Why not?" Fred said.

Wind, seagulls and salt air. Not far away was the regular clinking rattle of tackle against aluminum masts. The foghorn had shut up, since there was nothing left in the atmosphere to complain about. Meg walked quickly downhill toward the center of town.

"What happened to your former leader?" Fred asked. "Fired, I heard. True? What for?"

Meg said, "I pay no attention to art historians. They do their thing, I do mine. Never did. Don't give a shit. Nothing they say touches what I know or do."

"Gotcha," Fred said. "Lonely life."

"Not for me."

"For the art historians."

"Critics too," Meg said. "If you can tell the difference between one parasite and the next."

"I'm with you so far," Fred said. Central casting hadn't hired enough extras for this scene.

"Except one," Meg said. She stopped and put a long hand on Fred's shoulder to stop him. "Talking about—can't recall the name—about how art was taught in the Paris schools a century ago and more. It got my attention. 'The study of the nude in the classroom atelier is as common to an artist as are calisthenics to an athlete. As a subject to command the attention of even an unruly student, the human body is hard to beat. It is straightforward, complex, varied, compelling, amusing, and measurable. And it is a valuable teaching tool since it either does or does not translate believably from three dimensions to a two-dimensional plane. Its skin exhibits a surprising variety of colors in an excruciating sequence of almost indistinguishable shifts.'

"It's the only thing I ever memorized except some of *Oh captain, my captain,* for a school play that I can't forget now mostly because I forgot it then and I still have nightmares about it. When I'm awake I remember, not when I'm asleep."

The town, the movie set, seemed uncomfortable, as if nothing about it was quite real. Williamsburg or Sturbridge were made fake by the addition of inappropriate wealth. Did poverty lead to the same feeling of unreality? Shouldn't poverty feel more real than wealth? Of the mixed age groups on the sidewalks, most were students or of student age. There were next to no children other than a single baby being carried in a pouch across its mother's chest. Where would a child go to school? There couldn't be anything closer than fifteen miles.

"Curious town," Fred remarked. "It's almost *Lost Horizons* except with Yankees instead of Tibetans.

"Bee gives us a back room," Meg said. They'd reached the tiny center of the commercial area where Bee's Beehive, on the opposite side of the road from the Stillton Café, had been closed last night.

Inside was a single room, twenty feet square, where students sat at tables or at the counter behind which a stout woman in red stripes and an apron must be Bee. A jerk of her head, crowned with white curls, motioned Meg and her guest toward an archway back of the counter, which led to a small room where four people sat around a table. A shuffling among them made two spaces.

"Stay away from the meatloaf," a man said, standing and holding out a tentative hand.

"This is Fred," Meg told the group. "He's with me but I can't vouch for him."

Wary introductions proceeded. The warning against meatloaf had come from Bill Wamp, a man of perhaps forty-five who taught second- and fourth-year painting. He was dressed more or less like Farmer Jones, in a red plaid shirt and bib overalls clean enough to have been purchased yesterday. He was heavyset and graceful, red faced and balding. And loud.

Arthur Tikrit, a small and dapper man whose fingers seemed never to be at rest, as if he were secretly tormented by musical composition, was responsible for first-year two-dimensional design, color theory, and illustration. Barbara 'I'm Bobby' Ballatieri did printmaking. She was in the middle of a speech, "No way can you call what we do here sculpture. Clay, plaster, fiberglass. That's it. You want to work in steel? Head for Kansas City or L. A. I'm not kidding. Don't waste your time here. We can't help you." Bobby held up her sandwich, declaring it "chicken salad and not half bad. On rye." She cut a frail blonde figure, in jeans and a black denim shirt.

Slowest to rise, slowest to hold out a hand, slowest to sit again, was Philip Oumaloff, who resembled a caricature version of that caricature of Brahms: thickset, square, and copiously hedged with fat white hair and beard.

"I am emeritus," Oumaloff proclaimed.

Chapter Nineteen

"Filling in for Morgan Flower," Fred said. "Temporary. So temporary I am almost evanescent, like a fairy's fart. But the school intrigues me. How the devil do you do it? I can't think of a more endangered breed."

"Smooth," Philip Oumaloff said. He managed to deliver the single word in a thundery warning rumble.

"Phil knows the place better than anyone," Bill Wamp said. "He's been around for—what?—fifty years?"

"Phil goes back beyond Basil Houel, anyway. Ask him," Bobby Ballatieri said.

The stout woman from behind the counter put her head in. Meg told her, "BLT on whole wheat. Ginger ale. To go. Thanks, Bee."

"I'll try the chicken salad, with coffee," Fred told her. "Bread as close to pumpernickel as you can get."

Meg slipped out of the room, leaving Fred stranded with his new companions.

"We will talk of the weather," Phil Oumaloff decided. The others in the remaining group showed no sign of circumventing his will, but nobody volunteered an appropriate weather-related gambit. They sat in awkward silence until Bee brought Fred's coffee in a thick white diner mug.

Fred said, "Why would the acting president offer me ten thousand dollars not to take Morgan Flower's classes for a couple of days?"

"It has been raining, but may clear," Phil Oumaloff intoned.

"So you say," Bobby Ballatieri challenged.

"It's a company town, is it?" Fred asked. "Everyone lives here?"

Bill Wamp had taken a mouthful from his plate of fish and chips. Still, he was able to say, "Nevertheless, what we experience today would have been, in former months, very possibly snow."

"Admittedly it's not the weather," Fred said. "But we could try a different neutral subject. Hypothetical. Say I want to dispose of a body around here, how would I do it?"

Even so, the conversation did not go well.

"What I want is a tour of the campus," Fred told his writing group. Even those who had collapsed most firmly rose as if they had been stung. "No. No. A virtual tour," he amended. "Exercise. We do it from where you are. Walk me around the campus—you call it a campus? Hell, walk me around the town. But in writing. To hell with your problems."

He looked around the room. Briefly as he'd been in town, some faces were familiar. The rosy young man who'd laughed last night in the Stillton Café, about the Meeker Method—that had to be Tom Meeker. From the lapsed Rotarian look of him, he might not be cut from true administrative cloth. No, there was a better prospect.

"You're Steve, yes?" Fred said to the male who had been cooking and mopping in the kitchen of the Stillton Café the previous evening—"since anyone can do this who doesn't have his head up his own hind end, you be the one who says, at whatever interval you want to, 'Shift gears.' That means, for the rest of you, writing, change paragraph, change subject, cross the street, go back in time, whatever. But change something. Meanwhile you are giving me the reader all the information I need to understand this place. Like, for example, what's over our heads here?

"Meanwhile…"—he had recognized the student who, in the early morning before classes began, had been answering the phone at the receptionist's desk. Not-Tom, though President Harmony had insisted on calling him that. "Your name?"

"Peter Quarrier, Dr. Taylor."

"I'm Fred." To the class, "Sorry. It's not important. Let me be Fred. That's what I'm used to, if you don't mind. Peter, you're off the hook. In a way. But on another hook. What I want you to do—pretend I'm blind and lead me around the place telling me everything. What's what, what's where, who's who, what it looks like, what it used to be—so I can compare—and we'll be back in a couple hours. Steve, you know when the break is so you can signal that too."

"This means I'm not writing?"

"Like hell. Peter, let's move."

Peter stood, gathering up a knapsack and hoisting it to his shoulders.

The foghorn had started again, moving so insidiously into the atmosphere that the beginning of the sound's recurrence had not been noticeable. A thin rain, which might be no more than settling cloud, had obediently followed. Fred turned up the collar of his jacket.

"You want the applicant tour?" Peter asked as they set off, heading toward a neighboring building that looked the same as Stillton Hall.

"I will go crazy if you give me the applicant tour," Fred assured him.

"I thought so. We'll get out of the rain. I'll draw you a map, we can talk, I'll maybe give you a line on what you want."

"You've spent time in the service," Fred offered.

"Marines." Peter led the way around Stillton Hall and into the large shed Meg Harrison had indicated earlier. It gave the effect of a low barn in which a colony of nudists was engaged in hieratic contemplation of the ineffable.

"Harrison's work," Peter explained. "Don't touch anything." Harrison's figures, either life size or three-quarters, stood in frank and simple poses reminiscent of, perhaps, the archaic Greek. They were oddly symmetrical, especially for this day and age.

If a right arm was raised, the left was raised also, in almost the same gesture. They were both male and female, adult or young adult. One, her arms bent upwards so that her elbows reached the level of the top of her head, could have been intended as a caryatid, holding a roof up. There must be a dozen figures, all apparently transfixed with expectation of the second coming; maybe the third.

"How the devil does she move these things?" Fred asked.

"Fork lift. And very carefully," Peter said. Each figure stood on its own wooden skid. Though they differed markedly from one another in stance, body type, and features, and even in the way the surfaces were treated, they seemed kin. "She says, in here we are in Plato's cave," Peter explained, "which means something to her. Maybe to you."

"And she fires these? At this size?"

"We could. The kiln's big enough. But she mostly lets them dry out, makes molds from them, sends the molds to New York to be cast in epoxy or bronze or plaster or whatever. There, over there's, the machine to grind clay, and all. But you don't care about that. Let's sit."

He led the way to a workbench and shoved tools and debris aside until there was space for him to lay out the drawing pad he pulled from his knapsack. They hoiked a couple of stools over and sat.

"There are buildings here and there. Some you wouldn't find, like printmaking. Photography we don't have any more. I'll be drawing the map while we talk," Peter said. "In case someone wants to know what we're doing. But, like I say, you don't care about that."

"What *do* I care about, Fred asked.

"Harmony knows shit about what she's doing," Peter said. "Tom and I, we put her on speaker half the time, if nobody's around."

Chapter Twenty

"Problem is, most of the time I'm in class. Also she's gone a lot. She goes to lunch. That's what presidents do, she says, like she's about to be crucified. Then comes back half in the bag. Or doesn't come back, more like."

"I can't quite see her at Bee's Beehive," Fred said.

"Are you kidding? Mix with the natives? That would be unheard of, as she would say. She drives to meet friends in Salem or Marblehead or Beverly or one or two places in New Hampshire. Or Boston."

"She lives in Stillton?"

Peter laughed. While he talked he had been drawing a map that seemed to include the entire peninsula. He was confident enough of his work that he drew with a pen. "That would also be unheard of. Nobody lives in Stillton." Peter managed to sound like Liz Harmony when he said this: Liz Harmony confiding to friends, at a distance, after a bout of golf followed by a more ambitious round of whiskey sours. "She sometimes sleeps in the director's cottage—here," Peter put an X on one of the rectangles drawn along the shore, not far from what must represent Stillton Hall, the admissions building and the other classroom building Fred was aware of. Printmaking was blocks away, in its own little world as someone had said. And the academy owned other buildings here and there.

"Three or four nights a week she'll sleep in town. But she's Boston. So, but, anyway, the questions you threw at her. I liked those."

"I'll bet," Fred said.

"She wants us to call it the presidential manse," Peter said. "Has the kids clean it for her. Do her presidential dishes and toilets, everything. And then won't stop complaining that it's never right. Throws cocktail parties for her friends there and marks the bottles. You know. The most they can do is maybe switch the Chivas for Seagram's Seven. As long as she has the Chivas bottle and the liquid matches the mark…"

"She invites faculty?"

"You're kidding. She's got them paralyzed. She'll fire anyone she wants to, and they know it."

The presence of so many witnesses, Meg Harrison's brooding figures, fostered a sense of almost random conspiracy, and Peter dropped his voice. "Everyone's afraid. Even the ones who hate each other hate her worse. And they can't fight back, because nobody's contract is worth shit, and Harmony makes it clear she doesn't value a one of them. You're not happy? Leave. See if you can find another job teaching art. Economy like this one."

"Peter, how much did you hear this morning?"

"See, what it sounds like, nobody has a contract. Or. Well, everyone has a one-year contract that is worth shit. Harmony can renew it or not if she wants to, or if she wants to fire somebody's ass, she will, and let them sue. Good luck finding money to pay a lawyer to get the rest of your year's pay. Do you see what I mean?"

"You're third year, right?" Fred said. "No. Scratch that. What I mean to say, you've been here all this time? Since first year?"

Peter said, "The people you should talk to are Rodney Somerfest. The director until they fired him. He might talk. Forget the faculty. Even if you got them drunk they're all so scared…Rodney might talk to you. But who I'd try is Lillian. No question about it."

"Lillian," Fred said.

"She did admissions. Also reception. That's her chair I'm in before class, and after until five-thirty; sometimes at lunch. Unless it's Tom. Or there's another…"

"Where do I find Rodney? He's still in town? Or Lillian? She's around? What's her last name?"

"They paid Rodney off to take a hike. He's not here, obviously. Before he was canned he was in the director's cottage, before it turned into the presidential manse. A manse is like a house. You probably know. I didn't.

"Listen. I want to graduate. I want my diploma to be worth something. In fact, I want my diploma to be a degree. I can't afford to start again. I wouldn't have started here in the first place except—well, that's a long story. Half the kids…well, hell, they're young."

Fred said, "How do I locate these people?"

Peter hunched closer and whispered, "Everyone's running scared. She'll do anything she wants to. It makes no difference to her. She's a volunteer. She's willing to fire the whole faculty. I've heard her say so. You think she won't expel a work-study student if she thinks I'll make trouble for her?"

"Let's walk," Fred suggested.

"Then, scared as they are, she gets the faculty in to talk to her one at a time," Peter said, rising and rolling the map he had been making. "She whispers and looks around behind her and makes everyone think she knows something. She's—we'll go through the back." He started leading the way through the far side of the building. Once in the rain again, they heard the foghorn more clearly, felt the rain more precisely, smelled the salt air and the general marine decomposition, heard the screaming gulls craving the loneliness each felt to be its due. Silhouetted against the sea was a sort of small, square arched building of yellow fire brick, about the right size for a playhouse—"The kiln," Peter said. And next to it, an open shed for the forklift on whose seat an elderly man sat smoking the stump of a cigar.

"Milan," Peter said.

"Fred," Fred said, walking over to shake the old man's hand.

"What can I do for you?"

Peter, shaking his head almost imperceptibly at Fred, told the old man, "Fred's the new guy. Teacher. I'm giving him the tour."

"Nice day for it," Milan encouraged them, replacing the cigar stump afterwards. His dress was black jeans with suspenders under an open jacket of stained, faded canvas. He'd set his black sou'-wester hat aside on the forklift's gear shift. Big square head with mottled, weathered features, and a full head of hair gone gray. He blew smoke at them that hovered in the wet air, neither rising nor dispersing.

"He's in her pocket," Peter said once they were out of earshot. "Some people, if they don't want much anyway, and they already have it, they get their entertainment making trouble.

"Not that she's likely to fire him, if she even thinks about anybody that far down the line. Because who else knows how the lights work? And the furnaces, the water, the rest of it? Who fixes the toilet some asshole dropped clay in?"

Their walk was taking them in the direction away from the admissions and administration building. "Even though she went out for lunch, I feel like her office is watching all the time. Like Nazis in some movie about that war they had back then."

"You've seen combat?" Fred asked.

"Not to talk about."

Fred asked again, "How do I find these two people, Rodney Somerfest and Lillian—what's her name?"

Chapter Twenty-one

"You could ask Tom Meeker if you want to, but I wouldn't. He's a decent printmaker but he's a good-time boy. I wouldn't trust him. He'll do anything for a joke. Also I don't trust the girl at the desk right now," Peter said. "She's a part-timer, she's new, she's dumb, and she let Harmony scare her into dressing up like a secretary, even though she's a student. I'll get you the info later if I can. I mean, I *can*, but only if it's there. Krasik is her last name. I heard someone had seen her here in town."

They'd reached a headland from which it was possible to see the lighthouse through the wreathing veils of whatever this precipitation was—fog? Rain? Steam rising from the gray surface of an ocean that could barely bring itself to lift the occasional modest swell. The birds were louder, and more varied, here.

A silence developed while they watched the weather.

"Since I'm a veteran," Peter said after a few minutes, "I've been around more."

"You know where I'm staying?" Fred asked.

"Sure. Everyone does. If they care. Flower and that girl. The first-year student…" He let the opening extend.

"Right," Fred said finally. "I've heard about that. Is there anything to it?"

"Them together, you mean?" Peter asked. He lifted his shoulders. A bead of rain dropped from the tip of his narrow nose. "I'll go back to Stillton B now and write your assignment. I'll stop by this evening if I can get something for you. The map…" he gestured to the chest of the poncho under which he was carrying his earlier work…"I'll fill in some more. Fred, whatever you're here to do I figure it can't make things worse. This place goes up in smoke, I'm out three years, all that tuition, and my grant. So, whatever you're doing…" He turned and walked swiftly in the direction of Stillton B.

"Tell the gang to leave their work in the classroom where I can find it, in case I don't get back in time," Fred called. "Under a rock or something so it doesn't blow away."

Peter, without breaking pace, nodded his head and waved what could be construed as agreement.

At this point, going to Clay for information would be more infuriating than useful. The nearest public library must be forty minutes away and, in any case, unlikely to offer anything like privacy. A room with a telephone, and with a door he could close, would be a handy thing. Fred needed either a cell phone, which he could not yet bring himself to subject himself to, or a safe house with a phone.

Clayton's voice at the Mountjoy Street end of the line was, as usual, made up of equal parts courtliness, impatience, and reticence. Still, he admitted being there, being substantial, and being in reasonable health.

"Acting on what you might qualify as impulse," Fred told him, "I took a room at the Stillton Inn. I take it on faith that you're after something. I can't work from where they've put me."

"You are able to speak freely?" Clay asked. He rarely trusted a telephone, dismissing them with the dark suspicion, "It lets them know what we are thinking."

"Parker Stillton has telephoned, greatly upset," he continued. "That attorney who appeared with him, what was his name? Baum? Has also telephoned. He undertook to volunteer

true identity as a research librarian is not concealed. And
ow that you have your laptop with you—because I handed
you at the airport. So—do you have a pencil?"

Both a pencil and a burning desire to get back into the pool."

There's no rush," Fred assured her. "But see what you can
that will reduce my ignorance about the man I am replacing,
gan Flower. Stillton Academy of Art, obviously. Abraham
n, attorney at law. Parker Stillton we know. The sculptor
Harrison. I'll have some other names later but I can't recall
e I wrote them down. This Elizabeth Harmony who's pre-
ing to run the place. You've got all this?"

What are we looking for?" Molly asked. "You sometimes
up an awful load of irrelevant…"

Themes and convergences," Fred said. "Something's not
here. Beyond the missing people. I'm curious."

Give me a couple of days. I'm on vacation, remember?
ss—is it an emergency?"

No rush. I'd say if it were."

lso there's something on tonight Mom wants to watch with
ildren. Some Atlantis kind of program, but with pyramids.
e to be there to reinterpret Mom's interpretations."

nd Josephus Stillton," Fred remembered. "The guy who
d this operation back over a century ago. Who was he?
did he do? I'd look it up myself, but…"

now. And are you really teaching?" Molly asked. "Standing
front of a class and all?"

have to tell you, I'm taken by surprise," Fred said. "I really
ie kids. All that energy. I'd forgotten. They're serious.
e even optimistic and idealistic. They're…well, in short,
eserve much better…"

lly said, "Go on to your faculty meeting. I assume you
aring those academic robes?"

ot 'till graduation day. Given how long I was at Harvard,
think I qualify for a robe that hangs much lower than
ples."

directions and instructions until I informed him that I was in
conference and, in any case, not at liberty to shape events. I
allowed him to conclude that you are uncontrollable."

The hotel room was so plain and simple that it likely would
not make the set designer's cut for that imaginary movie about
Stillton. Fred had taken a single. It boasted a single bed with an
orange cover, a single window, a single chair, a single closet big
enough to hang a single damp jacket in, and a single bathroom
with toilet, sink, and shower. The floor was wood, and grainy
underfoot with ancient etched-in sand.

Most important was the single telephone on the exceedingly
functional table next to the bed.

"I don't have much time," Fred said. "You can get messages
to me at this number. If anyone's listening at the switchboard,
I don't care.

"I'm no closer to information concerning the missing teacher
and the missing student. But that's not your concern. Also I'm
not hoping for much cooperation from the powers that be, but
I'm pushing on. What interests me is the larger setup."

"Tell me," Clay offered. "But use as few nouns as you can
manage. It's nouns that give the game away."

Fred had pulled the somewhat comfortable chair over to the
window from which—the room was on the second floor—it was
possible to see Main Street with its desultory traffic. Was the
town's problem that many of the buildings were vacant for the
drear months? The rain had not stopped. Rather, each individual
droplet was sitting in the middle of the air, awaiting the advent
of the power of gravity.

"You know it's not my field," Fred said. "In fact, I am allergic
to academia. To me, academia always seems…"

"I know your views on the subject," Clay interrupted. "The
impressionable in pursuit of the inexpressible."

"Your line, not mine," Fred said. "Still. Here's my impression
of Stillton Academy of Art, based on less than a day's exposure.
It's a real con."

"Indeed. An illusion in pursuit of the irrelevant. Or—perhaps the reverse is more apt: the irrelevant in pursuit of an illusion. Yes, of course. Nevertheless, there must be something…"

"With the exception," Fred pushed on, "that it's like a house being sold by a crooked broker. The house is real enough—the students, the teachers, the classes—with the exception that it makes no sense to me that they teach two-dimensional design without giving the students access to computers—but that's their business. Where there's trouble is there's a disconnect between the people doing the work and the people running the place, or pretending to. The volunteers on the board and the present acting tyrant Elizabeth Harmony. Whether it's merely corporate stupidity or active hostility, I wouldn't bet a nickel on the academy's chance to survive."

"All this talk about accreditation?" Clay offered.

"Without accreditation, the place is sunk," Fred said. "That's for sure. What do I know? But even if you reached blindfolded into the colleges that have to supply these visiting committees, you couldn't hope to pull out nothing but dolts."

Clay cut in, "As you say, this matter does not concern us. Fortune has given us a presence where I want a presence. I want you to look at everything."

"Just filling in the context," Fred said. "If you want a sense of the relations between Stillton Academy and its governing powers, think a few Belgians in the Congo a century ago."

"There was considerable wealth in the Congo nonetheless," Clayton observed.

Chapter Twenty

It was necessary to bring Molly in from the
rented the same apartment each winter i
Unless you were willing to get into a rent
was nothing but the pool to do, other tha

"Wait a minute. I'll stand on the towel.
said.

"In that scarlet suit?" Fred asked.

"Never mind. Sam, get away from th
you, not before eight o'clock."

"This time of day, is there anythin
shows?" Fred said.

"He's hooked up the Nintendo Wii
Dad sent him, bless his little heart. Sam
Swim or read a book. OK, Fred. Have y
you can talk?"

Fred managed a speedy outline of
had brought him to the single room at
I'll have you know I am not the only
old lady. I saw her on the stairs. They
summer it gets more lively. Also when
has graduation. I'm racing. Have to ge

"To think that I would ever hear
Molly gloated.

"Moving on," Fred said, "Even
carpet, and wearing your most ineffab

"Lovely thought," Molly said. "I guess that does it for me." She finished her end of the conversation with a click.

The students in *Writing about your Problems* were still, and quite unaccountably, at work. Didn't they know enough to take advantage of the instructor's absence and make tracks? All this obedience, in persons old enough to vote, and rich enough to own matching shoes, was deeply disquieting. Molly accused Fred of projecting menace. "When people look at you," she'd say, "they tend to think of all the bad things they have done." Even so, what could Fred do to them? One or two of these students might really care about the matter so artificially put before them—but it was impossible that so many would willingly toe the line. Wasn't it?

How phrase the question?

It could wait.

Fred had timed his return for the end of the period, and made a point of sampling the students' efforts as they brought them to him. He let Peter know, quietly, that by eight o'clock he could be found at the Stillton Inn. "That gives you some privacy," he said.

"Gives everyone privacy," Peter pointed out. "Whatever you are doing. If you don't see me, assume I got nothing."

Peter left. The room was gradually emptied except for a single female student who seemed so engrossed in the task that she was not aware that her tribe had left her alone to face the hostile ministrations of the enemy. Simply in terms of mechanics, the business of writing required significant physical concentration. The students had nothing to sit on but their clumsy "horses". Their paper must be balanced on the drawing boards they propped either on their laps or, more frequently, on the horses' necks.

This student was so involved, Fred let her work. He sat on the model's platform, next to the bowl of last month's fruit, denting the blue and orange draperies and wrinkling the sign Meg had left. The silence in his classroom studio magnified the concluding clatter in Meg Harrison's Stillton A, next door, where students must be covering their work-in-progress with damp cloths and shrouding them in plastic, so that they would be malleable when they were next approached.

Without looking up, the student said, "I'm Emma. It's true. He's sleeping with her. I hope they get him."

Her voice was frank and matter-of-fact. She still didn't look up. "It was me last year," she said. She kept writing while she talked, as if either the writing or the talking was governed by a force outside her body. "Which, to me, it seems like, now, he's a collector. It's all here."

She smacked the tablet she was writing on with her left hand while the right continued its work.

Fred ran his eye down the class list. Emma. Only one Emma. Emma Rickerby.

"If you want to talk, or need to," Fred started.

"It's all here," Emma said. The tablet was white, lined paper. She stood, brushed the seat of her jeans absently, settled a russet knit wool sweater, and shook the full black hair, wisps of which had become tangled in her glasses while she was concentrating. She unfurled the paper that had been turned back while she wrote, leaving a clean title page showing, "Morgan Flower."

Chapter Twenty-three

"Give this to him," Emma said, dropping the tablet on the seat of the horse and walking out. The rosy student Fred had identified as Tom Meeker had been hovering in the doorway, as if hoping for a quiet private word with the teacher after class. He fell in beside her as she walked past, jerking her head as if to signal either, "We're going this way," or else, maybe more likely, "Leave me alone, for God's sake, would you?"

His seat in the class had been directly behind her.

There was too much to notice. Anything could signal something. Keep your eye on the matter at hand. Whatever it was Clay wanted, which was not whatever Parker Stillton and Abe Baum wanted, which was not, in turn, what they had claimed they wanted, yesterday, in Clayton's parlor.

But as long as he was here, Fred had to be doing something, and that might as well be to continue the wild goose chase he'd started with: the missing student and the missing teacher.

Emma had left behind her in the studio a faint dusting of particles of charcoal, and the strong scent of whatever musk women her age these days were using.

"You're sure your name isn't Rosetta Stone?" Fred asked. His first instinct had been to follow the student herself; but the tangible document she had left behind her took precedence and, in any case, should not be left unguarded. And whether or not it was to her taste, she wasn't alone. Fred made his way through the vaguely concentric jumble of horses until he reached the one Emma Rickerby had vacated. He picked up her tablet. He'd look into it later.

Are you kidding?

The first page was all caps, angry, angular, but even: the repeated message: **FUCK YOU.** Fred flipped through the pages. Emma showed a commendable consistency. Neither the hand-writing nor the message wavered or varied. Neither her speech nor her manner had seemed crazed—but this? Fred slipped the tablet into the midst of the uneven collection that was his reward for the afternoon.

Not only did the teacher's life involve hours of aggressively administered boredom in the classroom—he also had to carry it home with him!

"Still, you don't have to be sane to tell the truth," Fred said. "In fact…"

But it was time for the faculty meeting.

If you regarded Fred as a member of the faculty, and Fred did not, the faculty present numbered nine unless you regarded Phil Oumaloff as faculty, which Phil Oumaloff obviously did, in which case the number was ten unless you left Fred out.

The group was gathered, buzzing and whickering and making assorted sounds of non-verbal guttural distress, in what Meg identified as the board room—a small room with a large table that seemed to occupy the remainder of the first floor of the admissions building, where Liz Harmony's office was. Meg had caught up with Fred outside Stillton hall, wiping her hands and face on a rag she tucked into a back pocket of her jeans.

"Sorry to bug out like that. There was something…you make out all right with the gang of four?"

"If you mean the luncheon conference, I think you can safely say that we are none the wiser. Your work, on the other hand—what I saw of it—has real presence."

directions and instructions until I informed him that I was in conference and, in any case, not at liberty to shape events. I allowed him to conclude that you are uncontrollable."

The hotel room was so plain and simple that it likely would not make the set designer's cut for that imaginary movie about Stillton. Fred had taken a single. It boasted a single bed with an orange cover, a single window, a single chair, a single closet big enough to hang a single damp jacket in, and a single bathroom with toilet, sink, and shower. The floor was wood, and grainy underfoot with ancient etched-in sand.

Most important was the single telephone on the exceedingly functional table next to the bed.

"I don't have much time," Fred said. "You can get messages to me at this number. If anyone's listening at the switchboard, I don't care.

"I'm no closer to information concerning the missing teacher and the missing student. But that's not your concern. Also I'm not hoping for much cooperation from the powers that be, but I'm pushing on. What interests me is the larger setup."

"Tell me," Clay offered. "But use as few nouns as you can manage. It's nouns that give the game away."

Fred had pulled the somewhat comfortable chair over to the window from which—the room was on the second floor—it was possible to see Main Street with its desultory traffic. Was the town's problem that many of the buildings were vacant for the drear months? The rain had not stopped. Rather, each individual droplet was sitting in the middle of the air, awaiting the advent of the power of gravity.

"You know it's not my field," Fred said. "In fact, I am allergic to academia. To me, academia always seems…"

"I know your views on the subject," Clay interrupted. "The impressionable in pursuit of the inexpressible."

"Your line, not mine," Fred said. "Still. Here's my impression of Stillton Academy of Art, based on less than a day's exposure. It's a real con."

"Indeed. An illusion in pursuit of the irrelevant. Or—perhaps the reverse is more apt: the irrelevant in pursuit of an illusion. Yes, of course. Nevertheless, there must be something..."

"With the exception," Fred pushed on, "that it's like a house being sold by a crooked broker. The house is real enough—the students, the teachers, the classes—with the exception that it makes no sense to me that they teach two-dimensional design without giving the students access to computers—but that's their business. Where there's trouble is there's a disconnect between the people doing the work and the people running the place, or pretending to. The volunteers on the board and the present acting tyrant Elizabeth Harmony. Whether it's merely corporate stupidity or active hostility, I wouldn't bet a nickel on the academy's chance to survive."

"All this talk about accreditation?" Clay offered.

"Without accreditation, the place is sunk," Fred said. "That's for sure. What do I know? But even if you reached blindfolded into the colleges that have to supply these visiting committees, you couldn't hope to pull out nothing but dolts."

Clay cut in, "As you say, this matter does not concern us. Fortune has given us a presence where I want a presence. I want you to look at everything."

"Just filling in the context," Fred said. "If you want a sense of the relations between Stillton Academy and its governing powers, think a few Belgians in the Congo a century ago."

"There was considerable wealth in the Congo nonetheless," Clayton observed.

Chapter Twenty-two

It was necessary to bring Molly in from the pool. Molly's mother rented the same apartment each winter in West Palm Beach. Unless you were willing to get into a rental car and drive there was nothing but the pool to do, other than miniature golf.

"Wait a minute. I'll stand on the towel. I'm dripping," Molly said.

"In that scarlet suit?" Fred asked.

"Never mind. Sam, get away from the television. I've told you, not before eight o'clock."

"This time of day, is there anything on besides hospital shows?" Fred said.

"He's hooked up the Nintendo Wii or whatever that is his Dad sent him, bless his little heart. Sam, you have two choices. Swim or read a book. OK, Fred. Have you got to a place where you can talk?"

Fred managed a speedy outline of the circumstances that had brought him to the single room at the Stillton Inn, "where I'll have you know I am not the only tenant. There is also an old lady. I saw her on the stairs. They say at the desk that in summer it gets more lively. Also when Stillton Academy of Art has graduation. I'm racing. Have to get to a faculty meeting."

"To think that I would ever hear you speak those words," Molly gloated.

"Moving on," Fred said, "Even while dripping onto the carpet, and wearing your most ineffable scarlet suit, I know that your true identity as a research librarian is not concealed. And I know that you have your laptop with you—because I handed it to you at the airport. So—do you have a pencil?"

"Both a pencil and a burning desire to get back into the pool."

"There's no rush," Fred assured her. "But see what you can find that will reduce my ignorance about the man I am replacing, Morgan Flower. Stillton Academy of Art, obviously. Abraham Baum, attorney at law. Parker Stillton we know. The sculptor Meg Harrison. I'll have some other names later but I can't recall where I wrote them down. This Elizabeth Harmony who's pretending to run the place. You've got all this?"

"What are we looking for?" Molly asked. "You sometimes turn up an awful load of irrelevant…"

"Themes and convergences," Fred said. "Something's not right here. Beyond the missing people. I'm curious."

"Give me a couple of days. I'm on vacation, remember? Unless—is it an emergency?"

"No rush. I'd say if it were."

"Also there's something on tonight Mom wants to watch with the children. Some Atlantis kind of program, but with pyramids. I have to be there to reinterpret Mom's interpretations."

"And Josephus Stillton," Fred remembered. "The guy who started this operation back over a century ago. Who was he? What did he do? I'd look it up myself, but…"

"I know. And are you really teaching?" Molly asked. "Standing up in front of a class and all?"

"I have to tell you, I'm taken by surprise," Fred said. "I really like the kids. All that energy. I'd forgotten. They're serious. They're even optimistic and idealistic. They're…well, in short, they deserve much better…"

Molly said, "Go on to your faculty meeting. I assume you are wearing those academic robes?"

"Not 'till graduation day. Given how long I was at Harvard, I don't think I qualify for a robe that hangs much lower than my nipples."

"Lovely thought," Molly said. "I guess that does it for me." She finished her end of the conversation with a click.

The students in *Writing about your Problems* were still, and quite unaccountably, at work. Didn't they know enough to take advantage of the instructor's absence and make tracks? All this obedience, in persons old enough to vote, and rich enough to own matching shoes, was deeply disquieting. Molly accused Fred of projecting menace. "When people look at you," she'd say, "they tend to think of all the bad things they have done." Even so, what could Fred do to them? One or two of these students might really care about the matter so artificially put before them—but it was impossible that so many would willingly toe the line. Wasn't it?

How phrase the question?

It could wait.

Fred had timed his return for the end of the period, and made a point of sampling the students' efforts as they brought them to him. He let Peter know, quietly, that by eight o'clock he could be found at the Stillton Inn. "That gives you some privacy," he said.

"Gives everyone privacy," Peter pointed out. "Whatever you are doing. If you don't see me, assume I got nothing."

Peter left. The room was gradually emptied except for a single female student who seemed so engrossed in the task that she was not aware that her tribe had left her alone to face the hostile ministrations of the enemy. Simply in terms of mechanics, the business of writing required significant physical concentration. The students had nothing to sit on but their clumsy "horses". Their paper must be balanced on the drawing boards they propped either on their laps or, more frequently, on the horses' necks.

This student was so involved, Fred let her work. He sat on the model's platform, next to the bowl of last month's fruit, denting the blue and orange draperies and wrinkling the sign Meg had left. The silence in his classroom studio magnified the concluding clatter in Meg Harrison's Stillton A, next door, where students must be covering their work-in-progress with damp cloths and shrouding them in plastic, so that they would be malleable when they were next approached.

Without looking up, the student said, "I'm Emma. It's true. He's sleeping with her. I hope they get him."

Her voice was frank and matter-of-fact. She still didn't look up. "It was me last year," she said. She kept writing while she talked, as if either the writing or the talking was governed by a force outside her body. "Which, to me, it seems like, now, he's a collector. It's all here."

She smacked the tablet she was writing on with her left hand while the right continued its work.

Fred ran his eye down the class list. Emma. Only one Emma. Emma Rickerby.

"If you want to talk, or need to," Fred started.

"It's all here," Emma said. The tablet was white, lined paper. She stood, brushed the seat of her jeans absently, settled a russet knit wool sweater, and shook the full black hair, wisps of which had become tangled in her glasses while she was concentrating. She unfurled the paper that had been turned back while she wrote, leaving a clean title page showing, "Morgan Flower."

Chapter Twenty-three

"Give this to him," Emma said, dropping the tablet on the seat of the horse and walking out. The rosy student Fred had identified as Tom Meeker had been hovering in the doorway, as if hoping for a quiet private word with the teacher after class. He fell in beside her as she walked past, jerking her head as if to signal either, "We're going this way," or else, maybe more likely, "Leave me alone, for God's sake, would you?"

His seat in the class had been directly behind her.

There was too much to notice. Anything could signal something. Keep your eye on the matter at hand. Whatever it was Clay wanted, which was not whatever Parker Stillton and Abe Baum wanted, which was not, in turn, what they had claimed they wanted, yesterday, in Clayton's parlor.

But as long as he was here, Fred had to be doing something, and that might as well be to continue the wild goose chase he'd started with: the missing student and the missing teacher.

Emma had left behind her in the studio a faint dusting of particles of charcoal, and the strong scent of whatever musk women her age these days were using.

"You're sure your name isn't Rosetta Stone?" Fred asked. His first instinct had been to follow the student herself; but the tangible document she had left behind her took precedence and, in any case, should not be left unguarded. And whether or not it was to her taste, she wasn't alone. Fred made his way through the vaguely concentric jumble of horses until he reached the one Emma Rickerby had vacated. He picked up her tablet. He'd look into it later.

Are you kidding?

The first page was all caps, angry, angular, but even: the repeated message: **FUCK YOU.** Fred flipped through the pages. Emma showed a commendable consistency. Neither the handwriting nor the message wavered or varied. Neither her speech nor her manner had seemed crazed—but this? Fred slipped the tablet into the midst of the uneven collection that was his reward for the afternoon.

Not only did the teacher's life involve hours of aggressively administered boredom in the classroom—he also had to carry it home with him!

"Still, you don't have to be sane to tell the truth," Fred said. "In fact…"

But it was time for the faculty meeting.

If you regarded Fred as a member of the faculty, and Fred did not, the faculty present numbered nine unless you regarded Phil Oumaloff as faculty, which Phil Oumaloff obviously did, in which case the number was ten unless you left Fred out.

The group was gathered, buzzing and whickering and making assorted sounds of non-verbal guttural distress, in what Meg identified as the board room—a small room with a large table that seemed to occupy the remainder of the first floor of the admissions building, where Liz Harmony's office was. Meg had caught up with Fred outside Stillton hall, wiping her hands and face on a rag she tucked into a back pocket of her jeans.

"Sorry to bug out like that. There was something…you make out all right with the gang of four?"

"If you mean the luncheon conference, I think you can safely say that we are none the wiser. Your work, on the other hand—what I saw of it—has real presence."

Meg had stopped short, though the meeting might already have begun.

"I like to look around," Fred said.

"You didn't…" Meg started.

"Touch anything? No. Not even the shrouded figure, which I wanted to unveil. Like Rodin's *Balzac.* No, I understand the theory. Keep it damp. I'll share my ignorance and tell you, your work makes me think how much Maillol missed, getting hung up the way he did on that one well-made girl."

"Who? Oh, Dina Vierny?"

"I guess," Fred said. "Since I'm curious, and you invited me, I'll sit in on the faculty meeting."

"Why am I not surprised?" Meg said. "In here."

Of the three seats around the table that were not occupied, Meg slid quickly into the vacancy between Phil Oumaloff and a weasely-looking man whose large, black-rimmed round spectacles gave the immediate impression that Harry Potter had somehow grown up wrong.

President Harmony was not visible. One of the two adjacent empties must be hers. Fred took the one that abutted Bobby Ballatieri, giving her an answering collegial nod. The female wraith who had been seated at the desk in the foyer stood in the doorway and made an elaborate count, pointing to each person as she mouthed a number, but forgetting where she had started along the ellipse.

"We're ten, if you count Fred," Fred helped. "I'm Fred."

"I'll tell Ms—I'll tell President Harmony you are gathered," the woman moaned. "You have the agenda? No. I do. I'll get it."

"Harmony sets the agenda," Bobby Ballatieri whispered. "We're always all on the edge of our you know whats."

Fred established his academic credentials. "That could be better than being on the edge of *her* you know what."

Bobby's respectful guffaw accompanied the reappearance of the female apparition with a fluttering sheaf of paper which she distributed, one sheet to each place, the final one being laid at the empty spot next to Fred, like a place mat. The typed page, Xeroxed in stone-age fashion—had they no computer anywhere?—was headed AGENDA. Only the last item was of interest: 6. Professor Taylor.

The clouds parted and President Harmony stood in the doorway for twenty seconds, waiting for the glum assembled company to stand. This failed to happen. She swept to her chair, noting both Fred's presence next to it, and the absence of an alternative. She looked sharply around the table, thought better of this approach, and instead rewarded the company with a smile that conveyed exactly the same warning. "Close the door, would you?" she asked. When nothing happened, she added, "Arthur? Would you mind? Anyone might…" she let the suspicious hint poison the air until Arthur Tikrit—illustration, 2-D and color theory—rose and scrambled around behind his colleagues until he could reach, and close, the door she had just entered by. In the windows behind Fred—therefore behind Harmony—the sea and the rain and the view must all be adding a backdrop of scenic importance to her appearance, but there was nothing to see through the windows on the other side, facing Fred. He noticed now that he'd taken the only chair with arms. No wonder. If he'd done it on purpose, he couldn't have made a better move. He'd taken her chair. For the first time in his life he could appreciate the thrill that results when the twin presidential cheeks are in firm contact with reserved presidential leather.

"There will be sherry," Harmony announced. "Despite the fact that our occupations lead some to adopt what might appear a Farmer Jones apparel, my office is glad to make the effort. Sherry will arrive. Caroline is arranging it."

The bad children were nevertheless being rewarded with a prize that would also punish them as they deserved. President Harmony uttered a small laugh and brought a ringed index finger to the first item on a trivial agenda.

"We'll start with number six," Fred said.

Chapter Twenty-four

Phil Oumaloff puffed and rose as if he would give off steam. The puffs voiced hasty words. "Personal privilege, hopelessly inopportune, outrageous." When he became coherent the purple flush in his large face subsided to a less dangerous crimson.

"Forgive the outburst," he instructed Liz Harmony and, by extension, with a wave of his hand that included the rest of the table, everyone else but Fred. He became courtly. "I speak as one, forgive me, if you will indulge, who is long familiar with the traditions and the practices of this academy," he portended. "Granted they are not written. Granted their long existence may not be law. Nevertheless, a tradition, by its nature, lends stability; and stability, by its nature, fosters longevity. It is my honor to lead the preparations for the academy's celebration of its first alumni reunion. As such, I believe that item number one, as well as the principles of order and collegiality...more to the point: This man is an impostor."

Oumaloff sat as suddenly as he had risen, as if the supply of steam had been rerouted. Shining before them all, and winking suggestively from the single-page AGENDA, was item 1: Preparation for Stillton Academy of Art's First Annual Alumni Reunion.

"The issues are priorities and proper precedence," Oumaloff propounded, and coughed a warning of an impending sermon. "Now, on the matter of the academy's invitation to Basil Houel..."

"Another time," Fred said. "What Oumaloff…"

"Not only is Basil Houel a distinguished alumnus, he has been unusual in maintaining his ties to the academy as well as to…ahem…an old mentor," Oumaloff insisted. "Even to the point where on occasion he has offered space on his studio floor in Chelsea to one of our students who has found himself caught short in New York. Houel is…"

"Speaking of time," Fred said.

"Please, Gentlemen," Liz Harmony started at the same moment as Caroline, after knocking, entered with a tray. The room fell into silence. Fred pushed on while the glasses and decanter were placed, in response to his beckoning gesture, in front of Bill Wamp, who started pouring and passing. He seemed a man destined to receive more than his share.

"What Oumaloff says is true," Fred repeated, disregarding Liz Harmony's frantic efforts at gesturing him to silence while Caroline was in the room. "I'm no professor. Never have been. Never hope to be. The first plan was I'd say I'm here to sub for Morgan Flower. It's true, but it's not all. Liz Harmony will tell you—I'll save you some time, Liz—no sherry for me—you have accreditation coming up. Are you ready? I think not. Everybody on a one-year contract? That's not going to fly. Salary scale? I don't know…"

"Your credentials?" Oumaloff challenged.

"I'm a trouble-shooter, and troubles you've got. What Harmony will tell you, I need access to everything and everybody. Can anyone tell me where Morgan Flower is? Since they're both missing, it looks as if he has high-tailed it with a student. That isn't news to anyone here. It's not a deal-breaker, though it is important how the place responds. If she's underage it's a criminal matter. But in the Commonwealth of Massachusetts, underage is less than sixteen. I don't know what they're thinking, but she's an adult. Probably not a big deal. Still. There's much more.

"You all know where I am. Morgan Flower's rooms until he needs them again. Unless I move to the Stillton Inn. One place or the other will find me. If you have information about anything I can use…when I'm done you'll get my report. Informally.

"That's about it for me. I'll be bothering you and you can come bother me. Anything that might help. It's a hard job you do here. I'm exhausted after one day of it. Enjoy your sherry."

He rose and, carrying the stack of papers he had earned, took advantage of the moment of silence he had engendered, and left his colleagues.

Caroline, at the desk in the foyer, was simultaneously administering lipstick and talking eagerly into a cell phone. She interrupted the flow and looked Fred's way. "Did she notice about the finger sandwiches?" she asked as Fred went past her.

"I'm not sure. For what it's worth, I didn't notice any finger sandwiches."

"That's the problem. She ordered finger sandwiches. What are they?"

"Try hot dogs," Fred suggested. "Hot dogs look like fingers."

"I hadn't guessed it could be that easy." She told the cell phone, "Be right back," and picked up the desk phone. "Oh, but, should I interrupt them? My friend says there's, like, a body on the beach."

"I'll take care of it," Fred said. "Best not to bother them. What direction, do you know?"

Caroline stretched an arm in the direction of the lighthouse.

"Hot dogs will keep them busy," Fred assured her. "Don't bother them with current events. I'll take a look."

The body, on its back on the sandy gravel, was being licked by irregular, and not very greedy waves. Naked and male, the corpse had not yet been much hacked at by its hungry marine fellows. But it had been in the water for a few days, from the bloated look of it. The water cold as this ocean was, it would slow the things down that make swelling. Rain was washing the sand from pinched features and a clotted, blondish mop of hair. The group of people gathering—there were fifteen or twenty by the time Fred joined them—was in a semi-circle, both to appreciate the corpse, and to wave discouragement toward the angry, circling gulls. Two uniformed men stood with the crowd, joining in the effort to distract the gathering, screaming birds. "His eyes are long gone," the stouter uniform was saying. "Eyes always go first. Softer."

"Let's move him up the beach," Fred suggested.

"Nobody touches him," the thinner uniform said. "Tide's going out anyway. Isn't it?" A larger swell lifted the body and rearranged its limbs. The gnawed penis flopped sluggishly.

"Yikes." A female voice. The crowd, as people will do at a beach, had stepped back instinctively so as to avoid getting its feet wet.

"It won't look good for you if you lose this body," Fred pointed out.

"Nobody touches nothing. That's an order. We called it in." The stouter one patted his sidearm.

"What kind of cops are you?" Fred demanded, looking more carefully at the uniforms.

"You see this." Another pat. "With the Academy. Stillton security. We don't need cops out here. Not normally."

Another wave lifted the body. It waved its hands and turned its head to reveal a dented place in back that was already occupied by alien life.

"Nobody touches nothing, is what they said," the thinner security guard said, drawing his weapon. Fred waded into the water until, up to his knees, he could stand between the corpse and open water. The foghorn hooed. It was cold, the Atlantic in March.

"Not making trouble for anybody," Fred said. "Just in case. So he doesn't get away. In the meantime, not to be obvious about it but—folks—we're looking at Morgan Flower, I presume?"

The gathering simultaneously shook its general head and jumped back from the next wave.

"Before my time. But I've seen photos. The former boss," the stout security guard said. "Somerfest. Boating accident, looks like. Guy didn't know from boats."

Somerfest went out in his boat naked? In March? What was Stillton Academy doing with security officers anyway? A place this small? What were these art students going to do to anybody?

"I guess he didn't know from boats," Fred agreed.

Chapter Twenty-five

Commotion wastes enormous amounts of time unless what one is after is a circus. The crowd was gathered around the beached corpse the way crowds have been gathering since the dawn of time, when anything edible, having lost the ability to defend itself, crosses from one eco-system into another. Add cell phones to the mix and the crowd grows fast.

Not until half an hour after he joined the group did state cops in a cruiser show up, sirens screaming—joined shortly by black unmarked vans holding technical folks and detectives. By this time Fred was in almost to mid-thigh and Rodney Somerfest's body, with each new wave, pirouetted on the points of its buttocks. The speedboats of harbor patrol and coast guard were slower, but were coming over the horizon by the time Fred was free to wade up the beach.

Caroline, holding steady, had evidently maintained the wall of protective silence demanded by President pro-tem Harmony, so that the Agenda in the boardroom could be followed in the magnificence of its fore-ordained sequence.

"Don't leave town," somebody yelled at Fred as he squelched through the crowd. He more or less recognized half the people as his students though others among the extras were well beyond student age.

Fred, moving faster, waved an assenting arm. Given the wind, the rain, and the Atlantic Ocean he had been standing in, he was wet through. He paused only to retrieve his loafers, and the stack of student papers he had handed to Milan, who had appeared from somewhere as he stepped into the drink. Milan had found a plastic bag somewhere.

"I reckon the boss knows," Milan said.

Fred nodded. "Gotta change."

Last night's garments were dank, if not still dripping. The Stillton Inn would have a dryer.

Even a robe. "I'll get one from the honeymoon suite," the woman at the desk said, looking Fred over with disfavor where he dripped on the rubber mat provided for that purpose inside the front door. She was well aware of the activities near the lighthouse, although ignorant of specifics, and, once Fred had explained his condition, she was happy to trade his information for access to the dryer. Her first coherent question had been, "How many bodies?"

Mrs. Halper instructed—the desk sign gave her this iden-tity—"Leave your loafers there on the mat. I'll stuff them with paper and we'll see. I'll find you something. I'll bring the robe to your room and wait while you get your things together." He'd had the presence of mind to leave his loafers on the beach when he waded in—upside down, but the crowd had kicked them upright and they'd filled with rain. At least they had not washed out to sea.

"Maybe a cup of tea?" Fred suggested. He'd been five minutes standing at the door, satisfying the top layer of Mrs. Halper's curiosity.

"Kettle in your room. Tea bag. Should be. Sugar. Coffee. Creamer. For the morning."

Fred plodded upstairs barefoot trailed by drops of disapprov-ing water, and accompanied by the overnight bag into which he'd stuffed the damp clothes from last night, in a garbage bag, as well as something to read from Morgan Flower's desk, in case the pile of student papers palled.

By the time Mrs. Halper's knock came, Fred had changed to a towel and could exchange the full garbage bag for a pink terry-cloth robe, lacking in size, that said *HIS* on it. Mrs. Halper handed the robe over doubtfully. "I couldn't find *HERS*," she said. "It's a joke we had. For the honeymoon suite. To break the ice in case the ice wasn't already broken long before. My husband thought of it, God bless him, he's been gone fifteen years. *HIS* on the girl's robe and *HERS* on the man's. So they get the idea. He was a big man like you." She held out a pair of white canvas shoes, much used. "I'll want them back. They don't look like much, but he was wearing them when…" she didn't finish, but continued standing in the doorway. Was she angling for an invitation to come in?

Fred made the exchange.

"You think they killed him," Mrs. Halper said. "Is that what you're saying?"

"Well, no, I didn't say that. It does look suspicious, the man being naked." Fred couldn't shrug. He'd lose the towel.

"Also, too, that head wound," Mrs. Halper added. "Not that I liked the man. He wanted to buy the inn."

Fred said, "I'd ask you in for tea, but I'm too old school. It makes sense, I guess, if the academy wants to expand."

"For himself," Mrs. Halper corrected him. "And he wanted it hush hush. I can't stay. The phone. People want a room now. I'm all there is. Or rooms. Reporters and that. Come down in an hour, your clothes will be dry. Or. No. I'll send someone up with them. I have to call someone anyway, give me a hand. People will start coming. There's the phone. It's what they do." She shouldered the garbage bag and took possession of the stairs.

The best he could do was to leave a message on the machine at Molly's mother's apartment. "Add Rodney Somerfest to the list. I don't know how he spells it. Correction. Spelled it. Past tense. He's been killed. So he goes at the top of the list. Former director of the place. Oh. This is Fred. You have the number."

◇◇◇

Then a hot shower and a cup of mournfully indifferent tea in the foam cup provided.

He had turned up the heat in the room, and stretched out on the bed to think.

◇◇◇

"God, Mister, I didn't know," the girl said, shocked, behind an armload of clothing, in the open doorway. Fred, springing upright at the click of hardware, had lost the towel. Even drained of its natural color, he knew that face.

"It's Fred," Fred said. He picked up the towel again and applied it.

"She didn't say…I mean I just thought…"

"It's OK, Susan," Fred said. The student's name had surfaced. First-year student. Missy Tutunjian's roommate. Susan Muller. "Sorry," Fred went on. "I couldn't do much with the robe. Put the stuff on the bed, would you, Susan? I don't want to lose the towel again."

"Hell, I don't care. I see guys naked. We have to. It's all those scars."

"Accidents when I was younger," Fred explained. "I'm more careful now."

"You sure woke up out of that bed fast," Susan said. "Like you were ready to shoot me."

Chapter Twenty-six

Telephone.

"Yes?"

"If you'll pay me back, if you want, I'll bring fish and chips."
Peter's voice.

"And a six pack if you'll join me," Fred said. "Fish and chips
for both of us sounds good. If you're hungry. I'm kinda stuck
here. My treat, obviously."

"Twenty minutes."

The canvas shoes of the late Mr. Halper fit as if Fred had been
breaking them in for the past five years. It was good, on the whole,
to be dressed and dry. It went with the general sense of ignorance.
Peter's entrance, with paper bags that crackled and steamed with
the smell of fish and frying oil, was equally welcome.

"Tell me about Rodney Somerfest," Fred demanded, wasting
no time as they unpacked dinner and arranged it and themselves.
Peter, sitting on the foot of the bed, left Fred with the table,
chair, and access to the phone.

"They took their photos, bagged him, and carried him off.
I heard to Rockport for a start."

"I don't care about that. Where was he living since he left?
You'd found an address?"

"Rockport. Rented room. I guess he liked the coast after all,
though he never stopped complaining about it."

"Where was he from? Wife? Family? Who was he friendly
with? What did they can him for?"

Peter lifted a big hunk of fish in his fingers, broke off a piece to eat, and studied the possible arrangement of Fred's questions while he licked his fingers.

"Concord, New Hampshire. He's been in cars. Somerfest Subaru. Then was working for a graduate degree in education, maybe from Suffolk? When they hired him. No wife or family I ever heard about."

"No ring on the finger. That doesn't mean much," Fred said.

"That crack on the head—I can't think of an accident that would do that, can you?"

"You don't buy boating accident?"

"Oh, please."

"Which brings us to the final question," Fred said, letting it hang while he opened a beer.

"I got Bud. That OK?" Peter asked.

"They're all from the same place. The final question?"

"Why they fired him? I don't have an answer. See, and I've heard President Liz say this a hundred times, the director serves at the pleasure of the board. At a certain point in time, the board stopped being pleased."

"And paid him off, you told me. How much?"

"What I heard is, a year's salary. I don't know."

"There'll be a record. Board minutes…"

"I've looked. Sure, they keep minutes, but they always go into executive session. That means they don't write down what anyone says or what they do. The secretary of the board types out a thing five lines long that says date, place, time, these people met, they went into executive session. Then they adjourned."

"You've given this a lot of attention," Fred observed.

"You mean, which you're not saying, for a *student*," Peter filled in. "It's true. I'm telling you. I have an investment in this place. Plus I think most of the teachers and the program are pretty good. We don't deserve to have the whole thing thrown away by a bunch of clowns.

"I started here fresh out of the Marines. I couldn't draw for shit. Still, I was older, and I knew my way around. That gives me a jump on a lot of these guys. I did my interview with Bill Wamp. He saw potential. I don't know what. Beyond, I wanted to paint and I didn't want any part of the city. After I started taking the classes, pretty soon something seemed off. I began looking around.

"They brought Rodney in halfway through last year."

"Before that?"

"Before that, my first year, it was like it is today. Acting director. Chairman of the board."

"Liz Harmony again?"

"No. He resigned. A name I don't remember."

"Where do they get the money for all this? A year's salary payoff for a guy who isn't working? Who hasn't worked even a year?"

"They threw him out and all of a sudden hired this security team."

"Where does the money come from?"

"They keep that really tight," Peter said. "I can't get a line on it. It would be easier to find out everyone's sexual preference."

"Less interesting, I imagine," Fred said.

"Just so it's not an issue. I was married when I started here. She was from around here, is partly why. That's over. I'm gay."

Fred ate a fry, and another. "Right," he said. "It's not my business."

"My partner's in Portland, Oregon. Also a vet. You're looking at things? You might want to know. This saves you time."

"And Rodney Somerfest. Single. Which way did the wind blow for him, do you know? What was the scuttlebutt?"

"Students this age, aside from thinking they can paint a masterpiece with a lighthouse in it, which nobody can, not even Hopper, for God's sake, it's just a lighthouse, all they can mostly talk about is sex." Peter ate fish.

"Of course, people can fool you," Fred pointed out.

"All the time. Not bad, the fish and chips, do you agree? Steve, at the Stillton Café. My point is, if there was a sex issue with Rodney, inside or outside the shop, with a student, teacher, hell, I never heard, and I would have."

"Between Morgan Flower and that student?"

"Oh, sure. Missy. She couldn't…"

"Let's talk about Missy Tutunjian."

"Didn't you want to know about Lillian Krasic?"

"Who?"

"Who ran the desk until they canned her. She's right here."

"Right where?"

"They send her monthly check here, to the Stillton Inn."

Chapter Twenty-seven

By ten-thirty the rain had thinned to a light mist. Peter Quarrier had left. "Homework. Color theory. Tikrit's a bitch." He'd taken the time to annotate his map, which he'd left rolled on Fred's table.

Fred studied it until he had the layout in his head. The academy's classroom and administration buildings were highlighted in yellow—a total of seven, of which he'd been inside only two.

"Milan locks them all at night. But you can get in," Peter said. "There's ways. Most all of them. I'll show you…some other time."

"They'll do me a tour when I'm ready," Fred said. "The reason I gave that assignment—if you've got problems, and who doesn't, don't make them worse by rolling around in them until you stink all over. Get over them. Move it along. Writing about your problems—that's just horseshit. It made me mad. That girl Emma…"

"She's already taking your advice," Peter said. "Moving along. If Tom Meeker would leave her be. Him she does not need. Listen, she's a friend of mine. If there's something she wants to tell you, she'll tell you. Otherwise, her business is…"

"Gotcha," Fred said, seeing him out. Reading between the lines, the student was simply working out a healthy derangement. The repeated FUCK YOUs had been so regular and balanced that even if it were Fred's longer term job to be concerned for her, there was no reason for it.

How much of Stillton could be asleep by eleven o'clock? The streets were almost deserted, most of the buildings dark. It made sense, of course, that Stillton proper would be mostly owned and occupied by summer residents. Except for earnest masochists, or poets, if there was a difference, it was a purely miserable place for winter or this early in the spring.

Fred stopped at his car, picking out some innocent-looking hardware and a flashlight. Television lights flickered like a cut rate aurora back of the closed blinds of Meg Harrison's bedroom window. Morgan Flower's green Toyota sat against the curb, not many lengths from Fred's vehicle.

The admissions building he'd seen. The contents of the desks and file cabinets, especially in Harmony's office, might prove interesting—but irrelevant to whatever Clay was interested in, and therefore irrelevant. Clay, for all his weirdnesses and eccentricities—or perhaps, rather, taking advantage of his weirdnesses and eccentricities—had an extremely canny nose for finding what he wanted.

Information was all very well; but what Clay wanted was *things*, and the things he wanted were beautiful or astounding or outlandish or, sometimes, questionable, works of art. He could find them where nobody else could; sometimes even under the very noses of his competition.

Clay preferred, when he could, to get a painting for a song, although its true value if measured in the symbolic scale of money, might be that of the maidenhead of the princess of one of the advanced western countries. His Turner *Danae* was a case in point. A hundred knowledgeable dealers and collectors at a country auction had handled it and let it go by unchallenged simply because it was not packaged as a painting. In fact, long separated from its stretchers, the canvas had been packaged as a package—the stained and shameful wrapping that contained the stack of lost Turner erotic works that Clay alone had recognized.

Though he would pay good money when he had to. Peter Quarrier had brought up Edward Hopper. Clayton's Hopper, a large oil of roofs in Truro reflecting the electric disquiet of a coming storm, had cost a pretty penny, although Fred could not name the sum. Clay had purchased it from a collector who knew what he was doing when it came to investing in art. The collector's choice to become a Lloyds of London "Name," however, had proved less happy, and he needed to be bailed out quickly by someone who wouldn't tell his friends about it. Since Clay told nobody anything if he could help it, he was the perfect choice. Presumably he'd gotten a deal, but nothing to brag about.

The thumb-box size Gauguin, however, and the Gericault, were evidence of Clay at his most expert hunting prowess. The Gauguin came from a flea market in Avignon. Clay had picked it out of a mixed bag of fakes and shabby academic or tourist pieces. Signed *PGo*, it had simply been overlooked by everyone who didn't know or remember that Gauguin was as happy to sign a picture that way as any other.

Not that Clay crowed about his acquisitions. He couldn't do so without spilling information. But Fred knew most of the ins and outs of the acquisitions he had participated in. In the case of the Gauguin, he'd been summoned to France to carry it out, along with the bill of sale identifying it simply as *Personnes dans un jardin, bois, artiste inconnu, 16 x 24 cm., E27,50.* Clay had a wedding to get to, on Lago Maggiore, and he didn't want the thing to muss his shirts.

Another element of his thinking might have been that, if the French customs agents had understood what Fred was carrying past them in plain sight, they would have exercised their rights, seized the painting as part of the cultural *patrimoine*, while reimbursing to the owner, as was also their right, the declared value—which Clay had insisted should be no other than the purchase price as represented on the bill of sale.

Fred, on the other hand, when he was not carrying something for his employer, preferred to travel light. In fact, it was the bargain he had made with the world, not to want ownership of much of anything. He loved a good painting—enough to leave it where it was.

Let Clay proclaim—truthfully, as far as Fred could see—that he was unmoved by the putative financial values embodied in his collection. In any case, those values fluctuated. The day's fashions could lead to ludicrous prices for despicable pictures. Take Allen Funt and Alma-Tadema or, if someone stepped a toe into the crazy quilt intrigue of contemporary art, how account for the almost Goldman Sachs, empty and illusory bubble of success enjoyed by Jeff Koons or Damien Hirst? The success was real enough in financial terms (as long as one got out at the right time). But apart from intrigue, fashion, and backroom dealings, what connection could there possibly be between high prices and questionable artistic merit?

Fred let himself into the back entrance of a second building that resembled Stillton Hall but did not seem to have a name. They stood side by side.

Chapter Twenty-eight

This building had been reconfigured so that the whole back side, the side facing the water, had been lifted, roof and all. A continual wall of glass, interspersed by structural members, had been set in between the roof's new drip edge and the top of the original wall, so that the resulting string of studios had three feet of daylight (in the daytime) along the entire outside studio wall. The original windows, meantime, had been filled in so that there was solid wall up to seven feet. Anyone desiring to take advantage of the view would need a boost.

The remodeling of the building resulted in a string of small studios, each of which was seemingly shared by two individuals. The parade of studios ran in either direction from the central corridor that Fred had entered. The studios were separated by partitions that reached seven feet in height, but communicated only with a corridor along the front, like that in Stillton Hall. It was a sensible, no-frills arrangement that would allow the academy to make the claim that third- and fourth-year students had "private" studios. The place smelled like a fire marshal's worst nightmare. And indeed, should a good fire get started, there wasn't much to prevent its sweeping the entire building briskly.

Something for the report.

Except there would be no report. The report was fiction teetering on the top of a fiction that rested uneasily on yet another.

Another time, if he'd been in the mood, Fred might have paid more attention to what passed for advanced student work at

Stillton Academy. But he was looking for something—although that something had not been defined. If what he was looking for was a painting, among all these student paintings, whatever it was, it should stand out.

Especially if it was an abstract. A Kline, Hoffman, or Rothko. Unlikely as Clay was to be looking for anything so recent.

As Meg Harrison had warned, the academy's tuition and examples seemed to cleave obediently to the nineteenth century. Using his flashlight dimmed by enclosing fingers Fred did a quick check of the studios. One end of the building was dedicated to third-year students. Though studio contents varied considerably, as did the studies and finished sketches and paintings stacked against the wall, or hung there, each partitioned cubicle held two versions of the setup that had intruded on Fred's classroom use: a nude young man, dark-skinned, half-seated on a stool, with all that hooraw around him—the blue crumpled cloth, the orange crumpled cloth, the gawd-help-us bowl of last year's fruit.

Other efforts—Fred was moving fast—included seascapes, still lifes, many portraits of the buildings visible in Stillton, the lighthouse in varying states of weather, and many self-portraits.

"Hold on. That's Peter Quarrier," Fred said in one cubicle. If everything on that side of the cubicle was Peter's, his version of the current classroom nude was as indifferent as all the rest. Unless you were really brave you'd never get past that clashing blue and orange without pulling both colors, raw, into the figure itself—presumably what Meg intended. But these students, so far, were too timid. Even though Matisse had shown them what to do a century ago.

"They're not looking at anybody," Fred complained. Something else for the report he wouldn't write.

The series of Peter's self-portraits, though, was sensitive, delicate, and strong. The one on the easel was wet, blocked out mainly in black and tan, with highlights of white that allowed for the appearance of either white or green. Maybe they could talk painting next time. Talk about Goya and Lucien Freud.

Fred kept moving, vaguely recognizing some of the students he had been with during the afternoon. Wasn't that Emma? The last cubicle along had a window, and that was surely Emma on the floor against the wall. On the easel, her version of the standing figure was well-drawn, just shy of being contorted, with similar contortions present in the fruit and draperies. She couldn't have seen Tamara de Lempicka, could she? And anyway, these contortions were not motivated by style, but by the way the head and the hand twist when the painter is struggling to concentrate.

The self-portrait that leaned against the wall showed a similar disciplined contortion. She'd put her hair back severely and against a greenish background, her green shirt, open at the neck, struggled to take precedence. As far as it was possible to judge in the pink glow Fred allowed to issue through his fingers, the colors in the head were red and green and yellow, like an autumn apple. The woman portrayed was ugly, as Emma was not. But in this self-portrait Emma was ugly, and it suited her.

In this cubicle, Fred searched more carefully among the trash, pinned notices, and scraps, in case some trace might lead to elucidation of an old connection between the student and Fred's predecessor. But there was nothing of interest.

The other end of the building had to be fourth-year painters. In these cubicles each student, using almost the same materials and inspiration, was seeking to establish an identity of style or subject matter in time to claim a unique thesis that might lead him to qualify for whatever passed for graduation requirements at Stillton. It was pitiful.

No way can they do this honestly so far from a big city, with museums and real galleries showing and selling good pictures and bad ones," Fred spluttered. "They have to jockey with collectors." He'd moved more quickly through the fourth year spaces, because they were disappointing.

The building held no basement. Heating came from a furnace room in the center of the building, where male and female restrooms had also been provided.

"Nothing here," Fred said, fighting to suppress the speech he was imagining, in which he raked his new colleagues over the coals for even pretending to teach painting so far from any examples of the thing itself.

"Morton" was three floors, with tiny rooms and garrets, clean, clean, clean. It was reserved for the studios, apparently, of students in the third and fourth years who believed they had gotten a good grip on reality and were devoting their talents to what the academy called two-dimensional design. So they had determined to sell their wares to commercial enterprises, and make their fortunes.

But they'd have nothing to sell. It might be that a painter can function with a nineteenth century mentality—though he won't compete with Damien Hirst—but the student who attempts commercial art without computer literacy is doomed. It might prove an interesting education, but the 2-D program was a fraud. Illustrations, arrows, bold logos in black and white—it was all pointless. Cut-and-paste crap. Most of them couldn't draw, either. Or if they could, they didn't bother.

Less pointless maybe, the top floor studios had knee-walls where the crawl spaces had been preserved for storage under the roof. And access to the crawl space back behind the work table of a student whose name seemed to be Rick Murphy—according to notes and messages—was impeded by a no-nonsense padlock that took Fred at least twenty seconds to open.

Chapter Twenty-nine

A king's ransom of dust and spiders. The space had been designed with an undernourished nineteenth-century servant girl in mind. The door hadn't been opened since before the room was painted in pale yellow. Fred's head and shoulders followed the flashlight in.

Odds and ends. Scraps. Shoes. A ski! Dismantled ancient cameras. Were those canteens? A riding helmet. The space might be four feet deep and ten wide. Above, the building's roof was irregular, interrupted by dormers. It looked like the junk families leave in the attic from one generation to the next so that the next generation but one will have something to disregard.

Wooden box in a back corner about right for a milk carton. Fred, wriggling backwards on his belly, dragged it toward him, making slide marks in the dust. Papers. The box was full of them—old and dry. Letters and envelopes, a couple of bound volumes—journals apparently?—Fred's survey was hasty. That musty smell was mice. Yes, mice had been at this. The smell was mice and old paper, with an undertow of dust and mold. This couldn't be what Clayton Reed was looking for, but it was something. And it would take a while, as well as decent light. Fred pulled the box into the studio and closed and padlocked the door, arranging Rick Murphy's work table and chair as they had been.

The box went into the trunk of his car. He'd driven the few blocks from Morgan Flower's apartment, having learned by now that rain was never more than a few steps away.

Lights still burned in the administration and admissions building, and six cars were parked in the vicinity, cars of sufficient polish and lack of ancient dings to suggest trustees. Likely Liz Harmony, though clued in tardily to the fate of her immediate predecessor, had called an emergency meeting. "What do we say to the press? He's nothing to do with us."

This could be a dramatic moment for Fred to introduce himself. But, then again…

The lighted window of the boardroom showed heads in silhouette, only two of which he recognized—Liz Harmony; Abe Baum. Liz worked for free. Did Baum charge by the hour? Where was this money coming from?

Three students, passing, recognized Fred as a fixture that belonged, nodded, and told him, "'Night." He was on foot again, walking the two blocks to the classroom building "where we do dry work," Peter Quarrier had said. "Classrooms. Like high school. The 2-D classes, small seminar kinds of things, reviews, and that class for fourth year students they ship a guy in for, called *The Business of Art*, which I can tell you is a half a joke. The first half. The half where you can't tell where the joke is going."

Eleven Sea Street was the building's only sign. True to his practice, Fred slid around to the back. However, there were lighted windows and moving shadows inside. Late night for someone. "Let's not start an affray," Fred advised himself. The 2-D offices were in that building also.

That left *Thirteen Sea Street*, next door, where painting and sculpture had their offices, and Milan's shop, behind that: a small shingled cottage overlooking the ocean that, were it not dedicated to this purpose, might well be offered at well into seven figures. Cunning little place to take the evening breezes, along with the gin and tonic, come August and July.

"Might as well start small," Fred said. "Holy smokes. He's got his private beach and everything."

"Figured you'd be around. The voice fell in behind him. "And don't say you were looking for me." The voice, a weary growl that sounded bored, was Milan's.

Fred slipped the hardware back into his pocket. "Busy night."

"If it isn't raining, it's going to rain," Milan growled. "You carrying heat?"

"Nothing much to shoot," Fred said. 'If I understand you. Oh, maybe you mean the flashlight." He took it out of his jacket pocket. "You never know."

Milan said, "We'll sit inside. Out here, if it isn't raining now, it's going to rain."

Fred followed the man up three steps and onto the porch and watched him open the door with a pair of keys. "Otherwise the kids borrow tools and you never see them again."

The light exposed tool benches, racks of hanging tools and equipment, pipes, wires, an electric heater, fans, horses needing repair, sawdust, a camp bed, a pair of narrow chairs at a cluttered table on which sat both hot plate and radio and the remains of a fried meal.

"The one I don't get is Phil Oumaloff," Fred said.

Milan said, "I'm having tea." He found a sink under some newspapers and filled a kettle he dug out of it. "Nothing hard about Phil. He thinks he owns the place." Milan put the kettle on the hotplate and switched it on. He'd pulled a single mug out of the sink also, into which he dropped two tea bags.

"Thing on TV. Did you see it? No. You're snooping around. I watch at the Stillton Café, upstairs. Where they prove the people from outer space designed the pyramids. *Pharaohs from Beyond the Sun,* they called it. You believe it?"

"Not really," Fred said. Milan hadn't invited him to sit, but he sat in the sturdier of the two chairs. "You?"

"Do I what?"

"Believe in these guys from outer space?" Fred said.

"Hell, I don't even believe in the Egyptians. Whole thing is a trick."

The kettle began to groan.

"Never say die. That's Phil Oumaloff." Milan chuckled. It sounded like water being disturbed in a flooded grave. "Used to be Rodney Somerfest too. But looks like he did."

"If he wasn't dead, I never saw a better imitation," Fred said.

"So. Who do you represent?" Milan demanded.

The kettle groaned faster, as if beginning to concentrate—to extend an inappropriate analogy that hardly suited the occasion—on matters below the waist.

"I'm independent," Fred said.

"In that case, just as a matter of interest, what's your offer?"

"My offer," Fred deliberated.

"I like to take her off before she whistles," Milan said, removing the kettle from the burner and pouring water over the tea bags.

"This whole place," Fred said, "seems to me the whole place is about to whistle."

Chapter Thirty

"Some names," Fred said into the phone. "Rosa Ludlow. Fitz Hugh Ludlow. Also Albert. Could be a given name, could be a patronymic."

Clay's end of the line held a silence that was interrupted by the discreet chatter of the Sèvres service he affected at breakfast time. Green tea. Clay had convinced himself that green tea did not include stimulants, which he abhorred and professed to eschew.

Fred, in turn, awakened; indeed, insulted, by the weak excuse for coffee provided by the room's electric drip pot, had worked through the contents of the box until, at seven, he'd found a passable, and portable, cup at Bee's Beehive. Bee had dug up a ham and egg sandwich for him as well.

"This is a secure line?" Clay demanded.

"Nothing anywhere is secure. The Pentagon isn't secure. I've told you that," Fred said. "The best you can do is be faster and smarter than anyone who might be listening. Most of the time we probably are. Or talk in Navaho."

"Levity," Clay reproved him.

"The names?"

"The names confirm my anticipation. I presume that you are leading up to something? What have you found? Explain these names, and their context. Say as little as you can. Perhaps—no, better for you to come. I am quite free."

"I am not free and not likely to be," Fred said. "Though I have no scheduled classes, I am required to stay in the area. This body's a monkey in the works."

"Monkey *wrench* is the *mot juste*, surely."

"An old box of papers. Letters, day books, jottings. Mice have been through it, and lived in it, and eaten a good bit, and my skimming has been pretty quick. I get those names, and some dates in the 1860s, and a general sense that one subject at issue is a trip west, maybe to as far from here as California."

"The material may well prove to be useful, provided...in the meantime, hold on to it, Fred."

"It is not mine," Fred said.

"One can hold something without owning it. Many do. You mention a body, Fred. Elucidate."

"Wild card. Rodney Somerfest. Director here very briefly. Fired last autumn. Killed, apparently. Recently. His body washed up last night. Very cinematic."

"Indeed." Clay hummed and tutted. A chink of Sèvres suggested a deliberative sip of the gruesome beverage. "Let us not be distracted by events," Clay advised. "Should events threaten to impede your efforts, bypass them. Keep looking. Look everywhere. Let no one know what you are looking for."

Fred let that one go. The obvious response would be too easy.

"One nice thing among the flotsam and jetsam," Fred said, looking at the item he had placed on the table next to him. "The only thing in our line. A card addressed to Rosa Ludlow, whoever she is. It's painted. A butterfly. Quite elaborate, even gorgeous in its way. The message, "Weather continues fine." No signature. Initials. AB. I do note that the A could stand for Albert, unless Albert is a last name."

A long pause on Clay's end. Then, "Aah."

"For me it rings a distant bell," Fred said. "But I can't find anything in my mind right now. My mind is like this mouse-eaten box of dreck. Too cluttered. A couple of hundred new people to sort through as well as two or three new people to pretend to be. Soon there'll be cops to dodge, who want to know

what brings me here and who I really am. Reporters are starting to turn up, and they're all staying here, at the Stillton Inn.
Nobody cares about Rodney Somerfest. But because the body
was naked, they hope there's sex to sell.

"Somehow there's always a market.

"Plus, there's going to be a manhunt now for Morgan Flower.
I took my stuff out of his rooms. The cops don't like a missing
person in the vicinity of a death by violence. They leap to conclusions. Therefore my primary, purported role is about to be
blown sky high. The headlines on AOL and Fox are going to jam
Missy and Flower and naked Rodney together in a messy *ménage
à trois* of leering speculation that lasts until the next governor
gets caught with his or her pants around her or his ankles.

"In short, the proverbial shit is in mid-flight, and making a
bee-line for the equally proverbial fan."

The butterfly card had been nibbled around the edges. The
painted image, though, was almost intact. Only the upper edge
of the right wing was damaged.

"All of this bustle could work to our advantage," Clay suggested. "It is certainly to our present advantage, at least, that
none of the searchers have the same goals as do we."

"Even I myself…" Fred started.

"Never mind. Keep looking. Look everywhere."

"Is it bigger than this breadbox?" Fred asked.

The expostulation at Clayton's end of the line, though faint,
nonetheless registered as, "Tchah!"

Outside the single window of the room, the day promised to
be clear and almost pleasant. However, the weather in Stillton,
Massachusetts, did not keep its promises.

"How much has Parker Stillton told you about this place?"
Fred demanded.

"Very little. Although we are distant cousins, by marriage, as
you know, that fact does not intrude upon his native discretion.
Nor on mine."

Clay's smirk could almost be heard from fifty miles away.

"Because it seems to me," Fred pushed on, "and knowing nothing about the way these things are done, perhaps caring less, if you ran a gas station or convenience store as sensibly as these people are running their academy, you wouldn't be able to see the place for the shadows of the vultures circling."

"My fear exactly," Clay agreed. "I may have put this off too long."

"I know you too well to suggest that you replace your pronoun with a noun," Fred said.

"Indeed. But I never saw an approach, a place of entry."

"A vulture starts with the eyes, then goes in under the tail," Fred helped.

Clay reproved him. "We may be wasting valuable time."

Chapter Thirty-one

"It can't be coincidence," Molly said. "Have you run into something called the Stillton Realty Trust?"

"Can't say I have."

"They're all of them in it. Maybe not all. But, listen," Molly said. *"Pharaohs from Outer Space*—that's what your mother was watching with the kids?" Fred interrupted.

"She believes every word," Molly said. "The kids think, since they saw it in her place, she gets to decide what's true. Of course the whole thing is that word we invite them not to keep saying. Scale model diagrams of space ships on the walls of Egyptian tombs and the rest of it. It was very convincing if you happen to come to it in a state of utter ignorance."

"It'll be perfect for my students," Fred said. "You mentioned a realty trust?"

"They all belong to it. Administrators, beneficiaries, whatever. That Elizabeth Harmony. I got the lineup of the trustees of your academy. They have to publish that somewhere, which means I can find it. Same names, anyway. The lawyer you mentioned? Abe Baum? He's in it."

"Rodney Somerfest?" Fred asked.

"Did you give me that name?"

"In a message."

"Oh. The light's blinking. No, I didn't get that."

"Never mind. Later. How about Parker Stillton?"

"Sure. I figured the trust must be named after him. I don't know how these things work. Unless you are burdened with money, you don't have to."

"What are the assets of this realty trust?" Fred asked. "Now you mention it, what *is* a realty trust? Besides—safe supposition—a tax dodge of some kind. What's this trust…?"

"Fred, give me a break. I've had a total of forty-six minutes to look so far. It took me until eleven o'clock last night to try to decontaminate Sam and Terry from this Pharaoh nonsense."

"This trust. There's an address in Stillton?" Fred said, his pencil poised.

"In Boston. P. O. Box. You want it?"

"Interesting," Fred said. "In other words, they prefer to remain anonymous. Can you find out what they own? Is this just another way to represent the board of the academy? Isn't a board said to own the institution it represents? Can you find out…?"

"Fred," Molly broke in, "I can find out a lot, and I'll keep looking. I'm also driving Mom and the kids to the beach, and making sandwiches beforehand, which they will all despise and reject before they eat them hungrily if not gratefully."

"I recommend devilled eggs," Fred said. "Nothing beats a devilled egg once it gets filled with sand."

"Noted," Molly said.

◇◇◇

"I'm interrupting," Fred said, interpreting the testy sound of Clay's response.

"I am on the other phone, waiting to bid," Clay said. "I have seven entries to wait until my number comes. Be quick, if it is important."

"Oh yes, I had forgotten the…"

"No names," Clay insisted. "Be quick."

"If you could trust Parker Stillton, I'd ask you to make him tell you about the Stillton Realty Trust," Fred said, "But he's part of it and my guess is you shouldn't trust him, so don't ask him. Have you heard of it, though? The Stillton Realty Trust?"

"No. And trust no one. I can't speak now." The click at Clayton's end of the line was not Sèvres, but hard plastic. If Sèvres had made a telephone, Clay would surely want one.

"The shoes are perfect," Fred told Mrs. Halper at the desk.

"That's lucky. Your loafers will be at least another day. I have them on top of the dryer where it's warm, but not so warm they'll shrink."

The vestibule, or lobby, or whatever they called the small place downstairs through which all guests must pass, this morning was enlivened by persons in teams who carried TV cameras and the kinds of cell phones that might also record what a person said, or take pictures. But there was nothing to record here, or to take pictures of. Everyone had already been to the beach to take pictures of the place where "Nude male body found." The body's name hadn't yet been released "pending notification of the next of kin" if any. At the beach, though, there could not have been much to photograph in the absence of the nude male body. There was the lighthouse, of course. And the lone seagull all of whose friends and acquaintances could be airbrushed or Photo-Shopped out.

Everyone wanted to know why the Inn didn't provide breakfast. Again and again, Mrs. Halper was obliged to refer her clients to Bee's Beehive, or to the Stillton Café. Once he had her to himself, Fred told her, "I'd like to meet Lillian Krasic."

"Why?"

"She's staying here," Fred said.

Mrs. Halper pursed her lips and shook her head. "She doesn't see people," she said.

"What an enviable position to be in," Fred said. "Unless—is she in solitary?"

"If you'd like to leave her a message," Mrs. Halper suggested.

"I'll phone her room later," Fred said. "After she's had a chance to start her day."

"Or you can leave a message for her with the desk," Mrs. Halper said. "The desk is me."

Fred told her, "Thanks," and strolled outside.

Main Street had taken on the look of the auction room before things get started. Strangers moved up and down, looking for an angle.

"You with the college?" a man of medium age and better than medium girth asked Fred, stepping into his path in front of the dark front door of the unopened barber and beauty shop.

"Not a college," Fred said. "We call it an academy."

"Explain the distinction."

"We make the distinction. We leave it to others to explain it. Who are you with?"

"*Boston Globe.*"

"What's happening over there?" Fred asked.

"We leave that for others to explain," Fred's correspondent said. "Can you give me some background on this place? Anything beyond what shows up on Google? Town looks like it died in 1863."

Chapter Thirty-two

The office of Homeland Realty in Rockport, Massachusetts, did not show extraordinary hustle. Fred sat in his car across from the entrance which, at ten o'clock, on this weekday morning, still showed no signs of activity. He'd already spent enough time surveying the colorful photographs displayed in the front window, of properties being offered at very attractive prices to their present owners.

The mist was heavy enough to qualify as fog, but not as rain. The added mist of his breathing, condensing on the inside of the windshield, did not decrease the general visibility.

"As Napoleon wisely might have said the evening before Waterloo," Fred said, "why not rehearse the disposition of our troops, the prospects of our opponents, as well as what brings us here? Are there perhaps anomalies and unknowns?

"One. We started in the deep end, and blindfolded. The academy, represented by Baum, comes to me, demands that I settle the issue of the missing student-teacher couple, and keep it all under wraps because of the primary goal, which is accreditation.

'Two. Fifteen hours later the academy tries to scare me off. But, three, they don't try hard. Then they try to buy me off but, again, four, they don't try hard.

"Five, they claim they want accreditation but, again, they don't try hard. I don't know anything about it, but it's obvious, if you have no admissions program and no real director and no attempt to hire one and no catalogue and no money, and even so you're offering an unnecessary lunk like me fifteen grand to go away, to be paid out of money you don't have (if it's true they don't have it…)

"Six. What does the happy handyman Milan mean when he asks me, first, 'Who do you represent?' and then, 'What's your offer?', and then clams up? Do I take an interest? Is he fishing? Making trouble?

"Interruption. Who is AB? Butterfly boy?

"Seven. We know two things about Rodney Somerfest. Three, actually. He tried to buy the Stillton Inn. He's fired. On top of that he's dead.

"There's somebody now."

Fred gave the woman a chance to decant herself from her yellow slicker, do whatever adjustments might be necessary to the resulting ensemble, start the office machines warming up, turn on lights, check messages, before he breezed in.

"Hi," Fred enthused, letting his extended hand lead him across the office. Cynthia Mangone was pinning the name tag over her left breast. Beneath the tag, as background, a floral print suggested hydrangeas against blue sky. An electric coffee pot back of her was already dripping thin tan liquid, but she hadn't yet turned over yesterday's page on the desk calendar.

"Cynthia," Cynthia said. She gestured toward a comfortable client chair. She might be forty-five or fifty. There was less on her desk than on the two other desks in the room. Noticing Fred's outstretched hand, at long last, she offered hers.

"Fred," Fred confided. He sat. "Thing is, I drove all through Stillton. You know it?"

Her eyes flickered assent.

"Great little place that seems to have caught the plague," Fred continued. "The phrase ghost town came to mind. Not even a McDonald's. Still, I like it. I'm intrigued. The people I represent—let's say I'm from the Middle West—I'm out here looking. That's enough to start. But I don't know the area. So I decide I'll drive through town, get a feel for the place, before

I select one of the local realtors to show me the ropes, tell me how the land lies, what's what, what's available, asking prices, recent sales, the rest of it.

"Thing is—and I couldn't believe the yellow pages or Google, all that—anyway, the way I am, I like to go by what I see—there's no sign of a real estate office in Stillton. Like the whole town has been dead and buried for a thousand years, along with Rip van Winkle.

"So, I get on the phone to a friend of a friend who's done business out here, and she recommends Homeland Realty.

"So.

"Here I am."

"You want coffee?" Cynthia said.

"I'll keep you company."

She rose and turned and occupied herself in a series of womanly gestures that served to mask whatever she might be thinking. Fred's opening gambit had been so broad, so vague, so pregnant with possibility, that she needed to analyze it.

The mug she offered, not Sèvres, was at least china, though it would require a good deal of effort to break it. Fred gestured refusal of adulterants. The coffee smelled bad enough already.

"We do business all over the North Shore and into New Hampshire," Cynthia said.

"What I want..." Fred started.

"Yes?"

"I like the feel of Stillton. I don't know why. Well, I do. Something about it, you know?"

"We handle properties everywhere in the area," Cynthia said. "I'll check, see what we have in Stillton."

"Also I was wondering," Fred said. "Maybe there's a town ordinance against it? I didn't see a single FOR SALE sign. I have to say, this day and age, where I come from, frankly that's just plain weird. Even if everyone knew there was an earthquake coming, like in San Francisco, there'd still be action. At least where I come from, there's always someone who figures he can make a pile and get out before the next bomb drops."

While he talked, Cynthia Mangone was going through the motions of scrolling through listings on her computer's screen. "No,' she said finally. "Strange. Tell me, what kind of place are you interested in? Waterfront? Commercial? There's a whole block of storefronts opening in Rockport, for example. A seaside mansion, summer cottage, acreage to develop—what is your pleasure?"

"We want to buy a town," Fred said.

Chapter Thirty-three

"And I wouldn't discuss the issue with just anyone," Fred said, "obviously. Which is why it is so important to check you out as carefully as our people did—discreetly—though you might have gotten wind that someone was asking questions—no?—well, good. Our people know what they are doing.

"You'll agree at this stage of the game I can't really say who we are, my firm, or who we represent. An overseas subsidiary of one of the big internationals based in, for example, Bahrain or Dubai. That's a for-example.

"So—for the moment—we don't mention the names of our principals. It starts talk, which is always counterproductive. Makes a mess in the market and costs money. And for what? After we look everything over and consider the variables—licensing restrictions, deep-water access, political climate—it's happened before—we could have the whole package wrapped up with a bow on it and the head honcho tells us, 'No, we think we'll go with the west coast. Find a town in northern California, Oregon.

"I'm boring you."

"God, no!" Cynthia Mangone managed. "It's just—we're moving sort of fast. It's just, in America…"

"We know all about America in Kansas City," Fred bragged. "Hell, you could say we invented America. Bob Dole. What could be more American than that?"

"Bob Dole?"

"Not to drop names," Fred said. "Sure, you start quietly, buy through straws—that's where a discreet operation like yourself comes in. Next, when you control a majority of the properties, there's eminent domain and rights of way and the condemning of blocks for the good of the community and so for a while mayors and town councils all have to be involved. There's always holdouts.

"Churches is a big one. Which is one of the big attractions of Stillton. Banks you can always buy out but a church is harder. You have to condemn the building, satisfy the congregation; often it's easier to work around the damned church, leave it as an island, attractive, church bells and all, people dressed up for Easter: but next to a casino it can be a real downer.

"Forget I said casino.

"And so—and also you can't sell liquor within spitting distance of a church, and as far as a place where girls might show a little, you know, because we're talking a *private*...

"But, and so I notice in Stillton there's no church, which is a plus. No school, which can be a problem. That is, if there *is* a school. Which there isn't, so there's no problem. It's like they saw us coming.

"If there's nothing listed in Stillton, how come?"

Fred threw out the question, leaned back in his chair and waited.

Cynthia Mangone said, "When Rockport got started, more than a hundred years ago—really got started—it was like Stillton. Bigger, sure. But the same idea. Now it's got everything. Tourists. Art. Motif number one."

"I'm wasting your time," Fred said, getting up.

"What I'm doing, I'm thinking," Cynthia Mangone said. "I talk when I think, but not necessarily about what I'm thinking about. It's a habit. Bear with me. How's your coffee?"

"Pretty consistent," Fred assured her. He sat and took another sip to prove it.

"Take an example. Say I wanted to put my toe in, start small," Fred said. "Which is a stupid way to do it but, I mean, imagine if the Hunt brothers, when they wanted to control the world silver market, started by picking up the odd tea set at yard sales.

But, for the sake of argument, say I decide to buy the Stillton Inn. Can you do that for me?"

Cynthia jabbed at her computer's keyboard and scrolled in several directions until she could tell him, "The tax rolls assess it at twoa million seven."

"OK. So we offer double," Fred said. "When the time comes. If the time comes. If it comes to that. What else does Mrs. Halper own?"

"Mrs. Halper?"

"OK. On the level now," Fred said. "And I have a good feeling talking to you. Obviously our people did a good deal of research before I came out here. Do I have it wrong? We show the title in the name of Mrs. Charles Halper."

"Odd," Cynthia Mangone said. Blue light from the screen bounced from her face. She had remarkably reflective skin. "The tax bill goes to Mrs. Lillian Krasic."

"Then there's been a transfer," Fred said smoothly. "Doesn't matter. We're talking a for-instance.

"We need a local Johnny-on-the-spot. I can't commute to Stillton and get involved in each little transaction, plus fly out to the conferences every six months in east who-knows, to report on progress, and all the while…

"I mean, we have some really big projects to worry about. The way I like to work, we sew this up in a week or two, nominate someone local to do the nitty gritty, which takes time and more patience than I have, the next time you see me might not be till the grand opening."

"GRAND OPENING," Cynthia Mangone said. Her mouth was so full of capital letters she could scarcely get them out past her teeth and lips.

"See, what I am, I'm the big picture guy," Fred said.

"And the big picture keeps changing," Cynthia Mangone said.

"I'm that kind of guy. Think big, there's always that next horizon. I move, the horizon moves. A horizon is like that."

"And you already own, or have an option to buy, seven eighths of Stillton," Cynthia said.

"Dream on."

"Don't bullshit me," Cynthia Mangone said, her voice turning businesslike suddenly, with an edge of canny interest. "What do you think these things are that you are dropping here? Hints? You think I don't know bullshit? So. Here you are and yes, I'm interested. Why me I don't know, and why care? It's no secret *what's* happening out there; just nobody could really figure out who, or why. Or how you get past the major holdout," she continued relentlessly, "being Stillton Academy of Art. And the Stillton Inn too, you mentioned, pretending you don't know who owns it; Bee's Beehive, which is a restaurant; a gas station that will cave when the time comes, and about six properties that are so tied up in estates and title problems it will take forever.

"So, what I want to know, Mr. 'the coffee is consistent,' what does the Stillton Realty Trust want to waste its time with me for?

"What do you really want? What can I do for you?

"And, by the way, what's in it for me?"

Chapter Thirty-four

"Start with a name. If you are who you say you are. I have 'Fred' so far," Cynthia Mangone said.

Fred said, "I started wrong." He stood again, explaining, "Crick in my back," and stretched. "The business you're in, I imagine you're used to a certain amount of misrepresentation. I thank you for the coffee. Also for your time."

He'd hung his jacket on the coat rack provided so that the mist could drip from it onto the realtor's artificial hardwood floor.

Cynthia proposed, "I might could help with the holdouts. But you'll have to be straight with me. See, because so far I could see you coming from a mile away and it wastes time. So—maybe a card? Something real, on paper, that I don't have to scrape up with a shovel after you walk out?"

"I believe I have attained what persons in my line of business call the hour of lunch," Fred said.

"If that's an invitation, don't bother," Cynthia said. "In my diet, the beef byproducts are strictly out. There isn't a…"

Fred said, "After I consult with my principals, I could stop back."

"Or telephone. That's better," Cynthia said. "Or e-mail. That's the best. That always finds me. Here's my card."

Fred, on his way out, had to turn back to take the card from Cynthia Mangone who, demonstrating her aggrieved state, as well as her femality, had remained seated back of her desk, the light from the computer screen struggling against the print of hydrangeas on her blouse.

"Your card?" she demanded.

"Could be in the car," Fred said.

"A good disguise, that car," Cynthia Mangone said. "Like the sneakers and the jacket. I didn't figure you out until you started talking guff. If I get a line on one of these holdouts, if I need to get in touch, what do I do? Just Google 'Fred'?"

"You've been a help," Fred told her.

"That P. O. box you people have," Cynthia said. "Nobody answers the mail."

"You may be right about e-mail," Fred agreed.

Rockport, for all its grand and complex history, is a place that seems to specialize in lunch. Lunch, ideally, with a marine flavor. Being hungry, Fred parked amid the worst of the beckoning but mostly empty tourist traps in the most touristic portion of the seaside town. It was the wrong kind of day in the wrong season for the blessing of strolling tourists from far afield to be crowding the sidewalks looking for souvenirs of Rockport, or sitting in the restaurants ingesting more edible souvenirs, such as lobsters imported from the sovereign state of Maine.

Among the inedible souvenirs—and probably the worst— were the tangible evidence of Rockport's chronic infestation by summer colonies of painters and sculptors.

As one looked to select the winning place for lunch one was obliged to confront, and to ignore as best one could, the gaping doorways of the galleries. Some even exuded that miasma of canned *pot pourri* meant to impair the sales resistance of those who wander, unaware, into gift stores specializing in objects of decorative uselessness.

Rockport's famous motif number one, whether that was a red barn or a lighthouse, was broadly represented both in watercolor and oil. Which it was—whether the barn or the lighthouse—Fred might never know. Those bringing themselves to tinker with an attempt at representing natural things did floral arrangements, floral patterns, or the lone seagull whose feet have become fastened to the lone bollard.

For the more ambitiously "artistically" inclined, there were varied but cruelly abstracted versions of the female nude either painted or, perhaps more pernicious, bronzed. Of those objects that sported color, the color tended to the garish. In these instances, sales must depend upon the willingness of the tourist to return to Dubuque with the object in question, and the rehearsed line, "I bought this in Rockport, Massachusetts. We stayed there. Ed had his eye on a seagull picture—over a breaking wave, you could see the reflection even, of the gull, and the sun setting and all, but I thought, 'No. We can remember that anyway with a postcard. Let's take the risk. Sure people will talk, but I'm like that. Something came over me. It's art. It's OK among friends.'

"If strangers come for drinks, or people from the bank, we can hang it upstairs."

Was this the hideous fate of the students who managed to persist in struggling through their painting courses at Stillton Academy, and who then must find a means to earn a bare minimum to subsist on while they churned out pictures that progressively, over the years, looked less and less like what they had imagined when they were young and ideals plagued them—and more and more like what all the tourists imagined they would find in Rockport's galleries?

Hell, you wouldn't have to look at, know, or be, a naked human being, in order to turn out stylized "nudes" like these. The "bronze" wasn't even bronze, but a congealed liquid like that cosmetic spread they used to sell called "Man-Tan."

Had all these painters been through a comparable train of study? Wasn't it all wasted? Even if she does it very well, is the ballet dancer's skill not misused if she spends her days walking people's dogs? Even though the occupation makes use of many of the same talents?

Bad as the student paintings might have been, last night, when he glanced them over in his quick look through the painting studios—at least they were honest. Give Stillton's teachers that much credit.

Even granted that the world did not exist for which they were training their students, at least they were training them for an imagined something and not to become automatons with no aesthetic scruples.

Fred's lunch might have been the moral equivalent of the seagull picture. However, it was tasty fish chowder, a tasty and resilient hard roll, and a convincing plate of broiled blue fish to follow.

◇◇◇

There were all of seven other diners. Each of them, even the little girls, was involved with either one lobster or a matched pair. It wasn't until his coffee that Fred exclaimed, "For God's sake, it's Albert Bierstadt!"

Everyone in the place looked at him, alarmed.

"It's OK, folks," Fred reassured his fellow diners—as well as the hovering waiter and the woman back of the cash register. "Perfectly OK. AB is Albert Bierstadt."

Chapter Thirty-five

Whatever the clues had been that led to Clay's suspicion, once again he had scented possibility. The box of papers Fred had skimmed through so haphazardly this morning, in his room, endangering the evidence with weak coffee, showed correspondence and familiar dealings between some persons named Ludlow and this significant nineteenth century American painter.

Bierstadt's paintings, whether tiny or simply huge, had reported an idealized version of the landscape of much of northern America as the United States was expanding into the west. New Bedford, where he had lived in his early years; the White Mountains of New Hampshire; Wyoming's Wind River Valley; Yosemite; the Pacific coast—Bierstadt had known and traveled them all, making sketches from which, back in his New York studio, he rendered finished paintings sometimes of monumental size, and even majesty.

To amuse his friends, he had also liked to make small, even postcard-sized versions of invented butterflies. That card, on the table in his room, even without the initialed AB, was solid proof: the issue on Clayton's mind was Albert Bierstadt.

Fred paid his money and made tracks for Stillton.

And was obliged, once he had arrived in town, to move with care. For one thing, it was a completely different town from the one he had left a few hours before, on account of what he had learned about it.

His instinct had been correct. Something was up. The place was either controlled by a monopoly, or under siege, apart from a few buildings. No wonder so much of it was vacant. His unwitting informant, Cynthia Mangone, had let it drop—in her unwise attack—that most of what the academy did not control, this other entity, the Stillton Realty Trust, whose members coincided with the academy's board, either owned or had an option to buy. If the Stillton Realty Trust wanted to own the entire town, only Stillton Academy stood in its way.

Massachusetts is a commonwealth, and not a state, as any fourth grader in Massachusetts will tell you. Fifth graders have mostly forgotten it. Nevertheless, the Commonwealth's police are called State Cops by everyone, even fourth graders. And it was the cruisers of the state cops, about six in all, that presently moved through the streets and lanes of Stillton.

A cruiser was parked in front of Morgan Flower's building. The car was empty. Uniformed figures passed in front of Flower's windows. A second cruiser idled in front of the admissions and administration building. One uniform behind the wheel. Presumably another uniform, of a detective type, was inside, talking with Elizabeth Harmony about her predecessor; perhaps interviewing faculty.

Fred left his car at some remove, down in the lanes by the shore where doomed fishermen, the unwitting tenants of the Stillton Realty Trust, congratulated themselves on the cheap rents that let them afford to follow this trade.

"Holy Toledo," Fred said, walking. "All of that silly fantasy I found in Flower's desk? The 'Inn at Stillton Sound' and the rest of it, whatever it was. The Spa. Condos and lap pools and the rest. That horse shit? Responsible luxury. All that? Maybe it wasn't fantasy.

"Maybe it *isn't* fantasy.

"If Dubai can build its own new offshore island in the form of a Dunkin' Donut, and fill it with parks and yachts and docks and arboretums, why can't the Stillton Realty Trust build and promote a New England Williamsburg-by-the-Sea, complete with authentic historic lap pools and casinos, and all the other luxurious responsibilities they can dream up?

"So. What is Flower up to, and who is Flower? Because if there's one thing I know for sure, that man's no teacher."

Four o'clock. The last third-year painters were packing up in Stillton B, Fred's classroom. The lean young man Fred recognized from some twenty-seven exercises seen by dimmed flashlight the previous evening, was buttoning his shirt.

"OK, Don. Thanks. Next week, then?" Meg Harrison said, handing the model an envelope.

Did these folks pay in cash?

Fred wandered through the studio, edging between the easels where students, reluctant to surrender for the day, were studying their progress. Emma's figure had become more contorted. The man's green penis now sported a lavender shadow. They suited each other. She'd painted out the bowl of fruit.

"It's better," Fred did not say. He contented himself with a nod.

"I'll recommend we put in an exhaust fan," he told Meg.

"Go ahead. I've told them for five years," she said. "By the way, I got your hint about the setup. I photographed it. I'll strike it. Take it down. I can put it up again, no problem. So it's not in your way."

Fred said, "There are students here majoring in sculpture? Whatever you do in that line here, you told me, that isn't metal or fabrication?"

"It's better without the fruit," Meg was telling Emma. "A better picture. Granted. However, the fruit is part of the problem. Put it back in. Paint the fruit the way you did the penis—straight on, here it is, get on with it—you've got something. Put it back in. Keep the fruit, take it with you. Bring it back next week. Even better, match it with something new. When you paint it, make it look like something you'd be interested in putting your mouth around; but scared."

"Like that penis," she might have pointed out.

The students had a variety of ways to pack and carry their wet paintings. They were too large to be stored in their lockers. Meg started to fold the orange and blue cloths.

"We have a couple of possibles," Meg said. "To answer your question, Fred. One third-year is wavering. Two second-years in figure modeling show promise, though don't confuse figure modeling with sculpture. And there's a genius in first year, but..."

"So. One of mine," Fred said. "Which one?"

Meg finished folding, tucked the cloth under her arm and hoisted the stool down to march it across the studio to place with the others. "Make sure these easels are back against the wall," she said to the room, "and stack the horses. Show some respect for the folks who have to clean this whorehouse. Some of those folks are you."

Emma had boxed her equipment and was carrying the wet painting into the hall where a sudden scuffle produced raised voices. "Lay off, Tom. You're on her like a ghost." That was Peter Quarrier's voice.

Fred stepped out for a look. Peter was standing in dangerous confrontation with Tom Meeker, who had appeared from somewhere with a portfolio under his arm. "What do you fucking care?" Meeker countered. "It's not like you could fucking want her."

Students, interrupted in their departure, were gathering in a loose crowd. Emma, both of her hands occupied, stood between the men. "I can talk for myself, Peter. You lay off too. And listen, I've told you a hundred times, Tom. I mean it. Lay off of me. Get lost."

"We know all about you," Meeker sneered. "You and the weed..."

"Keep this up if you want me to break your neck," Peter said quietly. His breathing was fast and shallow, and his face was white.

Fred eased into the mix, took Tom Meeker's elbow in a grip that could be disregarded only at the cost of a broken arm, and let him out into the air.

Chapter Thirty-six

Tom Meeker, fuming, might nevertheless be grateful for the force that had pulled him from the confrontation. If Quarrier had to, he could take Meeker apart in three well-trained minutes. "It's not like Quarrier could want her," Meeker complained. "He's queer."

"It's likely more a matter of what she wants," Fred said. "At least in my experience. Anyway, why don't you take the opportunity to cool down?"

"Show off. He has it all except he's queer. I'll show them. I'll show her," Meeker blustered. A few students had followed them warily out of the studio building and into the chilly air, in which the foghorn seemed to be causing hysterics amongst the seagulls. "You think I can't?" Meeker shouted. If he had friends among the gathered students, none admitted to the fact. Meeker glared at his audience a moment, then turned and went away. The hallway outside the studios had emptied.

Fred found Meg in Studio A, finishing up. "They can seem almost cute in the first year," Meg said. "Sorry about that. It's been brewing. Meeker. Talk about cute! Remind me, if we ever have time, to tell you about the Meeker Method."

"I'm going to check this building," Fred said. "For my report. That whole building next door, the painting studios, that's a fire trap."

"Tell me about it," Meg said. "It's been a long day." Her arms full of props, she hovered in the studio doorway.

Fred said, "I haven't even gotten to the printmaking studios. As far as this building goes, I've noted the need for ventilation, and you concur. Anything else?"

"Get me decent sinks and drains in the figure modeling studio. And in the annex out back. And a strong water supply we can depend on. If you can do that…hell, who am I kidding?

"The way these committees and commissions work, it's always the same thing. Like government. Form a group. Do a study. Face squarely and honestly your needs and shortcomings. Talk through them until you agree how to write them down. This after you've already wasted seventy-five institutional hours composing an utterly futile and irrelevant 'mission statement'. So, write your report. Then in five years, when it comes time for the next report, it's easier because if you can find the earlier study, you can just copy it, because the problems are still the same, but with additional leaks and financial troubles.

"And all the cracks you found the last time around have gotten wider.

"Sure, the painting studios should be brick or cinderblock. That means a new building. Or, let's go beyond buildings a minute—if we say with a straight face that we offer a major in sculpture, we should acknowledge that there is such a thing as metal. Casting. Pouring. Welding. Fabrication. That means the space, the tools, the hoists, the faculty.

"Good luck with your report. Me, I've had it, I guess. You could feel it at that faculty meeting, I know. Everyone's given up. We're so used to being treated like shit, we don't react any more. Why fight if there's nothing to fight with or fight for? I'm heading for the high ground. It's a shame."

While she talked, Meg had walked the length of the corridor, past the student lockers, to the swinging doors leading into the figure modeling room. She pushed into it and tossed her props into a corner. It appeared that no class had taken place here during the day. All was as it had been at the end of yesterday's class. "Go ahead, look around," Meg said. "Just don't fool with the students' work. Don't for God's sake unwrap anything. If it doesn't stay damp, they're screwed. Not that you'd have any reason to look at it."

"Heading for the high ground," Fred repeated her words. "You're looking for another position?"

"This place won't survive," Meg said. "It should. It has an impressive will to live. But it won't."

"Because?" Fred said.

"We'll see what your report says," Meg whispered. "Take it from there. I'm out of here. Turn out the lights when you're done. The doors will lock themselves. The kids will be coming in to clean, probably seven in the morning. If they remember. But they're pretty good about it."

The building had become his. Fred checked the men's room and the women's. Everyone in the world apparently had somewhere else to be. It was the space above the studios he wanted to get to.

The studio ceilings were ten feet high, generous, and that allowed for the easels to be extended to accommodate even large paintings—if any of these students could afford such extravagance. But the building had a long peaked roof. In its twin, where the third- and fourth-year studios were, the ceiling had been removed. The reconfiguration of the roof line included the shed dormer that permitted the extent of glass in the north wall.

But here, in Stillton Hall, the ceiling remained, with large square traps visible in both studios, painted as the ceiling was. That would be an immense space for something, though the roof's peak would be low.

Fred checked both traps, looking up from the studio floors. One or the other of them should offer a ring bolt into which the person below, armed with a stick with a hook in the end, could pull down the hinged trap and unfold the ladder—if there was a ladder.

Except that there was no sign of hinges, nor of ring bolt.

A tall stepladder would be useful. There had been a couple on Milan's porch, chained and padlocked to discourage borrowers—but never mind. The studio's furniture offered an alternative. He'd make the ascent in Stillton B.

Fred dragged the platform on which Don the model had spent the day, under the trap. On that he engineered a wide platform of horses, standing toe to toe; on top of that a further platform of horses on which he could place a stool. Standing on that, he was able to reach the plywood trap and, pushing it upwards, to free it from the latest coat of paint that glued it shut at its edges.

It lifted evenly; therefore had to be lifted high enough to clear the joists, then be slid to one side. Dust rained down and glinted in the studio's waning daylight. The stool allowed him to get arms and shoulders into the attic space. The stool, though, was uncertain enough that there was reason to hope that he would not finish this part of the mission in a comic debacle. If he'd had time, and help, he could have used the student lockers to construct a nifty set of stairs.

It was the best he could do. He hoisted himself upwards until he was in.

And he was surrounded.

By junk.

Light filtered upward through the opening. Wet daylight also muscled in through dirty windows at either end, under the roof peak. Fred could not stand, the peak being no more than five feet.

"They're crazy not to insulate this roof," Fred said. "Given in winter they have to keep the studios warm enough for a naked person to work in. And not the kind of work that generates heat. Presumably this floor is insulated. Still…" something else for the report he was not going to write.

Worrying smell of char all around, pervasive. Char and dissolving junk.

The building, like its neighboring twin, and like the rest of the town, had the feel of having been built no later than the 1880s. Though it had been remodeled, rethought, and recast, the bones of Stillton Hall were basically as they had always been. The building's original purpose, whatever it was, was consistent with its present use—except that, in this useless attic space, the Josephus Stilltons, or their survivors, instead of going the yard sale route, had stored all their impossible crap.

Chapter Thirty-seven

So much of it showed traces of smoke and burning. Fred shouldered through dismal heaps of furniture: the carved rosewood love seat in pink plush, missing three legs; the chair constructed of longhorns; nightstand with cracked marble; and underfoot—well, underknee, because up here locomotion was possible only on all fours—the enamel bedpan missing large bites of enamel; the cracked glass urinal for the patient's use; cane-bottomed chairs without their caning, and missing legs, arms or backs.

And throughout, the smell of burning. Most everything here had known the intimate touch of flame.

In the attic itself, its floors or rafters, there was no sign of burning. Just the smell, given the volatility of the building's contents, was alarming. No, what must have happened, and it stood to reason—supposing that the Josephus Stilltons had been bigwigs in their day, they must have had a mansion that was appropriate to the exercise of whatever level of bigwiggery they professed. And there was presently no sign of such a mansion in all of Stillton. It must have burned, and its contents, rescued, have been shoved into the attic of this building to be sorted through some day.

Piles of books, frayed, scabbed and charred. Trunks—Fred pried one open and found clothes, as much as remained after the moths and rot. He eased open the second trap, above the figure modeling studio, to get more light. This made the crap easier to see, but it was still crap.

Wait. Picture frames. Yes. Frames.

Empty. Broken.

Fred kept looking, crawling through the dreck and dust. There was enough broken glass to make the crawling difficult. Here was a large supply of horsehair left behind when its covering—it had stuffed a large cushion—was devoured by moths who despised the taste of horse, and stuck to velvet.

Take the masked ball, the big scene at the end of—who knows—some nineteenth-century operetta—*Die Fledermaus?*—and collapse it, stage, sets, costumes, lights and all. Set fire to it then, and put it out. Pull out the people and anything of value. Make sure the firemen tramp through everything and stir the remains. Then sift and sort and shove all that remains into the attic, against a better day.

Die Fledermaus? Maybe *The Fall of the House of Usher.*

What was that, rain outside? Beating against the windows, drumming the roof in a sad pavane.

Nothing here. Nothing of value or interest.

No. Wait. Under the eaves at the far end. In the dusk, more trash—but it didn't look right somehow. It was too flat. Fred crawled through the wreck until he reached the spot. It was not at all what it appeared to be—piled books, a trunk, split china crocks, a randy rocking horse with a missing ear, a spill of tattered clothing—but rather a painted screen of canvas hanging from halfway up the rafters, making an effective knee-wall ten feet long, on which these objects had been painted, as if for a stage set.

The canvas lifted easily and back of it were rolls piled one on another, that could be rugs. So infected had his search become by cumulative disappointment , as well as by the length of the rolls, that Fred immediately dismissed them as rugs that should, by now, have been eaten as badly as any of the other cloth up here in which an enterprising mouse or moth or mold could discover protein.

Except the rolls were canvas.

Canvas hidden with great cleverness and care.

◇◇◇

Mrs. Halper handed Fred a note while looking with disfavor at the state of his clothing. Only this morning he had been freshly laundered and practically blown dry. "Detective Seymour wants you to call him," she said.

"How urgent?"

"He waited half an hour and then left the note," Mrs. Halper said.

What had to be a reporter—one of several adults standing in the entrance room—demanded, "Where does a person get a drink in this town?"

"The Stillton Café. I've told you. If you want something stronger, there's Buster's Provisions, but he closes at seven. What's left is the Stillton Café."

"Stillton Café has nothing but beer and wine I wouldn't wash my socks in."

"I'm glad to hear it," Mrs. Halper reproved him.

"But you've got something in the kitchen, for sure," the reporter insisted. "A bottle of Scotch?"

"I do, but no license to serve it," Mrs. Halper said. "And not a great deal of patience either. The matter is closed."

"State cop?" Fred asked, waving the paper he'd been given. "Detective Seymour?"

"The only police officers in this town are security from the academy. Which it looks like to me is this new President Harmony's way of seeming important. Because we sure Lord never needed them in the old days. So he's state. Has to be. Call him. He'll tell you."

Susan Muller came by, her arms filled with towels.

"Susan," Fred said.

"Yes, Fred?"

"Just saying 'Hi.'"

"Hi. Oh, and if I can't make class tomorrow…"

"I'll know where you are. So be there. See you then."

◇◇◇

Call Seymour first.

"You left town."

"Not the area," Fred said. "Errands in Rockport. Lunch. What can I do for you?"

"Monday night you stayed in Morgan Flower's apartment. You moved out last night. How come?"

"Telephone," Fred told him. "In the room here. I don't carry a cell. I should but I don't. The reason you know to find me here is I told the officers how to find me. What can I do for you?"

"Let's do this in the morning," Seymour said. "I've been on for twenty-four hours."

"I'm in class at eight-thirty," Fred said.

"Seven-thirty. There's a place on Main Street. Bee's Beehive. You know it?"

"All too well," Fred said. "No, that's not fair. I'm grateful to it. She opens at seven."

"Seven-thirty," Seymour said firmly.

◇◇◇

"OK. I take back everything I didn't say," Fred told Clay. "It's a spectacular find. I'm sure of it. I couldn't really see it, but I'm sure."

Was that the sound of Clayton chuckling? Surely not. That was as likely as Brooklyn Bridge rising into the air of its own volition.

"Say nothing," Clay instructed. Then, "Tell me everything."

Fred said, "The background will have to be confirmed. I have no doubt it can be fleshed out from local records. My conjecture is based on a quick reading of the evidence I've seen. My conclusions are partial, and subject to the fantasy that inevitably attaches to the thrill of discovery."

Chapter Thirty-eight

"So I'll separate conjecture from hard fact, and start with conjecture."

"Must we?" Clay complained.

"Conjecture gives context. And it's my story. So, here goes.

"By a certain date, let's say 1870 or so, Josephus Stillton had real money. Maybe 1880. In order to prove it, he built his time's equivalent of a McMansion. Running water, kitchens, ballroom, dining room, parlors, the works. Here in Stillton.

"Supposing that there was a Mrs. Josephus Stillton, she pushed him to make it nice, as well as making it big. She should have pushed him to make it of stone as well, but I guess she didn't."

Clay interrupted, "I fail to see the relevance…"

"For the ballroom, or for the dining room, he, she, or they ordered an extravagant decoration."

"Yes? Yes? The painting?" Clay put in, in an agony of anticipation.

"No, not *a* painting. A mural. By one of the foremost artists of the day. Albert Bier…"

"No names! No names," Clay pleaded. "Did you say a mural? Not fresco!"

"Fortunately not. I can't imagine this guy ever painted fresco. If he—let's call him AB—if he ever worked color into wet plaster, you'd sure have to prove it to me. No, in this case he worked on canvas cut to fit the walls."

"Oh, God! And glued?"

"No. There we're in luck. Stretched. The canvas was cut and stretched and tacked around the edges, and then I'm sure with the tacking edge covered by a molding that would also give the effect of a frame.

"Then the building burned."

"But this is almost mortal anguish," Clay pleaded.

"Hold on," Fred said. "I should have mentioned that although the mansion is conjecture, the mural is fact. I've seen it. It wasn't easy, and I could only see a sample. The subject is a panorama of the Wind River Valley in Wyoming, either at dawn or sunset. The panorama takes in, if I am correct, the full 360 degrees of startling landscape visible from a certain point on a plateau."

"I am speechless, speechless!" Clay managed. "But, you say the building burned?"

"Yes, but not before the mural had been removed. Here again we enter the realm of conjecture. Suppose that by 1920 someone decided to replace the ballroom windows—or mirrors—with more modern equivalents. Or someone decided the room could be better used as a kitchen or nursing station. Or someone simply decided that the painting was too old-fashioned or too pink."

"I know that pink," Clay said. His breathing was quick.

"You are sitting?" Fred asked.

"Get on with it."

"For whatever reason, the panels were carefully rolled and put for storage under the eaves of the garret of a large structure I teach in. I can't guess what the building's original purpose was, but it is presently used as studios. Then, when the mansion burned—understand, the mansion is just a guess..."

"Never mind. Never mind."

"Who is Rosa Ludlow?" Fred demanded.

"He married her. Go on. Go on. The paintings. The mural. Describe it."

"What I managed to see was under conditions of intense discomfort and difficulty, and I've managed to look at only a sampling of the complete work, as I told you. Odds are it's all there, but I can't be certain.

"The tallest rolls are eight feet high; the shorter ones either three or four. What I guess, the taller panels were stretched above wainscoting and chair rail that would have been between two and three feet in height. Windows or mirrors would grow upwards from the chair rail, and the three- or four-foot sections—mostly sky with vivid clouds—were stretched across those, as above the doorways."

"Marvelous. Marvelous," Clay said.

"Of course I was worried," Fred said. "Nobody knows this or takes it into account. If a painting on canvas has to be rolled, the painted side should always be on the outside. Oil paint is willing to stretch, in reason. If it's on the inside, it has to compress, and if the impasto is thick, it cracks."

"I know this, for heavens' sake," Clay expostulated. "Why are you teaching your grandmother…"

"So I was worried because in all these rolls, the canvas was on the outside. People mean well. They think it's a way to protect the paint. Then, with the heat and the dryness and the possibility of mice or leaks or squirrels…as I say, I was worried."

"And?"

"On quick inspection, they look fine," Fred said. "I'd feel better if I could really see them.

"Then, when the building burned, as I said before," Fred continued. "I lost my sequence there for a minute. Everything broken or awful or ruined or simply unwanted that came from the wreck of the mansion, got shoved into the garret in front of the rolled mural that was being stored up there already, and time moved on.

"He married her?"

"Who? Who got married?"

"AB"

"Oh. Rosa Ludlow. She had been the wife of Fitz Hugh Ludlow, a writer. Also a dabbler in hashish and women on the side. There was a divorce. That's all footnote…"

"As Macbeth said, didn't he? The rest is footnote?" Fred said.

"Footnote to us," Clayton explained. "To Rosa and to AB himself, we can hope that the marriage was main text, as was my own brief marriage—a shining chapter in the book of life."

There was a significant pause as both men hung at the brink of the emotional chasm offered by Clay's unexpected outburst of candor. It was a chasm as filled by dangerous color as was Bierstadt's Wind River Valley itself.

Fred said, "The only way to be sure is to lay the whole thing out, puzzle it together. See if anything's missing. You'd need a big space, like the floor of a gym."

"Bring it to me," Clay demanded.

Chapter Thirty-nine

The chasm of emotion that Clay had opened filled instantly with his utter unreasonableness. The only sensible response was disregard.

"At the moment that might not be practical," Fred said.

He had covered his tracks as best he could, though he must have left trails and prints of his activities in the dust and the piles of displaced refuse. He was haunted, also, by the careful job someone had done—when?—of making a screen of camouflage in front of the stored rolls of canvas. When had that been done? How many years ago? And why? So far was he from making sense of it that he didn't comment on it. Sufficient unto the day.

Below, in the studio, once he had rearranged the furniture, he had been sweeping the dust that had settled below the trap when a student entered—one he did not recognize—a male, stout and red-faced.

"I'll do that," he said. "It's my job."

"Just getting ready for tomorrow," Fred said. "My class meets here. I'm Fred."

"I know. You teach. I clean. I'm Rick."

"Rick Murphy?"

"How do you know my name?"

"They give us a list. There's only two Ricks. The other one's in first year, and I've met him."

"What they think is we're going to wake the hell up at six in the morning and clean before classes start. Which, to hell with that. Gimme the broom, would you?"

"You're fourth year," Fred said. "If I remember correctly."

Rick, sweeping, nodded.

"So you're thinking about next year," Fred said. "What's your major? Concentration? What do they call it?"

"Your list doesn't say?"

"There's too much on the list. I'm amazed I remembered your name, what with all the rest of it."

"Graphic design," Rick Murphy said. He hadn't stopped working, sweeping the area from which the furniture had been cleared, making a pile in which Fred's incriminating attic dust was well mixed with empty cans, wadded paint rags, and scraps of paper. He dragged a black plastic barrel over from the corner and scooped the pile into it using a dented metal dustpan.

"Go to Boston, I guess," Rick said. "I haven't really thought about it."

"Grad school?"

"I have to work," Rick said. "Everyone's so upset."

Fred took a moment. "I don't follow," he said after he had tried and failed to find a connection between Rick's two observations.

"Not that anyone liked the guy," Rick said.

"Oh." Rodney Somerfest.

"It's like something that happens in the city. New York. I went to New York one time. Almost got killed. I stepped into the road. It was a taxi."

"What was he doing around here?" Fred asked.

"You couldn't pay me to go to New York again," Rick said. "I almost got killed." He started moving the horses Fred had stacked against the wall Meg Harrison had designated earlier, into the cleared area he had swept. "Being you're here, how do you want these horses?" he asked.

Fred showed him. Concentric rings around the model's platform. Tomorrow he'd use the platform for himself.

"Does anyone have a theory what happened?" Fred asked.

"Ran a red light. Or it was me," Rick said.

"To Rodney Somerfest, I mean."

"Everyone says he was killed. Or it was an accident."

"If he was killed, what for?"

"I think he had money. Looked like it. His car and all."

"He was robbed, is your thought?" Fred said.

"Nobody liked him. Still," Rick concluded, "Still you can't help being upset. And then cops asking questions and all. People say you're friendly with Morgan Flower."

"Nope," Fred said.

"He's another one."

Fred waited long enough to allow Rick to flesh out the thought. But Rick evidently believed the thought was complete. He continued moving the horses. The easels stayed against the wall. "He's another what?" Fred asked finally.

"Rich guy that acts like he pretends like he wouldn't know what to do if he had a hundred bucks in his pocket."

"What's he want with a job here?" Fred asked. "If he's rich already?"

"Rich as he is, he can do anything he wants. Like with that girl. Woman. Student. I had him last year. Writing about my problems. Well he's got a problem now. The cops are all over his car."

Rick started sweeping the area he had cleared of furniture. "Broke into it, I guess," he said. Dusted it for prints. Looked everywhere. Then towed it." He smiled as he swept.

"Does anyone know where they went?" Fred asked. "Suspect, I should say."

"If they went to New York, look out!"

◇◇◇

A good deal later, after he'd managed to discourage Clay from imagining the prospect of instant gratification, Fred was able to reach Molly.

"Sure," she said, "there's a trolley that runs right to the beach, but Prince Charles prefers the car. According to Mom. And her car's here, as you know, since she gets someone to drive it down. And the bargain I had to make is, OK, we'll take the car as long as I drive. Which also means I have to find somewhere to park. But that beats letting Mom drive. Anyway, Terry is thrilled to pick up after that dratted dog. It's good practice for her. Teach her how to grow up to be a woman.

"Anyway. Morgan Flower. That was one of the names you gave me? Wait. Listen. Your message. Someone was killed? Be careful!"

"Someone died," Fred said. "We don't know how. Killed is a possibility."

"Rodney Somerfest. You told me. I looked him up. The only Rodney Somerfest I could find is a car dealer in Concord, New Hampshire."

"That's him," Fred said. "With a career change."

"This other name you gave me. Morgan Flower. I can't find anything. You can Google Morgan Flower until the cows come home. Nothing."

Chapter Forty

"He's a missing person," Detective Seymour said. Seymour was a burly fellow, seasoned and less sleepy than he seemed, who was used to being disregarded while he took advantage of it, and until it was too late. He sat across from Fred, and over a plate of poached eggs and hash. His poised fork considered and plunged into the yolk of the left hand egg while Seymour, apparently oblivious of the choice his fork had made, continued.

"By missing person I mean this," Seymour continued. "Morgan Flower is a genuinely missing person. Meaning I do not believe that he exists. His car, or what is said to be his car, is registered to Benjamin Star." The fork with its bite of egg found an appropriate aperture in Detective Seymour's face.

"I'm just having the coffee," Fred said.

"My eloquent pause invites you to make a relevant comment," Seymour said. "Relevant, that is, to my inquiry."

"What jurisdiction?" Fred asked.

"Then my next question—tell me about Benjamin Star."

Fred said, "I am completely in the dark. I wouldn't know where to start."

Detective Seymour was in plain clothes, which translated as a light-colored tweed sport coat that probably fit him five years back, and khakis. His mien was utterly morose. His fork pointed again at his plate as he said, "This is yesterday's dinner. I was too tired last night to do anything but sleep. Then I couldn't do that."

"I'm not telling you your business, which you know and I don't," Fred said. "In your place, I'd ask the academy's office for his personnel file. Academic records, letters of recommendation, previous history. The drill."

"President Harmony first said that laws of confidentiality prevented her from sharing, failing the warrant that we've applied for, don't worry. Then when she was convinced that she might be proved in error, she and her lawyer, she went for it and discovered the file is missing too."

"Really," Fred said.

"Mislaid or stolen by the former registrar," Seymour said. "That's the claim. For spite, President Harmony suggested. Woman named Lillian Krasic."

"Don't know her," Fred said.

"She denies it. Lillian does," Seymour went on.

"You have his address on the car registration," Fred said.

Seymour removed yolk from his upper lip with an inadequate paper napkin.

"Which you are apparently reserving," Fred said. "You'll also have his bank. Look at the cancelled checks. Hell, you know how to do this."

Detective Seymour took another forkful of hash and eggs and shoved the plate aside. He reached for his coffee. "Tell me this," he said. "They paying you in cash?"

"I'm here for a week, helping out," Fred said. "I'm not being paid."

"In other words, yes," Seymour concluded. "It's great. As soon as the government controls everything, everyone lies. I'm not going to report you to the IRS. I've got better things to do than catch jerks cheating on their taxes. Never mind. And don't try to convince me. Moving along…"

Fred said, "I'm new to the academic world. In fact it's not my field at all. I'd have said it's unusual for a faculty member to be paid in cash. Unusual to the point of irregular."

"President Harmony's term was 'informal,'" Seymour said.

"Are they all…?" Fred started

"Benjamin Star is the only one," Seymour said. "Supposedly. Where I come from, cash transactions, especially regular cash transactions, look like trouble. Common, maybe; but for a place like this, yes, I think your word 'irregular' fits. Can you think of any reason for the practice that would not embarrass, say, Saint Theresa?"

Fred spread his hands.

"At least they didn't pretend the guy was a volunteer for the last year and a half," Seymour said.

"Truth is a tricky currency," Fred remarked. "So is falsehood. It's not my business, except as a citizen, it's a matter of public interest: We are assuming the possibility that Rodney Somerfest was murdered?"

"I'm Homicide," Seymour said. "Next question. You say the board's lawyer, Counselor Baum, invited you to come here and teach for a week?"

"I said nothing about it."

"It's in my notes. Do you deny it?"

"Not at all," Fred said.

"That's also irregular. Why did you agree?"

"It was a good time to get away from the man I work for. Who pays me anyway. Also, I was intrigued."

"Anything else you'd like to tell me about Morgan Flower, né Benjamin Star?" Seymour said.

"His taste in clothes and mine don't coincide. It doesn't matter. We're not the same size," Fred said.

"Oh, Sir, in the life room!" Susan's voice—Susan herself, from the Stillton Inn; his student, entering at a run. "It's Meeker."

Chairs clattered as people rose, as if Susan was entering with the warning of an approaching tsunami. Bee huffed into the room from behind the counter.

"He's fallen or, I don't know what." Susan waved her cell phone. "I can't hear."

"We'll take the cruiser," Seymour said. "Fred, you show me where."

◇◇◇

Students milled around Stillton Hall, their excited chattering clouding the damp air, and refused to go inside, where the news had to be bad. The cell phones were out in force, carrying worried fragments and conjectures. The cruiser's siren might have conveyed a brief hope that whatever was wrong inside would now be made right, until it became clear that the siren belonged not to an ambulance, but to a cruiser.

Inside, in Stillton B, only Meg Harrison had stood by the fallen man. "I opened up at quarter to eight," she said. "Milan should have done it. Meeker was here, like this. He had no business…He doesn't respond. I've tried…"

Tom Meeker's body lay on the paint-splattered cement floor, dressed as he had been yesterday afternoon, his round face looking more questions than it would now have time for. The thing in his throat had not produced enough blood to justify so much death. There was no reason to check for pulse, but you do that anyway. The model's stand was again beneath the trap, and a few horses lay almost randomly around, as if they had toppled all at once.

"A struggle," Seymour said. "All those students out front, I want them inside until I can talk with them."

"Looks like one of our scalpels," Meg said. "We use them the next studio over, for clay. For fine work."

"Get the students inside. Get them in that studio next door, then. Don't let them touch anything," Seymour said. He pulled the cell phone out of the holster on his hip.

Chapter Forty-one

Fred said, "You'll be busy a while. For now, I can help, or get out of your way. Your call. "We'll talk later. Whenever you say."

"Later," Seymour said, re-holstering. "I've got to secure the scene. I have work to do. Go ahead, do whatever you volunteers do."

"Officer?" Rick Murphy.

"Don't touch anything, kid." Seymour. To Meg Harrison, "You teach here, don't you? Do me a favor. Get all of those kids next door, in that big classroom."

"Studio."

"Whatever," Seymour said.

Rick Murphy persisted, "Officer, you should know this."

"Be fast."

"Him and this guy were fighting yesterday," Rick said. "Everyone knows it."

Meg broke in, "Fred broke up a fight between two students. Meeker and…"

"The dead man and who else?" Seymour demanded.

"Another student. Peter Quarrier," Fred said. "Just so you know, Peter was with me two evenings ago. Fish and chips and a beer in my room at the Stillton Inn."

"This man Fred," Rick Murphy said, trembling with the enormity of witness, "was here last night. He was cleaning up something."

"We'll take everyone's statements later."

Rick Murphy insisted, "This is important. You're letting him get away."

Seymour, moving the other occupants of the room toward the door by herding them before him as he moved, with his arms spread, paused, exasperated. "Was the body present at the time?" he demanded.

Fred kept his peace.

"I came to clean. I'm the one cleans the building."

"And my question is, you cleaned *around* the body? You left all these chairs or whatever they are upside down like this?

"Of course not."

"So I take your statement later."

"My name is Rick Murphy."

"Sure. Everyone wants to get on TV. Everyone, out! I want to talk to Peter Quarrier."

In Meg Harrison's studio no class was forming. The model, already robed—that is to say, already naked, and robed in readiness to strip for the first session—an older woman, corpulent, with big flat dirty feet—was standing smoking next to the platform where she was to have spent the best part of her day reclining, if Fred's interpretation was correct of the shapes under wrap on the modeling stands that had been circled in preparation for the day's work. The intended problem being, no doubt, for the students to discover bone and muscle that provided coherence to the assembled flesh.

Among the gathered students, many were Fred's, first year, *Intro to Lit.* There was Bill Wamp also, a faculty colleague.

Fred assumed a commanding position on the model's platform, next to the disappointed model, who had likely driven an hour to get here from some urban center.

"Whether we work or not, you get paid for the day, Bella," Meg called. "At the moment it's all kinda iffy."

The students being clustered in small groups, talking with concern—the dead man was one of them after all, and not of an age to die—Fred had to make some noise to get attention.

"For the ones of you who are my students in this morning's class, we can't do class today, obviously. I don't even have my books. I just…Two days ago, I know some of you got the idea that I was making fun of Emily Dickinson. A poet who makes up lines everyone can remember—she's always going to be mocked.

"The only thing I want to say. She was in this world to make art. You are here to make art. Tom Meeker was here to make art. Art lasts, and it outlasts us. After we're gone, art keeps us going. So, despite what the lines might seem to say, some lines of Emily Dickinson's are in my mind. They come back often. If I had made these lines, I would be proud.

> I reason, earth is short
> And anguish absolute,
> And many hurt;
> But what of that?

> I reason, we could die:
> The best vitality
> Cannot excel decay;
> But what of that?

"Accept no phony consolation. See you next week. Or, well, maybe not—but you be here."

He climbed down from his perch. Bella dropped her cigarette stub on the floor and stifled it with a flat bare foot.

Bill Wamp was next to the swinging doors into the corridor. Fred, on his way out, paused. "Peter Quarrier is one of yours, yes? Someone should get the word to him. Do you know where to find him?"

"Peter's third year. So he's Meg's. He'll be mine next year. If he's still here. It doesn't look good though, does it?"

"You know his work?"

"We all know everyone's work. Once they're in second year, they have their work reviewed by the entire faculty. So we know all the students' work. And the faculty's teaching methods too, by necessity, from seeing their students."

"Even Morgan Flower?" Fred asked.

"Even Morgan Flower what?"

"If the whole faculty meets for student reviews, does that include Morgan Flower?"

"What would he contribute?" Bill Wamp asked, genuinely perplexed.

"I'm going back to the Stillton Inn," Fred said. "If anyone wants me. I'll leave word at the desk if I have to go out."

"You're not hanging around here?"

"Gotta catch up with my bowels," Fred explained. "Men's room here—seems to me, in the vicinity of a crime scene, we ought to try not to contaminate anything."

Main Street. Opposite the Stillton Inn. There was no mistaking Clay's silver Lexus. He thought it made him inconspicuous.

Susan was behind the desk. Missy Tutunjian's roommate. His student. She blurted, "I figured, what with Meeker and all and everything…please don't…"

"Forget it," Fred assured her. "You guessed right. All bets are off. And Mrs. Halper needs you."

"They all cleared off last night. There was nothing to see or do. Nobody to talk to. Somebody started the rumor the big story is Rockport. But they'll come back now again. Because Meeker. Even though nobody liked him. Whatever he'd do, nobody liked him. It was pitiful in a way. He's a joker, Meeker. Never knows when to stop. Already the phone. And there's one…" She turned and reached into the set of cubby holes behind her, pulled out a slip of paper. "A Mr. Degas," she said. "Didn't need a room. He's waiting in yours. Says he's…" she looked up, worried, as she handed the paper over, "Is that OK? He really insisted."

"I know him," Fred said.

"I asked was he any relation, but he ran upstairs and didn't answer before I could explain I meant was he related to the painter. He looks…he looks like he ought to be related to *somebody* big."

Chapter Forty-two

When Fred opened the door, Clayton paused in mid-pace, expectant. He'd dressed to match the Lexus. The suit was as gray as Prince Albert's most dismal dream. The necktie, however, was almost Sonia Delaunay—so out of character it might have been intended as a disguise.

"Show it to me," Clay demanded, his lean limbs frozen in anticipation as if the springs had seized up.

Fred closed the door, crossed the small room and sat on the table. If Clay wanted to sit, he'd be glad of the single chair. Because of something someone had said to him in early childhood, maybe, Clay was unlikely to sit on the bed. Fred said, "The quickest answer is also the most candid. It's short. So listen carefully. *Impossible.*"

Clay said, "I can almost smell it. You know my instincts. Surely we can talk freely here. Where is it? The butterfly…"

"The butterfly's in a drawer. It looked like trash where it was. I don't want…"

"Of course. Never mind. I did not wish to pry."

"I'll show it to you," Fred said.

"No, no, never mind," Clay said. "It's of no interest beyond corroboration. Such bagatelles, if charming, were not well advised in terms of the artist's oeuvre as a whole. You say 'impossible'?" he challenged.

Clay sat on the chair and put his hands on his knees. His socks, exposed, were revealed as a uniform pale green. No calf appeared. It wouldn't.

Fred said, "By this time the building's cordoned off and filled with techies. One of my students was killed there. Last night or early this morning."

"Gracious!" Clay rose, dithered, and sat again.

"The next thing is for you to get back to Boston. If you are found to be here, you are likely to stay here."

"I am incognito," Clay protested.

"Your car is known by anyone in the art world locally. There are quarter-page photos of you in the *Globe,* the *New York Times,* whatever they have in New Haven."

"I was powerless to prevent that. When the museum appointed me…"

"I said you would come to regret it. The point is, until this moment, although the interest of the press has been considerable, it has not been intense. That will change. *Student Killed in Life Room.* It's catchy. Two deaths look like a trend. That's catchy too. And if you are spotted here, and identified, it will be assumed that you are on the trail of treasure. Which you are."

"My very point," Clay broke in, exasperated. "Bierstadt is the point."

"Your motive is not necessarily the prevailing motive," Fred said. "In the great scheme of things. I need coffee. That has nothing to do with the fact that you came here on your own and I want you out of town."

"I am not following. What does your wish for coffee…?"

"Exactly. Now, the reporters who left town last night, disappointed, are on their way back. You will be seen. When you are seen you will be recognized. When you are recognized it will not be assumed, it will be *known,* that somewhere in this town is a painting, or a collection of paintings, that is worth—let's just say modestly—your attention.

"Until this morning I had assumed, or hoped, or imagined, that a total of two people knew about the mural, yourself and me. Already that's in doubt, but I'm not sure. I don't have time to go into it. There are several issues demanding my attention. One dead student and another I'd like to talk with before… My point is, once it is known that you are in town, the big fish start to take interest. And while I have often heard it said that nothing is healthier for the marketplace than competition…"

"I have *never* said that." Clay had gone almost as green as his socks.

"Plus, once the people doing the stories get wind of a painting—it's always a 'masterpiece' once they get started—worth what, if you sold it right, a good hundred million dollars and change?"

"Stop! Stop!" Clay said.

"You think this woman in Arkansas doesn't have agents sniffing the breeze all the time for a chance like this? And you think Hiram Parks wouldn't bid her up and up?"

"You are known. I repeat. If you are seen here the water is instantly filled with bloody chum. Then the sharks circle in."

"Show me at least the building," Clayton begged.

"Again, impossible. Get out of town. Leave now. In fact, I'd say—that profile of yours, that white hair—take my car. Anyone who sees my car discounts the driver. Likewise, anyone who sees me in the Lexus is going to discount the Lexus."

"At least describe…"

"The best I could do was to undo the first three feet or so of each roll, and even that was damned near impossible. Plateaus. Broad space. Clouds. A lot of pink rock and water. Chasm upon chasm. Cloud upon cloud. Now. Go. Here are my keys. Put gas in it, but not until you are well out of town."

Clay eased his car keys off the ring and dropped them on the table.

"Put my jacket on over the suit," Fred said. "I'll pick up another one somewhere."

"You think—the academy's board has no suspicion?" Clay pleaded.

"They're after more obvious game, in my opinion," Fred said. "But I can't read all the signs. Clay, while I'm dealing with you I can't work with the matter at hand."

"Is there a back way out?" Clay asked, finally catching on.

Fred pointed to the window and its wooden fire escape. "If you want to be noticed, that will do it for sure. Just walk out like anyone. Give my car three minutes to idle before you put it in gear. Damp weather…"

Susan Muller was on her way out when Fred, after waiting a decent interval, came downstairs, imperfectly dressed for the Stillton weather. "They've picked up Peter Quarrier," she said. "They've taken him away somewhere. Nobody knows where."

Too late, then.

"Let me buy you a coffee," Fred said.

Susan was pulling a heavy blue sweater around her. It already glistened with mist. The same mist settled eagerly on her short red curls. She swung her canvas bag and strode swiftly. "I could use that," she said.

Chapter Forty-three

The Stillton Café was abuzz. There wasn't a table free, or room at the counter. Susan greeted colleagues who otherwise kept their distance, due to her present attachment to a representative of the occupying forces.

Once they'd got their coffee and Susan had dressed hers with sugar and cream, they sparred and parried with the crowd, looking for quiet.

"I wouldn't mind talking with you," Susan said. "But here it won't work."

"Is there anywhere else?" Fred said. "Given it's raining—I guess that's rain. Don't know anything else to call it. You have a studio, maybe? We can't use my room, obviously. People would—an older man—student—all that…"

"Don't get studio space till your third year. That's what makes it so hard and all. We'll go to my place. Besides, I have this effing drawing to do."

"Whatever you say," Fred said doubtfully.

"It's OK. There's always people around. If you're thinking, like, virtue and safety and reputation and parents and danger and rape and all that. Come on.

"Because if I know Meg, she's not going to let us off the hook. The drawings are due in over a month but tomorrow we have a crit of the work in progress.

"It's terrible about Meeker. But it gives me an extra day."

She'd already walked Fred out of the café and into the chilly street, sparkling with damp. The State cruisers were back, nosing around town, frightening everyone with aggressive reassurance. The moving citizens, or students, seemed, if Fred read the signs correctly, to be stricken by this sudden and ominous equivalent of a snow day.

They walked downhill toward the classroom and administration buildings, but turned right when they reached the edge that overlooked the ocean, and moved through lanes separating small cottages, humble, appealing, shabby, that were destined to be worth many millions each, once Stillton Realty Trust had its way. Wasn't that the plan?

"We're in here. Second floor," Susan said, walking into a cottage. Its door was not locked. Nor, upstairs, was the door into her rooms. The layout was akin to Morgan Flower's apartment, though smaller. The sitting room was almost devoid of furniture. Most notable among the furnishings, propped against the wall by an open bedroom door, and next to a full-length mirror clipped to another door—a closet door, she'd said?—was the study in question, palpably and believably Susan Muller, Fred's student, nude, but as if she was only barely, and slowly, coming into focus.

"If you're quick, as soon as you get here in the fall, you get your plywood from a second-year student," Susan said, dropping her bag.

The head of the figure was almost fully realized, shaded with lights and darks and half-tones, as if it had been worked up from the plaster cast of a Greek nymph. Then, as your eye went down the body—the neck, the shoulders, the breasts not quite symmetrical, the forearms—she'd chosen to represent her hands hanging straight at her sides—the farther down the body the eye moved, the less the shading had been finished. From the knees down there were only a few marks.

"It's like she's appearing out of a heavy ground mist," Fred said.

The drawing was on heavy white paper, much scuffed by erasures and second thoughts. The pubic area, below a plump belly and navel, was trimmed, with the start of a decorative patch above that might, in time, be as curly as the curls that were so finished around the face, depending on the trim.

"It's the effing feet and the effing ankles and the effing knees I have to get to now, and how do I get down there?" Susan said. She was stepping out of her jeans.

"Let's keep the door open," Fred suggested. "You know. Thinking about all those things you wisely mentioned—virtue, safety, reputation, parents…rape we don't have to worry about right now. But—in general—maybe you want to start locking the street door? Just—with all that's going on?"

He went to the apartment door and opened it.

Susan was laughing. "Sorry. Don't worry. I stop at the jeans. I'm just going to figure out the effing legs and feet. If I can. See, I can't help moving. Have to squat to get down to the feet, and once I squat, where are they? It's effing impossible."

She'd pulled the plywood away from the wall. Behind it was a rudimentary contraption of two-by-threes that folded out to make a sort of easel. "I got this from the same guy." The heavy blue sweater hung halfway down her thighs.

"Maybe stand farther back, you can see more," Fred suggested. "And find a way to put the drawing higher?"

"Then the scale gets screwed up. I'll figure it out," Susan said. "You wanted to talk. Put a chair where it doesn't reflect. I'll get confused."

She had already started to draw, bending or squatting as needed to get marks as far down as she had to. Her sensible underpants flashed white.

"Your roommate, Missy Tutunjian. How far has she got with hers?" Fred asked. "Does she go at it the same way?"

Susan said, "She took it with her." She had set her feet into marks painted onto the floorboards in white, about eight inches apart. "What the Hag says: you are always drawing from memory anyway. You have to look away from the thing before you look at the paper. But this, this is effing lunacy." She spoke standing, then squatted to work on a foot, from a foot that had become obscured as soon as she went down.

"The sweater doesn't help," she said. "Wait." She disappeared into the bedroom. When she came back she was belting the sweater at the waist with a pink scarf.

Fred said, "Speaking of parents, tell me about Missy's Dad."

Chapter Forty-four

"It's all you came for," Susan complained, stepping back into the marks again and looking back and forth between her drawing and her reflection. "That's what everyone says. Missy."

"You don't think much of her," Fred hazarded.

Susan shrugged, then went to work on the inner edge of a knee. "After I'm sure of the outline, then it's still effing weeks of shading," she said. "What I want to know is, why?"

Fred said carefully, "That's what I want to know, too. Why?"

"Your why and my why aren't the same why," Susan said, looking into the mirror. Had Fred placed himself so she could see him? Hard to say. "What I want to know, why do you want to know anything about Missy? It's all you would talk about, that day in class."

She bent, made a line, cursed and started wiping it out again. "What people say, her old man hired you. To find her."

"Therefore I'm asking you about him," Fred pointed out. "That makes sense."

"To put me off."

"She took her drawing with her," Fred said. "Anything else? Books? Clothes? Does she plan to come back, would you say? She pregnant, maybe? It could happen. Because they say she was having a thing with the teacher, Morgan Flower."

"That's not against the law. Is it? That's better." She approved the newly delineated knee. "I don't think much of Missy and I don't think much of Flower. So."

"Missy's father. He's supposed to be a big donor to this place. Big contributor. How much is your rent?"

"It's in the tuition. I don't know. It's mixed up together. I work, and I got a loan, and my folks help some. My big sister. She's working."

"Missy say where she was going?"

"Missy and me don't talk. Not about anything. Beyond, 'We need milk and this sock has to be yours.'"

"It never occurred to me," Fred said. "Where do you all do your laundry? I haven't seen…"

"Laundromat. Back of the gas station. Open all night. Good place to meet people you don't meet in class. It's like Stillton Academy's social life. Her old man? Mr. Tutunjian? He moved her in. She's from Lowell. Mercedes van. So what? She's got money. I don't. He's short. He's big in the chest. Smokes a cigar. Drove the van up but didn't move shit."

"How come he isn't all over the place looking for Missy?" Fred asked.

"He's got seven kids." She erased the knee. "I can't work in this effing sweater. If you don't mind…" She turned and stood, waiting for him to leave.

"Maybe lock the doors now for a while," Fred suggested again.

"He looked through her things," Susan said. "Him and that lawyer, Mr. Baum? If they found anything, ask them. I have to work."

"Aram Tutunjian. Lowell," Fred said into the answering machine at Molly's mother's apartment.

The painting department's office might be an office by name, but it was more of an unholy grab-bag of a random mess, in which an ancient wooden desk provided an academic flavor. Bill Wamp's feet were on it and the remainder of Bill Wamp was tilted back dangerously in a hefty wooden chair, talking with

Phil Oumaloff, who was standing but looking like someone who wasn't going anywhere. Around them in the room were most of a hanging human skeleton, paintings stacked against each other, lumber, a tall gray metal file cabinet whose open drawers spilled props rather than paper, plastic fruit, stained plaster casts missing noses or fingers.

"Make yourself at home, Fred," Bill Wamp said.

Fred removed the contents of another chair—the best that could be said of the contents was that they were not damp—and sat.

"Terrible. Terrible," Oumaloff said. The same words had been in the air when Fred walked in.

"Tom Meeker," Fred said. "What do you think…?"

"It's not Meeker I'm thinking about. There are a million Meekers. It's a shame and all, but there wasn't much talent there. No, it's Quarrier I'm mourning. He's been arrested. He's ruined."

"He told me he had been in the service. Peter Quarrier," Fred said.

"Terrible. Terrible," Oumaloff said. He was twisting a plastic eggplant in his hands, or fondling it, or polishing it, or worse.

"I did his admissions interview," Bill Wamp said. "You don't always remember them. But that one I remember. For one thing, Quarrier was older."

Phil Oumaloff interrupted with an explanation. "We have rolling admissions. A practice I instigated."

"Rolling admissions…" Fred repeated.

"Meaning," Bill Wamp said, "You can apply any time of the year and we can admit you at any time, for the next year or the next semester. Until classes are filled. No deadlines.

"Basically, we look to see if they're any good at anything. They don't know a thing about art before they come. How could they? Public high school in Lowell or Malden? What they think artists do is draw girls with big breasts and a cape, or G. I. Joe on steroids zapping the Ayrabs.

"Basically, they're coming from nowhere. But maybe they're good at rebuilding a truck engine, or one girl sewed her own clothes, which I only learned at the end of the interview."

"Basil Houel is one of ours," Oumaloff put in. "Before your time, Bill."

"He's not unknown, even to me," Bill Wamp said.

"He's all over the art magazines right now," Fred said. "A big success. New York. Acacia Gallery. Tight, hard-edged Romantic nausea pictures that sell. But he's the only alumnus name I've heard anyone mention. Is he one of a core group, or an anomaly of success?"

Oumaloff put the eggplant down and started doing it to a plastic grapefruit instead.

"But of course Peter Quarrier had been out in the world. Overseas. That fight yesterday with the dead man. So many witnesses. How could it be hushed up?" Oumaloff said.

Bill Wamp continued, almost in a reverie of mourning, "His portfolio—he had the crayon drawings of fruit left over from high school, sure, but there was also—I still remember them— tall vertical panels he'd drawn, like Chinese landscape, with a brush, of camps where he'd been overseas, with the trucks, the flags, the barracks, all seen from above and broken by clouds."

"Terrible," Oumaloff said. "Terrible. And over a woman!"

"Emma's not a bad painter either," Bill Wamp said.

Chapter Forty-five

"Quarrier could have been our next Basil Houel," Oumaloff mourned, after a pause he may have thought was pregnant.

"No classes today at all?" Fred asked.

"By decree," Bill Wamp said. "Respect for the dead. Also there's yellow crime scene tape everywhere, unless the students have already run off with it. If any of the students are working, they'll be in their studios."

"What I can't understand," Fred started.

"Two deaths," Oumaloff said. "Not meaning to crowd you, Fred. But let me speak. Two deaths, by violence. It will strike at the heart of Stillton Academy's reputation."

"If any," Bill Wamp muttered. "Sorry, Phil."

Fred pushed on, "What I don't understand. It's schizoid. What I see so far. Tell me if I'm wrong. What I see, as an outsider—let's say the teachers and the program are on the up-and-up. The buildings are hanging together. You have enough students. Sure, there are problems, like a respectable schedule of contracts…"

"That is a gray area," Oumaloff interrupted loudly. "There are two sides. With so small a faculty, imagine the problems if everyone started to expect tenure."

"Not only do I not have a dog in this fight, I don't even have a dog. So I really don't care," Fred said. "My point was only going to be, to me it seems the ingredients are here for you to survive. Even make a real play for accreditation. Except…"

"Supposing good will amongst all or most of the adults

involved," Bill Wamp put in. "Sorry. Of course the customers, the students, are adults too, after they reach sixteen, which they all are around here, by law. My point is…"

"Good will. That's what I wonder about too," Fred said. "Here's my question. Does the board want the place to survive?"

"Good question," Bill Wamp said.

"What's the financial situation?" Fred asked. "The board does fundraising? One board member or another springs for a memorial roof he can put his mother's name on? What's the endowment? Where's all this cash coming…"

"Not the faculty's business," Oumaloff declared firmly. "I can tell you. I've been thirty years at this academy. It's never…"

"So I'd assume," Fred said. "Why haven't they seized on a good thing? It's right there in front of them. Why don't they put Phil Oumaloff on the board?"

Oumaloff turned purple. His wattles shook back of that white beard.

"Watch it," Bill Wamp cautioned. He took his feet off the desk and sat straight. "You're on tricky terrain."

"I resigned from the board," Oumaloff said. He said it as if under torture.

"How come?" Fred asked.

Oumaloff, holding center stage, took the occasion to exchange his grapefruit for a bunch of plastic grapes. "At least in my day we would never allow the students to paint from these," he said. "The color is uniform. The size and shape are uniform. A painter must observe natural color. Real color. In natural light. Daylight. Although for drawing…It is no secret. I resigned in protest of the appointment of Rodney Somerfest as director."

"Phil had chaired the search committee," Bill Wamp said.

"Our workings were meant to be open, democratic, and transparent," Oumaloff said.

"Except there were no faculty or students included," Bill Wamp said.

"Open, transparent, and democratic to its own members," Oumaloff insisted. "Especially to its own chairman."

"I have never known where the candidacy of Mr. Somerfest originated. All I can say is that he was not among the applicants I knew of. His nomination was instigated by a faction of the board. His material simply appeared at a board meeting and, by the time of his interview—which I opposed—his appointment was a foregone conclusion."

"Phil wanted Basil Houel," Bill Wamp said.

"Indeed, Basil was outstanding among the applicants. That is no secret. An alumnus of confirmed success who stands out for an almost filial devotion...

"At any rate, I resigned," Oumaloff said. "It was clear how the votes would go. It amounted to a palace coup. A coup. Most of those on my search committee resigned at the same meeting."

"So," Fred said. "Since you've been on the board, you know the finances."

Oumaloff shook his head. He took this moment to exchange the grapes for a plastic orange.

"How should I read your negative?" Fred asked. "Is it refusal or emotion?"

"When I left the board, the financial picture was already weak. The endowment had dwindled drastically, or been foolishly invested. Buildings that had not been mortgaged were now under mortgage to banks from as far afield as Lowell, Massachusetts.

"The rationale for the palace coup was this. The academy's financial status had become so tenuous that only a businessman director could save us. My argument, that such a talent could be brought instead into the board, was laughed out of court.

"Rodney Somerfest had experience buying and selling cars. That was felt to be sufficient. And he was a candidate—as it later turned out an unsuccessful candidate—for a higher degree in education. Of art he knew nothing. It was his impression that Matisse was a men's cologne. It was obscene."

"So, Phil resigned, which I understand," Bill Wamp said. "But ever since, we have not had a shred of information."

"So," Fred said. "That brings us to the Stillton Realty Trust."

Chapter Forty-six

"Ok. So. They maneuvered you off the board," Fred summed up.

Neither Phil Oumaloff not Bill Wamp had responded to the stimulus. The name of the entity Stillton Realty Trust had produced no more than blank stares.

"You and how many more?" Fred went on.

"How many what?" Oumaloff asked.

"How many on the board resigned?"

"I was the spearhead of an impressive movement," Oumaloff bragged. "We were three in all who resigned in protest. Three out of seven."

"Leaving the way clear for those who remained to stack the deck in the darkness that resulted," Fred concluded. "I don't know how it works. Never been on a board. But however it works, the resulting board is working against its own best interests, that is to say, the best interests of the academy, and in favor of the self-interest of its individual members.

"What it looks like to me—and again, what do I know?—the Stillton Realty Trust is looking to buy up all of Stillton; whatever the academy doesn't own already.

"There's enough cash floating around that my guess is they're putting their own money into the payoff to Rodney Somerfest for example, although that's over now. Meanwhile the academy is mortgaging property in order to keep the operation going. No way could tuition cover it. So at the same time as the academy gets weaker, the Realty Trust gets stronger. Already it has options on or owns most of the town.

"What happens next? Say you don't get accreditation?"

Oumaloff handed the pair of plastic plums he'd been fondling to Bill Wamp, who held the warmed objects in his hand a moment before he deposited them on the desk with a grimace of intimate displeasure. They rolled, in two directions, but both to the edge and off, onto the dusty floor. They lay there.

Bill Wamp pointed toward the plums. "There's your answer," he said. "We fold. If we don't get accredited our students don't get government grants or loans. The work-study program is out the window. Neither the state nor the US Government gives us the time of day. Our loans are called back. We're dead."

"And then?"

"And then? You mean, after we're dead? After we're dead, we rot," Bill Wamp said.

Oumaloff had found a chair, cleared it and sat.

"Sure. *You* rot, and the *students* rot. That's obvious," Fred said. "But what happens to the entity, whatever Josephus Stillton named and defined when he drew up the documents that led to what currently exists as Stillton Academy of Art? There had to be a paragraph that said, if ever the board concludes that this academy can't hack it, anything that's left—whether buildings or bank accounts or wooden horses or plastic fruit—whatever's left, what happens to it?"

"Good question," Bill Wamp said. "I never thought of that."

"Whatever these jokers are doing they want to use the law as a tool on their side," Fred said. "Not my field. I mean, for example, something I overheard. Boston's King's Chapel, which I like to refer to as the Chapel of George the Divine. Christian Unitarian. Bear with me. Church downtown. Tremont at about Park Street. Freedom Trail. All that. Their situation, if they ever go soft and relinquish their Christian forms of worship, not only do they lose their major endowment under an 18th century will, but—at least this was true until not too long ago—they could even wake up one morning and find that control had been snatched away from their own board, and they must submit instead to the tender mercies of Harvard University.

"So, Phil, my question: Say the academy goes belly up, I repeat, what happens to what's left? Who gets it?"

"I have those papers somewhere," Oumaloff said. "Off the top of my head…"

"If you think of it, let me know," Fred said.

"You're saying they're not just clowns," Bill Wamp recognized. "Not stupid, but malicious. This board, in effect my employers, are actively working to sabotage the academy?"

"And profit from the wreckage," Fred said. "That's my theory. A theory I'm not spreading around right now, if you don't mind. No point starting talk."

"Who's in this? How does it work?" Phil Oumaloff demanded.

"I don't see that anybody in this room is involved," Fred said. "Beyond that…"

Oumaloff said, "It's preposterous! It's also possible. I'll search for those papers. It might take me…"

"I'm at the Stillton Inn," Fred said.

"Everyone knows," Oumaloff said, making for the door.

Fred cautioned, "They've been working to keep this very secret. I suggest we do the same. I wonder about the death of Rodney Somerfest, for example, in the light of the desire for secrecy."

"A nonentity," Oumaloff grumbled. "I knew it as soon as I saw his file. 'The Death of a Nonentity.' Good title for a 1930s movie nobody has seen. If Somerfest knew anything other than cars, ever, he hid it well."

Fred and Bill Wamp watched a plastic pear spinning on the floor in the wake of Oumaloff's departure. Bill Wamp stretched and yawned.

"You don't happen to know where Peter Quarrier lives?" Fred asked.

"Not a clue. Beyond everyone lives around here. There's really no choice," Bill Wamp said. "I should go check my fourth-year painters."

"Lillian Krasic. Any ideas?" Fred asked him. "Like how come, and when, did they shove her out, and how come are they still paying her?"

"She'd been at Stillton forever. Did her job. Knew everyone. Family in Stillton back forever. Meaning parents, grandparents. Fishermen. She isn't married. But your other questions—you got me."

"What happens to you if this place bites the dust? You singular. Bill Wamp."

"I'll tell you one thing. I'm not waiting to find out. I'm looking now."

"You'd be a fool not to. I'll walk with you," Fred offered.

"It's raining," Bill Wamp pointed out. "You're not dressed for it. You haven't been in town long enough. I've got an extra jacket you can use." He reached behind the office door and pulled out one of those red plaid jackets that is supposed to make any man look instantly like a man's man.

"It's a knockoff," Bill Wamp said. "Don't worry about it. It makes me look like Ralph Kramden going hunting." His own jacket was green waxed cotton, padded and very worn. The red baseball cap sported a big W.

"They give you a studio?" Fred asked as they walked along the sea view. Fog horn again. How long had it been moaning? It was so chronic a condition, a person forgot to notice when it stopped and started, like a dull itch.

Bill Wamp said, "For me it's either paint or eat. So I've been teaching. Summer I give lessons at a place in Maine. I still call myself a painter."

A lone seagull flew past with a limp gray something in its beak. Seventeen other lone seagulls flew behind him, screaming to tear it away.

Chapter Forty-seven

"If you want, I'll run you through the building," Bill Wamp offered. "Show you around."

"I'll figure it out," Fred said. "I guess, since I'm teaching third year students, I'll head for those studios. Just point me in the right direction."

"You want that end of the building," Bill Wamp said, showing Fred the direction he already knew to go.

The voices behind the closed door of Peter Quarrier's studio were Meg Harrison's, with an intervening rumble that was familiar: Detective Seymour. The cruiser out front had prepared Fred for this eventuality. In due course the studio itself would be cordoned off with yellow tape. For now Meg Harrison, Peter's instructor, was doing what she could to explain the week's classroom assignment, or the series of self-portraits, or the sketches on the wall, to a man whose disciplines were suited to the interpretation of evidence, and to questioning everything.

Quarrier's studio partner, whoever that was, was out of luck for the next week. He'd have to work somewhere else. Or she. And would the forces of law and order allow anything to be removed—even the studio partner's works in progress? As long as Peter was in custody, his effects would be in limbo.

"Tell me this," Seymour's voice, the challenge tinged with discomfort. "I know you people do this, I've been around. But why is the guy naked? Seems like, if you're trying to hand the students a puzzle to work with, a fancy robe…"

Fred proceeded along the hallway.

Emma, at work in her studio, had arranged the bowl with its still life of dilapidated fruit, on a table. Yesterday's class studio nude was on the easel and she, standing in front of it, was mixing paint on a crusted palette. Light furred by the rain, entering by the window at her right, made a distracting cross work pattern over the face of the painting she was engaged with. A self-portrait of Peter Quarrier, the one Fred had taken special notice of in Quarrier's studio two nights back, stood on the floor looking into the room.

Emma had her dark hair pulled back severely, as in her own self-portrait, which was missing. The green work shirt, a man's, was splotched with paint and hung outside black denim trousers. The rubber clogs on her feet were no one's fashion statement.

Emma's nod acknowledged Fred's entrance. Her face was wan, and streaked with tears.

"I guess you lucked out in a way," Fred said. "All the other studios get crowded by this time of the year."

Emma said, "You mean there's nobody else in the studio. I'm not the easiest person in the world to get along with, maybe." She held the brush poised, a dollop of lavender paint on its tip. "That shadow along the guy's dick. That's a lie," she said. "The way everything twists. Also a lie."

"Is it a good thing or not, working alone in the studio?" Fred asked.

Emma gave the orange on her canvas a garish lavender shadow. She'd already roughed in the bowl and its contents again. "It's a lie," she repeated. "A dick that green, you'd carry it to the doctor. Mary Louise couldn't hack it. My studio partner. Left at Christmas. It's good. So I've got space. And she took her goddamned radio with her."

She lifted the same lavender up to the model's chin and slashed it across, making a mark that was both vicious and poignant. "It's a lie, and I like it. Poor Peter." She put her hands to her face and shook, weeping. The brush with its remnant of paint, still clenched in her right hand, twitched like an antenna above her head.

"Well, I mean," Emma said, "poor Tom. Color and life are the same thing. It's what Peter always said. Poor Peter."

Fred cleared a place to sit on the room's single chair. There was also a busted horse, but the splotches of paint on it might not be dry, and the coat Fred was wearing belonged to Bill Wamp. "What do you know?" Fred asked. "Do you mind if I watch you work?"

"Sure," Emma said. "I don't know anything. Except they picked Peter up, which I didn't learn from Peter because obviously they wouldn't let him telephone. A friend of his told me. Early. They got him maybe even before he knew about Tom. Unless…"

"Stick to what you know," Fred said.

Emma said, "Anyway, last night, Tom came by. I was working. Though it's stupid to work at night. The color's all wrong."

With a wide soft brush she laid in a thick red mark at the base of the blue bowl.

"Peter's self-portrait," Fred said.

Emma started and looked away from her work, into Fred's eyes. "Peter wanted one I was working on. He walked me back to the studio yesterday, after the thing. Told me to stop, not make another mark on it, it was done. When I wouldn't, he took it. Then he said, 'Wait,' and went away with it. Came back with his.

"I told Tom I didn't give a shit where he was. Couldn't care less."

"'He,' meaning…?" Fred prompted. "I'm not following."

"The son of a bitch asshole." Emma turned to her painting again. "I'm fucked with the small brushes," she said. "When I get out of here, *if* I get out of here, I'll never use anything less than an inch wide."

"Why wait?" Fred said.

"I called Aldo right away. Peter's lover. He'll come. Peter's going to need friends. Help. Money.

"What they don't know, what they don't think about, most of what we do when we paint is an exercise in using the tools and supplies of poverty. And all the time we're trying to make it look like we're not poor. Because who wants to look at a poor person? What fun is that?"

"Morgan Flower," Fred guessed.

"Sure. Morgan could eat anything he wanted. We'd go out, he'd buy steak, or a lobster. For him, for me, he didn't care. I wanted a bottle of wine? Presto! A couple of times we drove up for the weekend to Lake Sunapee. The place. It seemed like he owned it."

"I saw that car he drives," Fred said.

"So Tom asked me. There he was again. How could I keep him out? Him all excited and revved up for self-justification. I thought he came to apologize. Fat chance. He said, and why should I doubt him? Because he'd listen there, in the office: Did I want to know where Morgan Flower is? Because Tom will do anything to get in my—to get on my good side. Which he didn't have a prayer.

"I said, Shit, no! No, that's a lie. I said, Fuck, no! Tom said, was I sure? I said, What does it sound like? The one thing more I want from that guy, I got. Forever. Which is a passing grade."

Fred said, "I like your work."

"It's student work. It's shit."

"OK. They're going to ask you about what Tom said and did. His visit. Then they're going to ask you about Peter," Fred said.

A pause. "Should I hide his painting?"

"I wouldn't. It's yours," Fred said.

"Tom saw it here. It looked like he was going to kick it. Should I hide it?"

"Don't confuse them," Fred said. "The one you gave him…"

"Peter took it," Emma said. "But I wouldn't want it back anyway. Not now. It's his now. Even if he…"

"They're in his studio," Fred said. "They'll see it. Meg Harrison and the detective. They'll, at least Meg, will recognize it."

"Shit. Nobody knows, only you, how last year Flower and I—I mean the students know and all, but not—what do I tell them?"

Her bravado had dwindled to be replaced by the single practical question.

"Because the fact is, Morgan treated me like shit," she continued. "And I don't want to go into it."

Fred said, "What I suggest, tell them Peter walked you back. That's true. Whatever the time was—don't lie about that—and when he left. Then Tom stopped by and while you were talking, he mentioned he thought he knew where Morgan Flower was."

"Listen, Fred. There's no chance, is there? Could Peter... could he have done that to Tom?"

"Not if I read him right. What do you think?"

Emma's shoulders shook and the tears came again. "Sometimes Peter would say he didn't want to live," Emma said.

Chapter Forty-eight

"That'll do it?" Emma insisted.

"They still want to talk to Morgan," Fred said. "After they talk to you, they'll be more eager."

"One thing's sure. If they find Morgan, he won't brag what he did to me. So I'll just be here working when they come. If they come."

"If you *can*," Fred said. "In my judgment, it would be worse not to be easy to find."

Her responding look was either guilty or cornered.

"Just be here," Fred said. "Working on something else, maybe, where you don't have to think?"

◇◇◇

It was a person Fred had not seen before, in the admissions and administration building; an older woman with the look of the seasoned professional. She was dealing briskly and implacably with incoming phone calls. The emperor Nero, enjoying the circus, could not have turned down his thumb more quickly than she instructed each caller, "Not at present," "She's in conference," or, "The academy will issue a statement."

She looked up with a "No" in her eyes.

"I work here," Fred said. He walked to the silent door with the new *ELIZABETH HARMONY, PRESIDENT* sign on it. "She in?"

"Not since she set me up this morning."

"Temp?" Fred guessed.

She refrained from the obvious reply, picked up the phone and told it, "Stillton Academy of Art. Good Morning."

"That would be a yes," Fred concluded. "So she's with the student's family?"

The woman said into the phone, "The admissions office is closed temporarily. Please call back next week." She hung up and told Fred, "She left no instructions."

"Schedule's shot to hell anyway," Fred said. "You know how I can reach her?"

"I'm doing the phone. That's it," she said, and proved it.

The room's phone rang. Fred, coming out of the shower, grabbed it. Molly.

"Gotta be quick," Molly said. "Vacation like this, there's not time for anything else but fun. Got a pencil?"

"Affirmative."

"These names," Molly said. "It would be easier if you'd stick to a single century. You're all over the map. Between people living and people long dead. But here goes. You listening? Ten minutes, Terry! And put that down!

"OK. Fitz Hugh Ludlow. If it's the one you want. American. Author. Nobody cares what he wrote. His claim to fame—in 1863 he was a member of the party that traveled the American West in the company of the German-born American painter Albert Bierstadt.

"Josephus Stillton. Born 1830—no, that was Bierstadt. No, yes, I guess they were the same age. Born New England. Massachusetts, in fact. Old family. Went west in the 1850s to seek his fortune. And he found it. Wyoming. Copper and silver. Big strike in the region of the Wind River Valley. Came back to Massachusetts as an older man. Bags of money. I haven't found an obit so I can't tell you about descendants if any. It looks as if there was a wife.

"You getting all this? Rosa Ludlow. Or Rosalie. She's a foot-note. Being a woman who lived in the nineteenth century, who's surprised? That's her *married* name, Ludlow. Because she married Fitz Hugh, the author. You following?"

"I'm with you," Fred promised.

"She didn't stop there," Molly said. "Fitz moved on to other things, there was a divorce, and she married the landscape painter Albert Bierstadt!"

Fred let Molly have the triumph that comes when disparate paths of research coincide. It was little enough reward for the work she was doing. "So Rosa Ludlow is Rosa Bierstadt," Molly finished.

Molly's voice changed. "Listen. I know you're running around, but I also know there are terrible things happening up there. You're on the national news. You and Governor Crabtree, though Governor Crabtree's been on for some extra-marital fun he's been having. Listen, I'm sorry about that student…"

"So even I can notice this set of coincidences. Have you got your teeth into a Bierstadt painting? In the middle of all this? What's it like? Never mind, tell me later.

"Anyway, you didn't ask me to but I did. It's one of those things everyone knows, but they don't know the dates and then, when it comes right down to it, they don't know the facts either, do they? So I looked up Albert Bierstadt."

"Good," Fred said. "And thanks. I am indeed rusty."

"Born near Düsseldorf, Germany, in 1830. Family moved him to New Bedford when he was three. By the time he was twenty he was exhibiting paintings. Three years later he's in Düsseldorf to study painting, then in Rome. In Europe he paints all over. Landscape. The kind of landscape that makes you stand there and shout, 'This proves there's a God!' Clouds, rainbows, storms, the works. Wildernesses."

"I know Bierstadt's paintings," Fred reminded her.

"Of course you do. I get him confused with all those other transcendental, hurray for the American scene painters. Anyway, by 1857 he's back in the USA.

"Two years later, 1859, he has a chance to join up with the famous Lander expedition. All the new territories opening up in Kansas, Nebraska, out to the Rockies. He made sketches and photographs that he works from after he gets back to his big New York studio. People start wanting his stuff and he paints big time and for big money. People can't decide if he's an artist or P. T. Barnum, but the money doesn't care what he is. It wants his stuff.

"So, he goes west again, as I said, in 1863, with Fitz Hugh Ludlow and that bunch, as far as California—how much of this do you need?"

Knock on the door.

"Be right with you," Fred called. "You have dates of death?"

"For Stillton, no. For Rosa, no. For Bierstadt, 1902."

Knock on the door, more insistent.

"Thanks, Molly. It's open!"

Chapter Forty-nine

"What does this kid Rick Murphy have against you?" Seymour said, coming into the room. He was being disarming. He carried two cardboard cups, and the smell was coffee.

"I'll get us another chair," Fred said. He took one from the arrangement on the landing where the management had provided for the possibility that guests would sit and exchange sweet nothings while contemplating the corpses of dried flowers on a table that forced them to sit so far apart they'd have to shout.

The chair Fred had found was the better one, but Detective Seymour was already seated, in the window, so that his backdrop could promise unpleasant weather. Fred sat in the better chair.

"To answer your question," Fred said. "You can choose. A. I don't know. B. Maybe the kid either is a good citizen or likes to make trouble. Or, C. Both or all three. To answer your underlying question, I went into that classroom to teach on Tuesday, and it was a goddamned mess. Dust and trash everywhere. Also, that life teacher, Meg Harrison, had a complicated setup in the middle of everything, stage set, for her painting students, with stools and cloth and fruit and the rest of it, and a big sign on it saying, 'Don't move it.' And that made me mad.

"It was as if my class did not exist. As if I didn't exist. So I was pissed and I didn't want it to happen again."

"Well, but you didn't exist," Seymour pointed out. "If I understood correctly, nobody expected you, right?"

"True. But the *class* was expected. The *class* was scheduled. Maybe Flower doesn't care—I'm calling him that. It's a habit— but *I* do. And I let Harrison know it. I came by last night to make sure the room was ready for me to work in this morning.

"It was dirty. I swept it. Next question. No, first an observation. That puncture in Meeker's throat. It could be lethal if it hits the jugular or severs the windpipe, but there should be blood. And struggle. I hear you picked up Peter Quarrier. I understand that, but I wonder…Anyway, there should have been lots of commotion, even after that wound."

Seymour looked Fred over with speculation a few seconds before he said, "Not really your business. I wondered too. The autopsy is started and it will take a while. If the scalpel had been withdrawn, there would be blood. A lot. If the wound itself isn't fatal, the guy could have died of shock. It could come on quick. Instantly.'

"You don't think of shock," Fred said. He took the lid off his cup.

"The fight between them," Seymour said. "Over a girl, I gather?"

"Emma. My reading, after two days here as a teacher— Quarrier is a friend and looks after her; Tom was a pain in the ass making unwelcome moves."

"But you are not actually here to teach," Seymour prompted.

Fred became expansive. "This chairman of the board, Liz Harmony, acting president, is not the brightest bulb in the history of the known universe. You have probably noticed. Not bright enough to give you the same story twice, true or false. Their lawyer, Abe Baum, and a friend of the institution, Parker Stillton called me in to troubleshoot. What they really wanted I don't know. The rationale they presented was disingenuous at best. Maybe they just wanted a wild card here to foment a ruckus.

"Place was already on the brink of collapse. The institutional life force is strong, but there is only so much insult the system can stand. I'm thinking shock, again. Parker and Baum asked me here undercover to find Flower. I'm calling him Flower. And this student everyone assumes he's run away with. Or vice versa; to find the student, I think now."

"Melissa Tutunjian," Seymour put in.

"Like a fool I said yes before I recognized that their cunning plan also put me in a straight jacket. As a substitute teacher I couldn't ask questions. Worse, my time was locked up. While you're standing in front of a class, you can't do anything. But talk. And I'm not much of a talker."

"You're doing OK. What was Quarrier doing when he came here that night?"

Fred kept going. "So I told Liz Harmony—she was against it—my cover would be I'm looking at the whole institution to see if it can measure up to accreditation. That way I can ask questions. While I'm looking to deal with Flower. Peter had office contact. And he is bright. And curious. He cares about the place and he's been around enough to see how vulnerable it is. I asked him to help."

Seymour took a ruminative sip from his cup of coffee. "I see a man who's frank and helpful and probably slippery as hell," he said. "My instinct is to invite you to collaborate with us, and to be equally frank with you.

"My instinct is also to remind myself, who are you kidding?" Seymour said. "What does this guy really want? Every time he opens his mouth, what he's really doing is looking for information. Your car is registered in Charlestown. Care to comment?"

"I have a house there," Fred said. "But I live with a woman in Arlington. She has two children. I keep my options open."

"And you work?"

"For a guy in Boston. It's an old-fashioned concept but he's an old-fashioned guy. I do research and odd jobs for him and he pays my wage"

"The obvious theory is Quarrier wants this girl Emma for himself."

"Peter Quarrier told me he has a lover in Oregon. In Portland."

"He's flying in," Seymour said. "That's what I mean. That was another question."

Seymour reached out and picked up the butterfly card from the table where Fred had propped it. Something to enjoy. "Nice," he said. "What did you, buy it from one of the kids?"

"It's old," Fred said. "Look at the edges. That's mice."

Seymour turned it over and read it. "The weather continues fine. I guess this card was not sent from Stillton. It's a pretty thing."

"I pick things up," Fred explained.

"And what progress have you made looking for Morgan Flower? That Benjamin Star thing—that was a blind alley. Flower borrowed the car, it looks like. Star is in Tibet or some damned place. Him we are not going to locate for a while. So. Flower is still a blank. Unless you have something."

"You don't have a home address for Flower," Fred said. "Something beyond this apartment they gave him in Stillton?"

"That's another question."

Chapter Fifty

The talk in the Stillton Café, where lunch was still in progress, was all of the deaths of Tom Meeker and of the former director, and Peter Quarrier's arrest. At such times, the presence of an interested stranger, even just passing next to a table, caused voices to drop, making everyone in the place seem a conspirator. But the occasional overheard word made the subjects at issue clear as they were obvious.

It was late for lunch, but the day was unusual in every other way as well. Fred sat by himself at a table—the lone instructor—and nursed a truly indifferent grilled cheese sandwich, along with the six potato chips, two pickle slices, and ginger ale. The conversation at the neighboring tables had fallen to whispers.

Meg Harrison entered, went to the counter and spoke to Marci, who was working in the café again today. Then she surveyed the room, saw Fred at his table of isolation, and came over.

"May I?" she said.

Fred swallowed. "Please join me. It's a god-awful shock to the place. A one-two punch. The students, especially. There's no way you can't feel…"

Meg nodded.

"Even the best of them," Fred said. "It's a hard world. How many of even the best of them can stick with it after they leave?"

"It's not like we're teaching dental hygiene," Meg said. She'd rolled her sleeves back as she sat. The muscles and tendons of her forearm popped with stress. "Try something else, would you? Let me eat in peace."

"Sorry," Fred said. "That remark sounded like me doing my project. Sneaking up. Asking with a trick, do your students get jobs at the professions you train them for? Whereas I just mean to be offering sympathy for a hard business.

"I'll change gear. That TV program Tuesday night? *Pharaohs from Beyond the Stars?* Did you catch it?"

"I was out. I heard about it."

"I'm in the same boat," Fred said. "Problem is a lot of the students saw it. Got convinced. They don't have any history to compare it to. A program like that makes it so easy. How do you counter it?"

Meg said, "All those programs about UFOs and other mysteries, they all begin by assuming that human beings are as dumb as mayonnaise. How could a mere human being ever be smart enough to figure out a pyramid? Well, I'll tell you a good way to start. Don't fry your brains watching TV."

Marci stopped at the table with a tray from which she unloaded two cheeseburgers, a huge pile of fries, and whatever was in that glass; a dark soda with ice.

"Ketchup?" Meg asked.

"You got it." Fred shoved the plastic squeegee bottle across the table. "Imagine if we could take all the time first-year students in any program, not just here but everywhere, spend watching TV, and make them use that same time drawing instead," he said.

"And keep them from watching TV *while* they're pretending to draw? You'd be amazed..." She squirted ketchup onto her plate.

"Of course I forget all the stupid things I've done," Fred said. "Try to."

"Why I joined you. In spite of appearances, there's a group of us working underground, trying to save Stillton Academy," Meg said. "In spite of itself. And at the same time as we have to protect our own asses."

"Good luck," Fred said.

"We need people outside."

"You're working against your own board," Fred pointed out. "The way I read it. Who's in your group? Phil Oumaloff?"

"That blowhard? God!" Meg's voice had dropped to a whisper that was not unlike the whispers being exchanged at neighboring tables. "He's like one of those battery-powered toys. Runs along the floor eagerly in any direction until he encounters an obstacle, and immediately he turns and runs exactly as eagerly toward where you're going. Or the other way.

"What Phil figures, he's always going to be the figurehead, whatever direction the ship is going. Simply because he's been around so long. He deserves it."

"So who?"

"Arthur Tikrit. Bill Wamp. Bobby Ballatieri from printmaking. You met her? We can't say anything to Phil. He'd go running to Harmony with it before it got cold."

"Rodney Somerfest?" Fred asked softly.

Meg said, "We haven't got long. What we really need is someone from the outside. Someone with heft."

"Everyone mentions this alumnus. The painter Basil Houel," Fred said. "In fact some, like Phil Oumaloff, won't stop mentioning him. I begin to feel the place is haunted by him. His shadow casts a pall across the rain."

"The last thing we need is another artist," Meg said briskly. "Even if Basil happens to be well known. And I guess he is connected, in a way, at least to the collectors his gallery sells him to. Those connections could help if they weren't all New York. But as far as Basil himself goes, artists know as much about staying alive in this world as a handful of grasshoppers. Now, you…"

"I haven't got heft," Fred said.

"You might know someone out in the big world, I was going to say, with enough money and connections…"

"Peter Quarrier is with your group," Fred said. Not a question. Meg had taken a large bite of her cheeseburger. The operation of chewing gave her enough cover to avoid responding directly.

"The theory is that some drawings in the tomb of I forget who, which are so bad they had to be by the ancient Egyptian equivalent of a second grade boy, because nobody can make them out, must describe the space ships and the extraterrestrials. Then a professor with a beard and an accent comes on and confirms it," Meg said. "And no, Rodney Somerfest never had anything to do with our group. He barely had anything to do with the academy while he was here. He did something, I guess, but I don't know what. He was an extraterrestrial himself."

"Reaching around in the dark," Fred said. "There's this guy. Tutunjian. Is he with the good guys or the bad guys?"

Meg was eating dipped fries. She said, through a mouthful, "Tutunjian is pretty much with Tutunjian. Sure his bank gave a good contribution last year, to the endowment fund. But at the same time they hold paper on some of the buildings."

Chapter Fifty-one

"Paper meaning mortgages," Fred said. He reached for a fry. "May I?"

"Fries I got," Meg said.

"Your first-year students. I can't get their attention," Fred said. "All they can think about is the big crit on their life-sized drawings. At least, until this morning."

"What he wants is the loans paid up or the buildings foreclosed. That's whose side Tutunjian's on.

"It's the first hard work most of them have ever really tried. I thought I was hungry. I guess…Marci? Could you wrap this other burger and the rest of the fries, to go?"

Marci, passing the table, swept up the dishes and reversed course.

"I've been thinking about what you said," Fred said.

"Yes?"

"How you had one first-year student who's brilliant working in three dimensions. I'm trying to guess who it is. Of course, I don't know them."

"The drawings will all be posted tomorrow. We'll do it in Stillton A. Stillton B I don't trust. Who knows if they'll take the tape off. Everyone lies. So, I'll have to get Stillton A cleaned up somehow. Anyway, come take a look if you want."

"You can tell from a drawing? A drawing's in two dimensions. You can look at a drawing and say, There's a sculptor?"

"I can. You can't. Come at lunch, when we break, if you're interested. The crit lasts all day.

"Also, it can't help that their idea is, Let's get high while we watch it. It's not like they're looking for information. If you want mystery, there's nothing like tossing a few bricks into the machinery. Thanks, Marci."

Meg went out with her package.

"He won't leave his name," Mrs. Halper said, holding out a folded slip of paper.

Phone number written there. Fred's line in the office on Mountjoy Street.

"Also your shoes are dry. They should be OK." She took the loafers out from under the counter. They were stuffed with rolled newspaper. The lobby area was still interrupted by adult strangers who had the look of those who either collect or manufacture news or its broadcast adjunct commentaries. Fred brushed past those who seemed as if they might harbor the intention to corner him and chat.

He'd kept the better chair from the landing and it was still in his room, although someone had been in and remade the bed. The result was less military and more house and garden. Fred hung Bill Wamp's jacket to dry over the back of the inferior chair and sat in the better one, his feet on the bed, the phone on his lap.

"It's the Wind River Valley? You're certain of that?" Clay started. It was easy enough to picture him down there, sitting at Fred's desk, all the relevant books and catalogues spread out.

"Not Yosemite?" he continued. "I'm trying to date—and truly you make it difficult—I have next to nothing—because representations of the Yosemite can be very similar. There is Cleveland's big *Yosemite Valley* of 1866…"

"Look," Fred interrupted. "What we need, to evaluate that painting, that mural, is to get it out of the attic where it is, to lay it out in a dry, well-lighted place, and to study it for two weeks. We can't do any of that."

"And all without letting anyone know," Clay agreed.

"I said Wind River Valley," Fred said, "because that's what it made me think of. In the half light, under the roof, with the back of my shirt full of spiders, and listening for footsteps below.

"It would make sense. If my other conjectures are on target. It's where Josephus Stillton made his fortune in mining. Why wouldn't he want a souvenir?"

"Fred, you haven't been talking about…"

"Relax, Clay. I've been talking with Molly, over the phone," Fred said. "The painting is real. It's good. I *think* it's Bierstadt. But even to nail that down, if you wanted to, you'd have to let a whole conference of so-called scholars and experts stand around agreeing and disagreeing with each other for about a week, drinking your liquor, then writing papers, and like as not afterwards Cameron would disagree with all of them, on both sides, then…"

"I know Bierstadt's work," Clay cut in.

"As far as the question goes, is it the Wind River Valley? You know as well as I do. The way he made those big monsters, there's always a generic aspect. It's not like he took a covered wagon with him filled with ten-by-twenty foot canvases, and set himself up on a plateau at sunset fighting off wind and birds and Indians. He had that huge Tenth Street studio in New York where he could work calm and dry, making up amalgams from his sketches, his photos, his imagination, and some wishful thinking.

"I'm guessing it's a New York production. That would make sense. Of course, if it was executed during his long stay in San Francisco, in the 1870s, he had to have the room's measurements with him, work to those specs, then roll and ship the paintings by boat, around the horn, yes?"

"My darkest fear," Clay began. He was seldom without a darkest fear. Disregard.

"So there are a number of imponderables," Fred said. "I have a question. What made you think there might be any such treasure here?"

"I have studied," Clay said. He made it sound like the old lady in the soap opera announcing, as the organ music swells to the commercial, "I have suffered."

"You're the one with the time and space to do research," Fred argued. "While I'm stuck out here with more lone seagulls than Robinson Crusoe could barbecue in a lifetime. Have you found any textual reference at all that Bierstadt ever executed a mural? I don't know what there is in the record. Order books? Correspondence, studio records? Correspondence with Josephus Stillton would be nice. Any sign of Stillton in the index to Hendricks' big book? You have it. Ideally, a letter from Josephus telling him, 'Dear Al, please make me a mural for a room yay by yay by yay high, which will represent a panorama of the area surrounding the strike where I started my Wind River mine. That would be helpful.'"

Chapter Fifty-two

Clay said, "I am still utterly unprepared for the news you have brought me. Aside from these most regrettable deaths…" he paused. "Not casting either blame or aspersion, Fred," he continued, "Please forgive my annoyance. I must know. I must know. And no, it was not instinct that led to my suspicion, although what I expected you might find—no matter…"

The elastic silence was broken by the intemperate tapping of what must be Clayton's pencil against the surface of Fred's desk.

"Shall I tell you my darkest fear?" Clay asked again.

"If you must, now that the subject has been broached."

Clay's anguished voice squeezed out the words, "William Bliss Baker."

"Name doesn't ring a bell," Fred said. "Not the remotest chime or clunk. Who is he? Agent for that lady in Arkansas?"

"You know the name, for heaven's sake, Fred. Think! He was a painter. A younger man. Student of Bierstadt. Good gracious. I am saying the name aloud. On the telephone!"

"I had meant to bring back with me the butterfly you found, as well as the box of correspondence, to study; but my departure was unpremeditated. In your haste to sequester me, I neglected even to look at the butterfly card," Clay said.

Fred pried off the canvas shoes belonging to the late Mr. Halper and wriggled his toes, his feet still stretched out on the bed. "Next question," Fred said. "Following an observation.

Even if this material was lying around in plain sight, and nobody knows what it is, and nobody cares, it still belongs to somebody."

Long pause. Fred wriggled his toes. With his free hand he began un-stuffing his loafers, tossing the crumpled paper at the wastebasket in the far corner of the room, next to the door.

"You do not suggest that I would connive at thievery?" Clay said.

"It would be a change," Fred said. "But we haven't discussed it. In fact—and here's part of the matter that is distracting me—my own instincts run in the direction of pretty simple. What was *your* plan."

"I intended to do as I always have. To respond to those events which I am not able to instigate or to anticipate, but to respond, if respond I must, before anyone else has a chance to do so."

"Here are the problems I see," Fred said. He eased his right foot into the right-hand loafer. It went, but required force. "Let's say the mural is Bierstadt's work, as I think it is. If I had to steal it I could, after things die down over there, and provided I wasn't beaten to it. But we agree that stealing is out. Supposing it is for sale, what is it worth? In this economy? Would the seller be better advised to wait?

"Next, supposing the work were for sale, and at a fair price… as an aside I just mention that in all the years I have known you, I have never known you to put the kind of money on the table that I think it has to be worth. In this case I doubt you can.

"Next…" He took off the loafer. Forget it. "Suppose you owned such a work as the mural in question. Where would you stick it? What next? What do you do with it? Does the phrase 'white elephant' not come to mind? It's beautiful, sure. Then what? We design a new wing in the big side yard you do not have on Mountjoy Street? We make sure that the available wall space accommodates the panels, once we have figured out what the dimensions had to be of the room they were made for?"

"I am listening, Fred," Clay said impatiently. "Yours are not the first footprints on the road of this intellectual exercise.

But your summary is clear, and it is useful that these issues be expressed between us. It saves time."

"Next," Fred said, "I can't for the life of me see, if this were for sale, who you would buy it from."

"But that is the simplest element," Clay said. "Surely. The owner of record must be Stillton Academy of Art itself. This means, as you know, its board of trustees. A speedy transaction, unannounced to the world. As we both are aware, the institution is presently experiencing a certain financial stress."

"You don't know the half of it," Fred said. "Hold onto your hat."

The loafers would go to Goodwill.

"Yes? Yes?" Clay's impatient voice competed with the orchestral accompaniment provided by graphite on planed and well-scuffed oak.

"I'm sure you must be right that if anyone can sell that thing, it has to be the board, acting for the academy. But my guess is that any major financial undertaking this jolly gang of pirates executes is not only going to be scrutinized by the Attorney General, it may well be reversed in court."

"If there are legal questions, we simply consult Parker Stillton. He is in an ideal position to assist, being a friend to both parties," Clay said.

"Like everybody else, Parker Stillton acts for himself, his own best friend," Fred said. "And I think that he and his other best friends are going to jail. Or they would, or they should, if the eyes of Justice were not blinded by dollar bills."

"Explain," Clay demanded.

Fred said, "If I could see the books, and I can't, and if I did I couldn't understand them anyway because that's their main purpose, I'd be able to show you what I suspect, and I think it's true. Bear with me. The board purged itself of dissenters at the same time as it hired this former director, Rodney Somerfest."

"The dead man," Clay recalled. "Please spare me, Fred, from board politics. They are the worst kind. Nobody ever has anything to gain other than status."

"Moving on," Fred said. "Right. Rodney Somerfest was the first dead man. The one who was not my student. Meanwhile they've mortgaged the academy buildings to a bank in Lowell…"

Clay interrupted, "Whistler was from Lowell. Though he famously chose not to be."

"Meanwhile the same members of the same Stillton Academy board have formed an equal and opposite realty consortium, the so-called Stillton Realty Trust…"

"Spare me, Fred. I really don't care," Clayton objected. "This is miles from the subject at issue. What concerns me, therefore *us,* is already sufficiently complex. The academy owns a work of artistic and historical importance."

"And worth lots of money," Fred mentioned.

"Never mind. They don't know what they have. Or even that they have it. Recognizing that they are a not-for-profit corporation, and that I have obligations as a citizen, how do I get it? How do I do so fairly? And advantageously?"

"And legally," Fred added. "That's my point. If these jokers are all in jail, because they are selling the academy's assets to themselves, which is how I simplify the situation—or if they are merely threatened with jail…wait a minute. I'll have to call you back. There's the door."

Fred tucked the butterfly card into the top drawer of his dresser.

"Tell them to wait," Clay almost shouted.

Fred told him, "My deal with the cops is, I'm on call. I'll call you back. Take care. For the time being I think we're screwed."

Chapter Fifty-three

Phil Oumaloff pushed past Fred into the room, puffing. He managed to get out, "Close the door. No one must know." He tossed a stained broad-brimmed hat of wet leather onto the bed. His starched white hair shook as he searched for a place to put his wet trench coat.

"Still raining?" Fred asked.

"It's letting up," Oumaloff claimed.

"Seems to me it's been letting up almost constantly for the last three days," Fred said. "Give me your coat."

Against Oumaloff's protests he took the coat out to the hall and draped it across the remaining chair on the landing. When he got to his room again Oumaloff had used his capacious buttocks to stake a claim on the better of the room's two chairs.

"No one must know," Oumaloff repeated. He was laboring under the strain of enormous self-importance. But that condition, like the weather, seemed to be a constant. In Fred's bedroom, Oumaloff worked to regain composure. Outside the foghorn hooed a warning so regular it was noticeable only if you paid attention.

"I'd offer you something, but there isn't—well—I can make tea or coffee. It's easy to tell which is which. You just read the package."

"Stop putting me at ease," Oumaloff said.

The two men sat in silence while Phil Oumaloff glared around the room. "What do you know about art?" he asked finally.

"People have been known to come to blows over it," Fred said. "But there are seldom fatalities."

"You make light of these deaths?"

"Despite your request, I am putting you at your ease," Fred explained, "by giving you the moral high ground."

"When a man is pissing downhill," Fred did not say, "he feels taller and stronger than he does when he is pissing uphill. Also his feet stay dry. By the same rule, a higher man with dry feet is a more confident man; and the more confident a man is, the more he tends to brag. This gives him away."

"I have known this academy, and been a good part of it, for over two dozen years," Phil Oumaloff declared. "When I began, we were forty-seven students, with a program that would have shamed Bunker Hill Community College. Or any other.

"Through the years we have been continually beleaguered, even assaulted. I make no apologies. Through my interventions, and those of a few others, and by the fortunate appearance of some worthy students, over the years we have managed to make the academy's reputation. An emeritus now, I am in a position to step away from the daily rough and tumble, and to take a deserved pleasure in contemplating the institutional history of which I may say I am a proud part."

"Oh yes," Fred remembered. "The alumnus reunion. Basil Houel. All that."

"The case we will make," Oumaloff said and corrected himself, "The case *I* will make, is one of a distinct and honorable tradition. Stillton is not, and never has been, the isolated backwater it appears to be. Fishing village yes, perhaps. And the earliest Stilltons may have been merchants, sea captains, even privateers. No matter. You point to Basil Houel?"

"Everyone else seems to," Fred said.

"Speaking of Basil Houel, at this very moment, and in this very town, under my roof—but no, it must be kept in strictest confidence." At the brink of unwelcome further expansion, Oumaloff pulled himself back and tried a diversion. "Never mind tea or coffee," Oumaloff said. "The case I will make refers to a much deeper tradition. I ask what you know about art. The question is too broad. Specifically, do you know anything of the work of Bierstadt? Never mind. They teach nothing. Nothing. My story begins with the death of Josephus Stillton. By fire. Specifically, and most likely, and tragically, by cigar.

Oumaloff took a breath and continued, "You, as another in a long series of fly-by-nights who sweep through town telling us our business, and vanish again into the wilderness you came from—everything vanished! Smoke!"

Oumaloff paused for effect. Or for applause.

"Smoke," Fred prompted.

"There is now no remaining trace of Stillton House, not even of the foundation. We know that it stood on the corner of Main and Sea Streets, where Main meets Sea in a perpendicular gesture. Of course. It overlooked the bay."

"Josephus Stillton," Fred said. "Wasn't he the founder of Stillton Academy? So, you found those papers defining the bequest?"

But Oumaloff's course was set elsewhere. "We know that among the furnishings of the home, Stillton House, the mansion, I suppose we can call it, were three paintings by Bierstadt. We still have what must have been their frames. Sadly charred. Sadly charred. In the jumble above Stillton Hall's studios. I have examined them.

"No. Not I myself. My figure has never been such…But some years ago I prevailed on a student to look through the material up there, and to measure the frames. They were among the flotsam and jetsam.

"And what's more, we can read in the record—these matters are never of interest to those who pass through, you might as well be insurance adjustors or efficiency experts—Bierstadt paintings that have not been accounted for. They were exhibited at the Academy. It is all in the record. We have their names, their titles."

"The titles of paintings get changed," Fred said.

"What was the name of the student you sent up there to measure the empty frames?" The question, unspoken, hovered in the air like a distracted butterfly.

"Exhibited at the academy?" Fred prompted. "Here at Stillton? For the widows and orphans?"

"Not Stillton Academy." Phil Oumaloff was exasperated. "People know nothing of history. Stillton Academy did not exist until after the death of Josephus Stillton. No. You could not know. By 'exhibited at the Academy,' I meant the National Academy of Design in New York City. The foremost venue in its day for the painters of the nineteenth century."

Chapter Fifty-four

"I will take tea," Oumaloff conceded. His oration had deflated him somewhat. Or it was a tactical move, to edge Fred into a servile position.

Fred said, "I'll be mother." He filled the kettle in the bathroom and did what was necessary to the electric brewing machine. "Bierstadt," he said. "I've heard of him. Aubrey Bierstadt."

"Not Aubrey. Albert. It was a tragic loss. Sugar, please. I'll put it in myself. *The Golden Gate, San Francisco,* 1863, perhaps the one that at one time belonged to John C. Frémont. *Storm in the Rocky Mountains,* also of 1863—its provenance has been murky; as well as a final painting from the same year, *Western Landscape—Mount Ranier, Mount Saint Helen's*—a small picture, perhaps one foot by two."

Fred carried the envelope of sugar to his guest, along with a feeble plastic stirring wand. Let Oumaloff have something tangible to fondle while he waited for the water to boil. "We'd put a hypothetical question earlier," Fred said, "talking with Bill Wamp in the office."

"If you had milk or cream I would take it," Oumaloff said. "But not that white powder."

"The question being," Fred pushed on, "if Stillton Academy, for whatever reason, is forced to shut down, what becomes of the assets?"

Enough steaming water had dripped into the kettle. Fred poured some over a tea bag and handed the foam cup over. Mission accomplished.

"It is all in the public record," Oumaloff said, as if reassuring himself. He dunked the teabag and kept it moving. "Yes. When we were inducted into the board, we were given a folder. Recent minutes, financial reports, what pass for the articles of incorporation, sections from the last will and testament of Josephus Stillton, all very moving and ponderous stuff."

"Which nobody reads," Fred said. "Like the text of any and all picture books. I've probably leafed through books about Aubrey Pinkham Bierstadt, but if I have…"

"*Albert*, not Aubrey," Oumaloff insisted. He opened the packet of sugar and dripped half its contents into the cup.

"You found the folder," Fred said.

"As an emeritus I am allowed an attractive rent on the cottage I live in." Oumaloff tasted the liquid. "When I resigned, I was made to understand at the same time that it might be more comfortable for me to leave town." He stirred and tasted again. "I declined. The cottage is filled with memorabilia."

He was determined to take his time. Give him a chance, he'd always be the middle part of one of those interminable shaggy dog stories.

"One concentrates on the future," Oumaloff said.

"Especially in a shaggy dog story," Fred said.

"I don't follow. Never mind," Oumaloff pushed on. Josephus Stillton died in 1890. Legal documents of the day, as perhaps you know…"

Fred shook his head. "Widow? Children?"

"There was provision for a wife if she survived him, but she perished in the same conflagration. There was no issue."

"Issue meaning children," Fred confirmed.

"The estate, after a few bequests, went to the trust that expressed itself as Stillton Academy. The intent was for the academy to provide instruction in useful domestic arts to the widows and orphan daughters of seamen, as you apparently know. Based on this rationale we have become, more than a century later, Stillton Academy of Art."

I know, I know, I know, Fred did not need to say. For the love of Mike, get on with it!

"Now." Oumaloff took another sip, considered, found it wanting, and added the remainder of the sugar. Stirred. Tasted. Whoever had killed Tom Meeker, had taken less time to get it done. "I did discover the folder," he said. "It stands out. The leather cover is embossed with gold. If I understand—in answer to the question we were debating—perhaps this should be brought to the attention of Mr. Baum. He is the board's attorney..."

"Yes?" Fred prompted.

"Because I cannot believe it is legal. For the remaining assets of what had been a charitable corporation to devolve to a private individual, or private individuals plural—it seems incoherent. Were she not so pressed with recent tragic events, I would bring it to the attention of President Harmony."

"She's not on your side," Fred did not say. "If you have a side. She hates you. Who wouldn't?"

Oumaloff shook his head grandly. "It is there in the public record. But there is much in the public record that the public ignores."

"Like the Bill of Rights," Fred agreed.

"Should the trust be obliged to liquidate," Oumaloff said, "the fallback legatee is to be any and all living members of the Stillton family, bearing the Stillton family surname, who reside in the Commonwealth of Massachusetts at the time of the liquidation, provided he has resided in the Commonwealth for at least five years prior to said liquidation.

"Forgive me if I speak in tongues. A legal document is infectious, though the infection produces incoherence. Incidentally, I've heard there may be a Stillton somewhere."

"Sounds like the potential for a complication," Fred said.

"Potential for an extreme conflict of interest," Oumaloff said. "That's what it sounds like."

"Except the only reason to liquidate the thing," Fred speculated, "is that its assets have become worthless and it may even be in debt for more than it's worth."

Oumaloff fixed a severe glare on Fred. "I had meant to begin with this observation. Given your own personal confidential relationship with the board, as an advisor on matters of accreditation—that *is* your role?"

Fred's nod was modest.

"I would have thought you might receive the same package."

"President Harmony has been quite worried and preoccupied by these deaths," Fred said.

"All of us are. All of us," Oumaloff said. "But then I considered. What was this man, Josephus Stillton, thinking? I have never even considered it. Knowing that the man died without issue, it never occurred to me to wonder. Are there other Stilltons living in Massachusetts? If so, might they be induced to appear at the reunion celebration? It would be a moving addition to the program, if they are respectable. It is not a common name, surely, with the two L's in the center…

"Fred, for your confidential report—and don't mention my name…I want you to deal directly, frankly and openly, and with all diligent secrecy, with this matter," Phil Oumaloff finished.

Chapter Fifty-five

"Well," Fred agreed.

"First, I do not believe it is legal. But it is possible to put an illegal wish in a will. Second, whether it is legal or not, it could lead to years of litigation."

"Not if the assets are gone," Fred pointed out. "At least all the lawyers I know keep asking for money."

"It must not be closed. It cannot be closed. It will not be closed," Oumaloff proclaimed. He stood and drained the remainder of his cold tea, as Patrick Henry must have done on the floor of St. John's Church in Richmond, Virginia, at the end of his speech to the House of Burgesses, after delivering the line—if indeed he did deliver it—that would be all anyone ever remembered of him, if they remembered it.

"There will always be a Stillton Academy of Art," Oumaloff announced—stepping on his own exit line. It was both an impotent threat and a hopeless promise. "Where is my coat?" He picked up his hat from the print it had left on Fred's bed. "Once litigation begins, the damage is done. Regardless of its outcome. Tell them."

Fred opened the door—his visitor seemed to expect that—and pointed along the hallway to where Phil's coat dripped onto the landing. The corpses of the dried flowers would be glad of the moisture and welcome new life in the form of mold.

The phone rang in Fred's room. "Desk," Mrs. Halper said. "Message for you."

Fred went down in his socks. The lobby was empty. Had the story of Tom Meeker's death dwindled so quickly? Where was everyone?

"Big fire in Boston," Mrs. Halper said, giving an answer to the unspoken question. "But the rooms have to be paid for. It's too late to cancel."

"I want to talk to Lillian Krasic," Fred said.

"She won't sell," Mrs. Halper said. She handed a small envelope over with the return address *The Stillton Inn*. "I said you were with someone. It was true. But I would have said so anyway. I don't want that in the rooms. I don't care how times have changed."

"That's what I want to tell her," Fred said. "What I want to tell her is, don't sell."

"She knows it. She won't."

"Thanks for what you did with my shoes," Fred said. He held up the envelope. "A student?"

"Not one I know. Female."

"Well, then, and thanks for that," Fred said. "These days a man can get in trouble without even opening his eyes. Much less his door. You look out for your guests, and I appreciate it."

"What was the murderer doing in your room? A couple of nights before?"

"You are speaking of Peter Quarrier? He was and is my student. And we don't know he is a murderer. Therefore we shouldn't say it."

"Whatever. Not my business. But you might as well know, I told that detective."

"So did I," Fred said.

"I like everything to be on the up and up."

"You took the words out of my mouth," Fred said. "Is there a place in town that sells shoes? Sneakers?"

"The loafers…"

"They'll be fine. But for someone else," Fred said. "Someone smaller. Thanks for this," he waved the envelope. "And thanks for watching my back. Girl comes to a guy's room, the next chapter is going to be trouble. Even when everything's square. In this country, these days...anyway, thanks."

"I'll tell Lillian," Mrs. Halper said. "That you want to see her. She doesn't see anyone. She saw that detective, but how could she say no?"

"I'll be in my studio. Later. E. Rickerby."

Fred folded the note again and put it back in the envelope, then busied himself with the household tasks of cleaning up after Oumaloff. "E. Rickerby? E?" He riffled through the sheaves of names from the past few days until he found her. Emma.

"Listen," Fred said.

"Where were we?" Clay answered. "It is all happening so fast, and yet nothing is happening. Suspicion is everywhere."

"What I want you to do," Fred said. "Get the book. Find a Boston address for Liz Harmony. Elizabeth Harmony. Can you do that? I'll wait."

"You have one down here?"

He'd answered his own line, but that rang on Fred's desk as well, so that Fred could deal with it if Clay happened to be attending a wedding.

"Under the thing," Fred told him. "Thing on the right side. Third shelf down."

"Very well," Clay said. "Harmony, Elizabeth."

"While you're remembering your alphabet," Fred said, "There's this much of a record. Josephus Stillton did own paintings by AB."

"Yes," Clayton said. "There are three that I know of. So, you have found them."

The exhalation at Clay's end of the line was pure triumph. "Fred, I congratulate you. Given the extreme difficulty of your search caused by intervening events."

"Hold on, Clay. I found nothing, I only have word of them."

"Well? Well? The biggest one, the best. *Storm in the Rocky Mountains...*"

"I'm telling you, Clay, I haven't found anything. I said 'There are three paintings.' I should have said 'were'. All three are said to have burned in the fire that killed Josephus Stillton. Also his wife."

Long pause at Clayton's end. Then he said, his eagerness barely suppressed by disappointment, "*Storm in the Rocky Mountains.* I was certain I had tracked it down. Bierstadt had taken it to Europe and toured with it, even showed it to the Queen—Victoria that would be—in 1867. Big painting. Said to have been sold in Paris to Sir Morton Peto. Twenty thousand dollars. According to Hendricks. But nobody can find it and then there's the contrary report, also recounted by Hendricks, that *Storm in the Rocky Mountains* burned in a fire at Earle's Gallery in Philadelphia in 1869, but still...then a *Scribner's* article from 1872 claimed that *Storm* was owned by a J. W. Kennard, but the artist's niece claimed that the owner was Peto, though he could have sold it to Kennard, but in any case..."

"In any case," Fred said, "the word here is, however it got here, it burned."

"What evidence is there?"

"I've seen charred frames. If that's evidence, and I don't think it is, it's not specific. Any paintings, though, that might have been inside the frames, would have gone first. They'd be nothing but cloth and petroleum and, of course, the workings of the highly flammable human spirit. They'd have the chance of a butterfly in flame."

"Dreadful," Clay said.

"But I see part of your trail now, anyway," Fred said. "From whatever records, you'd learned that Stillton had purchased these paintings..."

"Not from any *published* records," Clay said smugly. "Gordon Hendricks is all very well, as far as he goes. However..."

Chapter Fifty-six

Another lengthy silence, fraught with disappointment.

"You believe it to be a dead end, then," Clay concluded. "I confess, I was prepared for another triumph."

"I can't tell you more than I have," Fred said. "I don't know what there is, I don't know what there was, I don't know what there isn't. That pretty much sums it up. Did you find that address?"

"Still," Clay mourned, "we have the mural."

"In a manner of speaking," Fred said. "If by 'we have' you mean 'the mural exists.'"

Clay said, "I take your point. There is many a slip. Granted. Very well. You have a pencil?"

"I do."

"Good gracious! She is almost my neighbor." Clay gave the address. Harmony, E.'s address was Beacon Hill also, though tonier than Clayton's Mountjoy Street digs: on Louisburg Square. "Where a person chooses to live, a person who has more money than imagination," Clay scolded. "And whose friends and acquaintances, also lacking imagination, require an easy reference point to remind them of the overriding wealth and importance of the individual in question."

"Or you could be the live-in maid. Still, I'm glad you explained that to me," Fred said. "Being originally from the mid-west, I still miss some of the social niceties.

Therefore Senator and Mrs. Kerry..."

"And her telephone number," Clay said.

"Person this classy, I'm amazed she allows herself in the white pages."

"Tchah! What do you take me for? This is the *Beacon Hill Register*. As it happens, I had it with me, concerning another matter. Letter of condolence. One does not like to send such a thing to a man's office—nor to a post office box.

"Fred, what is your plan?"

"Following your advice, I thought I'd either anticipate events or respond to them."

"Those three paintings, the origin of my quest—you are certain?"

"Of course I'm not certain. The charred frames are the right age. How do I know what was in them? I didn't see brass plaques if that's what you want to know. But I wasn't looking for them. It was a nightmare up there. It was like looking for a particular issue of the *New York Times* in the Collyer Brothers' place."

"Absence proves nothing," Clay said. "Like most of history. The majority of the map should always be marked *terra incognita*."

"As in 'Here be dragons,'" Fred said.

"I surmise that the time is ripe for me to telephone Parker Stillton," Clay speculated. "Not volunteering information you understand, but..."

"Let's try to summarize what you'll say," Fred offered. "'Good afternoon, Parker. Lovely day.' I presume it's lovely in Boston? It's raining here. Well, more like a soup you'd send back. 'So, Parker, just to let you know. Stillton Academy owns something I want. They don't know they have it. I want to buy it. It's worth enough money to turn the place around, but naturally I can't, or won't, pay that much. I'll do the decent thing, naturally, but at the same time...' Are you following me?"

Clay breathed heavily. "Honor," he lamented.

"More critical, as I tried to warn you, Parker Stillton is not to be trusted."

"No one is ever to be trusted," Clay observed reasonably. "We know that."

"Cast your mind back," Fred said. "Parker arrived on your doorstep with this lawyer, Abe Baum. The academy's lawyer."

"He telephoned first," Clay said.

"Granted. Parker said—didn't he?—while I was in your parlor, watching them drink your sherry—that he was a friend of the academy, and had been considered for, or was considering, accepting a position on the board."

"An appropriate consideration," Clay said. "Continuity. The name. Reassurance. Tradition."

"But that he had decided against accepting. Did he say that? Is my memory playing tricks? Am I reading between the lines?"

Clayton's pencil tapped. "Tell the truth, I don't recall. My energy was directed to the suppression of my exultation at the fact that I now perceived an entry point in the bastion that had long appeared to be closed to me."

"Here's what I've learned," Fred said.

"Is it relevant? Much of what you have told me so far is not," Clay complained.

"I don't think so. I am trying to look at the big picture."

"Yes. Yes. So am I," Clay fretted.

"Speaking in metaphor. The board is placing the academy in such financial jeopardy that it may not survive. Meanwhile another entity, with the same people involved, has been buying effective control of all the town's other real estate. With a few holdouts."

"This is what I mean, Fred. You are making it too complex. They have something I want. Period. There must be a way."

"If the board of trustees in its wisdom decides that the academy has to close," Fred pushed on, "as I learned today, whatever is left of the assets must revert to whatever residents of the Commonwealth happen to carry the family name."

"The family name."

"Of Stillton. Stillton. As in Parker Stillton."

Clay's pause could be read as either interest, speculation, or a dead faint.

"Stillton," Clay said. "Cousin Parker."

"Exactly. Trained in law as he is, he could see, as even I could, that to be part of a board of trustees that moved to award him the assets…"

"Are there other Stilltons?"

"Hell, I don't know."

"Goodness," Clay said.

Fred hung up the phone. "Exactly my thought."

Chapter Fifty-seven

Eight o'clock. It was well past the right time for a quiet drink and a look at the paper. Or, better, less solitary, well past the right time to prop himself in an out-of-the-way corner of Molly's kitchen, if he could find such a thing, and talk through the mutual day, as interrupted by Terry, and sometimes Sam, while Molly threw supper together.

Sam was inclined to keep himself to himself.

The rain had let up. The fog horn had stopped, leaving a persistent stain in the eardrums. Main Street was filled with salt air and a dingy grayness. Gulls fought over scraps in the gutters, and screamed with the quick succession of triumph, frustration, and envy.

The human population, taking advantage of the unexpected clemency of the weather, was, much of it, outside in the chilly air. Bee's Beehive was loud with customers, some of whom had stepped onto the sidewalk with sandwiches. The Stillton Café was packed inside, and customers came through the doors with sodas or take-out.

There was Arthur Tikrit, walking downhill away from the promontory that housed his workplace. He failed to see Fred's wave. Small town like this that was mostly academy people anyway, an instructor would quickly learn a way to ignore the impediments of unnecessary greetings. It would be like trying to live an actor's life in the streets of Hollywood. "Hey, do you know who *you* are?"

Outside the painting studio building a cruiser idled. Students, ignoring it, like bait fish in the presence of a sated shark, smoked in front of the building's entrance—but being careful what they smoked. That was Steve, wasn't it? Fred's student. Also a sometimes cook at the Stillton Café?

"Steve," Fred greeted him.

"It's big news. Have you heard? They're trying to keep it secret," Steve said. He dropped his filtered butt and stamped it into the wet grass. "Fred, you remember Carla?" he said, including the woman smoking beside him. Another of Fred's students? Yes, from the *Writing About Your Problems* class. Third row back if you could call them rows.

"Sure. Sorry. Carla. It takes me a while."

"What did you think?" Carla asked.

"It's terrible. Tom Meeker, Peter…"

"I mean my writing. Describe the campus. What I did, mine was the one from the point of view of a cat."

Fred told her, "I'm embarrassed. What with everything going on, I haven't got to them."

"You're going to like it. It's different."

"What news?" Fred asked Steve. "There's been so much bad news."

"So," Carla said. Steve had a hand on her rump. Otherwise, the floor was hers. "You think you're going to have to keep looking at everything from six inches above the ground, which is a real bore, cats looking *down* the way they do. I've tried it. But then the cat jumps up on something, and keeps climbing. You're going to love it."

"You're both painters?" Fred asked.

Carla's "No" accentuated Steve's "Yes." Carla, shaking her head vigorously, was going on, "Graphic Design. But they let me visit." She leaned against the hand.

"Anyway, everyone's working tonight," Steve said. "I'm taking a break. It's like, well, it would be…"

"A person you know," Carla said. "Presumed innocent and all. But you never think. I mean people you know, you don't think one's going to be killed, and another one's the killer."

"You never know," Steve said. "Then there's this next thing…"

"What we found out, which everyone now knows," Carla explained, "except you being new around here: Meg Harrison, that's our teacher—she's got a surprise visiting artist going to show up for the first-year crit."

"God, I still remember," Steve said. "First year. Life size. El nudo. I'll never forget it. In fact I still have it, somewhere."

"Worse for the guys," Carla said, giving Steve a maternal tickle at the waist line. "You guys, you're so cute. One, Lambert, he's gone, no way would he take off his boxers.

"Like, in a self-portrait, everyone's going to lie anyway, yes? It's human nature."

"It's obvious," Steve agreed. "The fat guy gets thinner—or *really* fat, like it's on purpose. Everyone knows."

"But the guys' dongs," Carla said, giggling. "First year, most of them have never been seen by a girl, not naked. Not, you know, *there*. What do they do? It's not supposed to be a contest, but with guys, it's always a contest."

"It's fun to watch them now," Steve said. "But I have to admit, I was the same."

"'Measure it' is Harrison's motto. Measure everything. Everything's a signpost, a milestone, and that's *all* it is. The nipple to the navel? Boston to Chelmsford. The point of the shoulder to the elbow. The knee to the groin."

"Ouch!" Steve said.

"That's what she'd say. Measure the knee to the groin, and all the guys are doubling up. It's like she doesn't notice."

"She's a mechanic," Steve said.

"When you're eighteen, you think about groins a lot, and you don't necessarily want everyone else in the world thinking about yours. Especially the guys," Carla said. "Skinny dongs, fat dongs, short dongs, long dongs, dongs that hang sideways, who isn't circumcised, who is, are the balls tight or loose…

"'We don't care if you don't look like Michelangelo's *David*' she told Lambert one time. Still, you'd be surprised how many guys come out looking like Michelangelo's *David*. Which he isn't that well hung in my opinion anyway, though symmetrical and all. *You* didn't," Carla told Steve, digging again at his belly.

"And we all know the guys, when they get together, are pretending they'll serve her right, get their revenge, do themself with a hard-on, like she's never heard of a hard-on, or seen one or…"

"What's the 'Meeker Method'?" Fred asked. "That was Tom Meeker, right? I happened to overhear…"

Carla, her laugh cut short by the tragedy that couldn't keep her from chuckling again, explained, "Tom Meeker. What he did, he figured a system with two mirrors, so all you got in his drawing was the backside. Ever since then Hag Harrison has to expressly forbid the Meeker Method, which everyone in the class used to call Meeker's Moon."

"That clears that up," Fred said.

Steve said, "Knowing this crowd, they'll call that gesture the Meeker Memorial now. No disrespect."

"Who's the surprise?" Fred asked.

"Anyway, Meeker did the assignment, to the letter of the law, and she couldn't deny it. Also she couldn't flunk Lambert. He told her he'd sue. Sexual harassment, he said. The boxers had stripes. 'Who's going to know?' we said. 'Lie.' But he wouldn't," Carla said, giggling. "Last I heard he's pumping gas."

"Basil Houel," Steve said. "He's a painter. Big time. He went here."

Chapter Fifty-eight

Steve explained, "The way it always goes when they have these visiting artists, they do the crit, probably in the morning. Sorry. A crit—critique—the first-year students have to come early, and their drawings are already pinned up when the big shot rolls in. Basil Houel's work—you can almost touch it it's so real."

"He does trash," Carla said. "Who'd want to touch it? It isn't for me."

"But the *way* he does it," Steve said. "Anyway, so he spends the morning in Stillton Hall with the kids, and he and Harrison talk about the drawings, and what works and what doesn't and all, and that passage from the buttocks to the breast, and then they have lunch somewhere. They come back and he'll spend the afternoon in the third- and fourth-year painters' studios, looking at our work. It could be…"

"So everyone's cleaning up," Fred said.

"Time goes on. Life goes on. It could be big. This guy, he's connected. Big-time gallery. Acacia. Everything."

"Good luck," Fred said. Steve was lighting another cigarette. "I'll be on my way."

"If he has time, and if he's not too much of a freaking art snob, he might stick his nose in the designers' studios too," Carla said. "Steve. Later." She planted a kiss on his cheek, blowing smoke along with it.

◇◇◇

When Fred had passed the lighted window of the end studio, where Emma worked, the blind had been drawn. The day had long since darkened into dusk and then some, not to mention clouds and drizzle.

Inside, the studio building bustled. Students worked while their radios worked against them, and against each other, or against those who sported earphones with iPods. Emma's door was closed. Fred knocked.

Emma's visitor was stout, clean cut and clean shaven, wearing khakis, a button-down blue shirt whose neck protruded from a heavy gray sweatshirt without identification or motto. The haircut was military; the look, stricken.

"They won't say where he is," Emma said.

Fred held out his hand. "I'm Fred."

"Aldo," The young man said.

"Peter's friend," Emma said.

"You got here fast," Fred said.

Aldo nodded grimly.

"You've seen Seymour? The detective?" Fred asked.

Aldo, shaking his head, "Not yet. I just got here. Don't know how, but I'm here. I have Seymour's number to call. If Seymour wants to talk, he tells me where Peter is first, and he waits while I line up a lawyer. Peter's house is taped off. His studio…

"He never called me," Aldo said. "They must have taken his phone."

"What would they want with his phone?" Emma asked.

"Quick way to see who he's been talking to, where he's been. The cops…" Fred started.

"He always carries his phone," Aldo said.

"Not now. The cops will have it," Fred said. "They get anything they want."

"That's Peter," Aldo said, pointing to the self-portrait. It was still where Emma had placed it that morning.

"I've been thinking what he told me," Emma said. "When he was here in the studio that last time. I talked to you, Fred, but I was just thinking about me. Me. How I'll miss him if. But all the time me. Then Tom asked me, Do you want to know where Flower is, and I didn't. Because Morgan Flower can't go to hell too soon is my opinion. But now Tom is dead, and I don't want to talk about hell, because Tom gave me a hard time and he's dead now and so. But also, too, and I didn't say this, Tom said, and he would do this, he'd been in the office. He listened in sometimes, or picked up things, and he had his own ways of getting into the buildings.

"Well, tell the truth, most of these buildings, anyone can."

"Security around here, it's a joke," Aldo said. "Emma said that building, what is it? Stillton Hall where they found him, was locked? So what? Everyone knows how to get in. And once you're in, the doors have these panic bars. Public buildings, you have to. Anyone who was with him, who killed him. It's the easy solution, tab A in slot B, because they were fighting in a way, and kids heard a threat…" he gulped and went on. "Why Peter and Tom were in there together, who knows? If they were. That's the story so far. But did anyone see them? Then, after Tom…is what they are saying…Peter opens the door and walks out after. Door locks behind him, everyone thinks, But the building was locked. Mystery of the locked room. But it's not."

"Did Tom mention anything else about the office, when he was here?" Fred asked Emma.

"I was maybe the last person that saw him," Emma said, "except…"

Aldo had been standing. Now he sat on a metal stool. Emma, standing in front of the studio nude, in which the fruit had become garish, kept looking back and forth distractedly between the painting and her visitors.

"Peter believed there was dirty stuff going on," Aldo said. "He's older. He's been around. The kind of guy Peter is, he sees something wrong, he won't leave it be. And anyone can…I mean, we don't think we can, but if there's one thing you learn in the service, no matter what your mother taught you…"

"Basil Houel's coming. Meanwhile, all I can think about is, poor Peter," Emma said. "Also, poor Tom, of course. But Tom's dead. There's hope for Peter maybe.

"Peter has a paranoid streak," Aldo said. "Anyone who's been in the service does. If people are trying to kill you, you get used to running around thinking, Hey, people are trying to kill me."

"Any hint what Tom found in the office?" Fred said. "They both worked in the office."

"All Tom said," Emma laid it out, "and he was laughing. That fucking Harmony. That fucking President Harmony!"

"Check in with Seymour," Fred told Aldo. "These guys don't like to wait. You have a place to sleep?"

"Emma's fixed me up," Aldo said.

Emma said, "I totally fucked that fruit."

◇◇◇

Peter's map of the academy buildings was back at the Stillton Inn, but the campus was simple, the town small, and in any case the whole thing was pretty much in Fred's head by now.

Clay's Lexus would not look out of place parked in front of Liz Harmony's presidential manse, so-called—even on the new sign that stood at the new-looking gate in the new-looking picket fence that made the whole thing, shingled cottage and all, look like Nantucket. Unlike most of the town's buildings, this one was large enough, and enough set back, with a big enough yard, that its inhabitant could feel both important and somewhat protected by isolation.

No need, therefore, to close shades or curtains on the ground floor.

Car in the drive. BMW. Deep green. The windows lit. Phil Oumaloff holding forth, a glass goblet in one fist. President Harmony turning toward Oumaloff from a sideboard, the decanter in her hand, saw Fred through the window.

Chapter Fifty-nine

"I was told you had left," Harmony said at the door. She had opened it and now stood in Fred's way.

"My job's not done," Fred said. "You and I haven't really talked."

"I am with someone," she whispered.

"I've got no secrets from Phil," Fred assured her. "Whatever he's drinking, though, I don't want any. Water will do me fine."

She yielded him enough space to allow him to enter, saying only, "I am prepared to have Security remove you."

"If you want," Fred said. "But for now they seem to be pretty busy buddying up to the real troopers. Ah, Phil."

Oumaloff looked balefully at him over the rim of the glass goblet. President Liz had been interrupted before she was able to fill it.

"Never mind the water," Fred said, sitting in a third of a chintz-covered sofa. Correction: Presidential Divan. "Phil, you were saying?"

"My visit does not concern you."

"Now, now, Phil," Liz Harmony soothed. She poured amber consolation from the decanter into Oumaloff's glass before filling hers again, and sitting in a Queen Anne chair that matched the one Phil sat in, on the opposite side of a fireplace over which hung a painting of boats and rough seas made not long ago by an extremely distant admirer of Winslow Homer.

"Phil comes with a much-needed welcome piece of good news," Liz Harmony said.

"Your work?" Fred asked, gesturing toward the painting over the fireplace. The oversized signature in the lower left corner made the guess child's play.

Oumaloff nodded gravely. "When I retired, the board honored me by making this purchase. The painting is an *homage*. It would be beyond you. Unfortunately the academy has neither proper exhibition nor storage space. Otherwise, one of my dreams has been to assemble, by requiring each student to give—but you have other business. I no longer keep…"

"News as unexpected as it is sure to be good for morale. These terrible times and days. Phil learned that, although he seldom is in this area, a distinguished alumnus was…"

"Basil Houel," Oumaloff rumbled. "You have heard of him, Mr. Taylor. I mentioned him to you myself."

"He is to be our guest tomorrow," Harmony broke in. "Guest critic. For a project the first-year students are doing, didn't you say, Phil?"

Oumaloff nodded. "And there will also be time for him to visit the studios of the more advanced painters. At this time of the year, especially, when things often feel slack, it is often salutary…"

"On another subject," Fred said, "there's the Stillton Realty Trust. There's Aram Tutunjian holding the mortgages on so much of the academy's property. Abe Baum and Parker Stillton."

"Aram Tutunjian is a good friend of the academy," Harmony said quickly. "He asks us to find his daughter. Quickly. Discreetly. It is the least we can do."

"Who told you I had left?" Fred demanded.

The question took her aback.

"Never mind. The girl Missy may be a fool. But she's of age. If she wants to do something dumb with a man," Fred said, "she won't be blazing a trail into unexplored territory. When I was invited to get involved, there was a strong suggestion of foul play, or even of double suicide. I learned fast enough that was horse shit. What you really wanted from me I don't care any more.

"Moving on. Here's my question. Why did you fire Lillian Krasic?"

"Lillian Krasic retired. After long and honorable service," Harmony claimed.

"She was forgetting things," Phil Oumaloff chimed in. "I recall one occasion..."

"She was remembering things, more likely," Fred said. "A bigger puzzle: You paid off Rodney Somerfest in cash. Where did the cash come from? What did he come back for?"

Liz Harmony looked away to concentrate on Oumaloff, and matters of greater importance. "I spoke with that nice detective. He promised to have the yellow tapes removed before Milan opens the building tomorrow. Perhaps not in the boy's studio, though, he said. A tragedy. Did you know, one of the two boys, Tom, worked in my office."

"Both of them did," Fred said.

A mist of confusion crossed Elizabeth Harmony's face. "Never mind, the detectives and the technicians will sort that out." She leaned closer to Oumaloff to deliver herself of a confidential whisper, "The student they have arrested—I forget his name—is under suspicion also for the murder of my predecessor, Rodney Somerfest."

Oumaloff said, "Because of tomorrow's schedule, we will be pressed for time."

"Bring him to my office first thing. We will have coffee," Liz offered. "Eight o'clock. I will arrange—although the woman they sent, if she understands how to serve coffee properly, I will be astounded. She strikes me as a person who has been brought up in the culture of mugs." Her facial expression was all at the same time tragic, annoyed, self-congratulatory, and trivial.

"I must see to my guest," Oumaloff boasted. He stood, checked the emptiness of his goblet, and held out his hand to Liz Harmony. "I did warn you, Liz. For whatever reason, this man Taylor is determined to make trouble. As if the academy did not have trouble enough already. I told you, and as you have seen, he is starting rumors about this entity he is calling the Stillton Realty Trust.

"Since he palpably knows nothing of art—I have myself tested him—what is his game? Real estate? He stays at the Stillton Inn and demands information concerning Lillian Krasic! Is this not a trend?

"We have had our differences, Elizabeth, and no doubt we will continue to have them. Honorable opposition. All in the nature of things. No hard feelings. I will warn you again, and in his presence—do not put faith in this man."

Phil Oumaloff's exit was not attended by the applause he heard in his head.

When the door of the presidential manse had closed behind the aggrieved emeritus, Fred grimaced and confided, "That man's seven kinds of fool, but he got it right that time. Do not put your faith in this man."

Chapter Sixty

Fred stretched his legs. The white canvas shoes belonging to the estate of Mr. Halper gleamed in a damp and dirty way that, in the present context, was fully satisfactory.

"Here's what I want," Fred said. "You can be thinking about it, and wrestle with it, and come to your own conclusions, and consult your attorneys and all the rest of it, but in the end I think you'll agree. I'm not going to argue now. I am sowing a tiny seed I expect will grow in your imagination.

"Call an emergency meeting of the board for tomorrow evening. Seven o'clock. Make it one of your favorite executive sessions. All hush hush. Special confidential report from the confidential presidential confidential emergency troubleshooter on matters related to accreditation.

"No. Don't talk. It'll save time if you don't. I want Aram Tutunjian here also, and your lawyer Abe Baum. Might as well bring in Parker Stillton. Friend of the family. I want faculty too—no, don't say it. My patience is thin.

"What we're going to be talking about is the Stillton Realty Trust, and present issues, and the future of Stillton Academy, and the role of President Harmony. Here, among friends, is better than on Fox News.

"Where was I? Faculty. Meg Harrison, Bill Wamp, Arthur Tikrit. Phil Oumaloff's going to come anyway, so why not ask him? Also students…"

"Wait. Wait. Wait," Liz Harmony was protesting. She had risen and was standing uncertainly, her hand on the telephone.

Fred went on. "Students should be here. I don't know who. Maybe four, maybe eight. Ask Meg and Bill Wamp and Arthur Tikrit who to include. They'll arrange it. I'll have my presentation ready."

"But your presentation is a myth," Liz managed. "In fact, it's a lie."

"I'll handle that part of it," Fred said. "It wouldn't be the first lie ever to be presented in the sacred confines of your boardroom. The Inn and Spa at Stillton Sound? Luxury Suites? In fact, all that responsible luxury? Marinas? Gold-plated haircuts?"

Liz Harmony, at the mention of the Inn at Stillton Sound, had turned pale, and sat down so suddenly that her chintz had expressed alarm. It was accustomed to a more deliberate speed.

"I'd suggest that you invite that nice detective, Seymour, also," Fred continued. "I know, telephone Abe Baum. Ask him what he thinks."

"You're goddamned right I'll telephone Abe Baum. Right after I call Security," Liz said. But her hand did not lift the receiver.

Fred cautioned, "Just don't forget. There's the good of the institution; then there's the good of the individual. In this complex world we live in, it is not always easy…"

"Get out."

"Until seven o'clock tomorrow evening, then," Fred said.

"What do you want? How much? You and your group. You want a percentage? You'll have to put in…"

"You know what I want," Fred said. "Just the one little meeting. I'm off. Gotta write that report. I'm at the Stillton Inn."

"We know where you are." She was staring, bewildered, into the mist of a long long sentence that was peopled neither with nouns nor verbs.

◇◇◇

Fred sang as he drove out of Stillton. Tight little charming seaside place that it was, Stillton, Massachusetts was a great little town to be gone from.

He made Boston by midnight. Clay's bedroom light was still on, on the top floor. Clay sat up in bed late, reading books that resembled sleeping: Proust, or Thomas Pynchon. He wouldn't notice his Lexus back in its accustomed place next to Fred's old brown car. But, if he *should* happen to look down from his upper window…

Fred parked further down Mountjoy Street, then went back up to his car, took the spare key from under the fender and got what he needed from the trunk.

Louisburg Square is designed for persons who are born to the feeling that the concept of the gated community is déclassé. Why stoop to hardware? The forces of birth, education, wealth, and breeding are enough to discourage intrusion by those whose genetic impairments render them unqualified for entrance for other than those menial tasks for which they are licensed or to which they have been condemned by the misjudgment of needing to work for a living.

There was no sign of an alarm. There might not be. But then again, if one lived in Louisburg Square, persons of the burgling profession, which is *not* licensed, would know they were not invited.

Fred fiddled with this and that until the door opened.

The alarm could be silent, if any. He waited on the sidewalk for a full five minutes for the sirens, the flashing lights, or the much more dangerous and sensible silent swooping arrival of the unmarked car with its armed and running silent occupants. Nothing.

With the flashlight hooded and crimsoned by his fingers, Fred began checking Elizabeth Harmony's Boston residence. No sounds of occupancy disturbed the building's quiet. No nephew, between meaningful occupations, was whacking at an amplified guitar in basement or attic.

Harmony's tastes tended toward the egregiously grim Bostonian, as if she had failed to convince even herself, but still hoped she might pass. Of course, it was after midnight. Still, everything in the way of furniture, rugs, draperies, the portraits of somebody's ancestors who seemed to have died of aggravated constipation or terminal angst—everything whispered, in the worst way: We are Boston: Beacon Hill. We may not like it but, by God, we *own* it.

Front parlor. Check. Back parlor. Check. Study. Dining room. Kitchen.

Upstairs. A little study for the telephone.

The bedroom. Master- or Mistress-bedroom. Fred eased himself into it and, in the dim glow from the flashlight, contemplated a man-sized hump in Elizabeth Harmony's bed. He sat in the comfortable armchair next to the door, after first taking from it, and depositing on the floor, the heap of male clothing that occupied it. He turned off the flashlight.

Chapter Sixty-one

After a little while Fred spoke aloud, reciting the lines that Mrs. Fortuney, way back in sixth grade, had promised, or threatened, would come in handy some day, bringing comfort or resolution when all else was lost.

"The robin is the one / That interrupts the morn / With hurried, few, express reports / When March is scarcely on.

"Think of me as your robin," Fred said softly.

The hump in the bed stirred. The room was heavy with the scent of sleeping man.

"The robin is the one," Fred continued, "That overflows the noon / with her cherubic quantity / An April but begun. Round two. Now Emily's got us where she wants us, softened up. Half beaten to death by the bird."

The lump spoke. "What the fuck?"

"The moral is still coming," Fred advised. "Wait for it. Wait for it. The robin is the one / That speechless from her nest / Submits that home and certainty / And sanctity are best. There, I couldn't have said it better myself. Except I would leave out the robin."

"For God's sake!" The lump sat up, reached out and turned on a bedside lamp. Strong smell of booze in here as well as the effluvia of humankind.

"Morgan Flower," Fred said. It hardly counted as a guess.

The man stared heavily. He'd sedated himself. Alcohol at least, by the olfactory evidence. A man of middle age, he had too much sandy hair that curled too much and, even in this dazed state, an insurance salesman's smile. Or a Realtor's.

"I want to buy into the development at Stillton Sound," Fred said. "That other stuff, about the robin, that was just supposed to break the ice. We haven't been introduced. Hi! I'm Fred."

"Holy shit! I'm not dreaming? It's closed."

Morgan Flower rubbed his eyes and added, "Get out! Get out!" His demand had no backbone in it. Likely his backbone was still in Stillton, Massachusetts, tossing worriedly on Liz Harmony's mattress, surrounded by the rest of Liz Harmony.

"As a precaution," Fred said. He crossed the room and checked under the pillows for hardware. There was nothing. The man was a confirmed civilian. Trained for white collar crime, he could harm whole communities at once, not limit himself to going after his victims in the blue-collar fashion, one at a time.

"So," Fred said, sitting again. "It's too late to buy in."

"Wait a minute. You're *that* Fred," Morgan Flower said, finally waking up. "Liz said you were onto…Where is she? She brought you? Why? No, she would have called. She would have told…wait a minute."

His movements were sluggish, but he was going to get up. Yes. Boxers. Striped.

"Like Lambert," Fred said.

"Lambert?"

"Before your time," Fred said.

"I'm taking a leak." Flower moved clumsily toward a door that must lead to a bathroom. *En suite,* as they'd say in the trade. So you can relieve yourself in the bedroom. Even the robin squirts off the edge of the nest.

"Keep you company," Fred said.

"What am I, under arrest?" Flower tried to joke. He was not sufficiently awake to make it convincing. His legs were too spindly for the upper body; the feet splayed.

"Not yet," Fred promised. He stayed beside his man, close enough to smell but not define the alcohol on his breath, and whatever else he was using to bring about this lack of vigilance. The bathroom was illuminated by a dim nightlight.

"That's all the light we need. Here's my question," Fred said.

"Wait a minute. Let me focus. I'm trying to take a leak."

"I see that. You can be preparing your answer. Try to convince me. John Steuart Curry? Are you serious?"

Morgan Flower finished with his business, fluffed, folded, and put it away. The small parade of two went back into the bedroom. "John Steuart Curry? Sorry. No bell. Not a name I know. He's with you?" Flower managed, standing next to the bed, in the dark.

"He's on your flaming lesson plan. *Lives and Loves of the Artists*. Why? He's a two-bit no-count regional American hack whose only claim to fame..."

"Oh, *him!* You're joking. Are you? That course. I got the whole thing out of one book. Practically the entire course. That Craven book. Scan the chapters and print them out big and read them aloud, bingo, there's your lecture. What do they know? They don't care. You want a drink? I'm going to have one."

"I think not," Fred said. "Not yet, anyway. Sit down. Let's try another name. Tom Meeker."

"Oh. Shit!"

Was that relief? Flower was watching as Fred first kicked the pile of his clothing under the chair, and then sat. Flower went to a dressing table and pulled out a small chair; turned it and sat, out of Fred's reach.

"He's a friend of a girl there. The girl's mental. Everyone knows it. Still, he's the friend of this girl, the student, and the girl claims...

"So he called. Couple nights back. How he got the number I do not have clue one. It's her private number here. Liz. Unlisted. I can't use the cell. The other one—for charities and salesmen and all that nonsense—that's listed and I don't answer that one. As she probably told you. Well, you know anyway. I need that drink. I'm keeping a low profile. I need..."

Fred shook his head.

"Meeker calls, I answer. What did I know? I thought it was Liz calling back. Meeker told me to drive out there and meet him that night, in my classroom.

"But what, did he think I was crazy?

"He wouldn't say why. Wouldn't trust the phone, he said. He's a no-count joker, but he's risky. I could hear it. He's that girl's friend. What was it, blackmail? Did he plan to shoot me? What did I know? Plus I had no reason to go out there. Plus my car—anyway, long story short, I said yes."

"Right," Fred prompted.

"I could use that drink."

"I see that," Fred sympathized. "You said yes."

"I said yes. Then I had a couple drinks and went to bed."

Chapter Sixty-two

"I'll get dressed," Morgan Flower said.

"That can wait," Fred assured him. "Meeker told you to come out. Why? Let's try this again while we think about that drink we're not having yet. I mean—what reason did Meeker give you?"

Flower's expression, on a five-year-old, would have signaled the advent of purposeful slyness. "Didn't give a reason," he said. "My word against his. He's dead anyway."

"What does Missy have on you?" Fred tried.

That startled the man. He turned belligerent. "Whatever he said, which I will deny, what he wanted to do, on account of that other girl, Emma, was beat the shit out of me. I could hear it. In his voice."

"Emma Rickerby," Fred said.

"Mental," Flower repeated.

"Maybe more light," Fred suggested. He stood and found a wall switch that lighted, simultaneously, multiple wall sconces. "Other names that are presently holding the interest of folks out there in Stillton. Rodney Somerfest?"

He paused long enough to sense that Morgan Flower had nothing to say. In fact he was presumably, by now, resenting the fact that he had said anything at all, about anything.

A blank. "OK," Fred went on. "Missy Tutunjian."

"She's got nothing…" Flower blurted, until intelligence caught up with him. But his silence came too late. Just this much response was enough. As far as Flower knew, Missy existed in the present tense. That was a good thing. She was also, presently, by the sound of it, no friend of his.

"Where is she?" Fred asked.

Flower said, "You come with a lot of questions. Why Liz gave you the key…I'm getting that drink."

Fred put him back in the chair again and loomed over him until the sudden starch had dwindled away. "I notice you have been using Elizabeth Harmony's bed," Fred said. "Is this a coincidence?"

Flower's mouth was tight. He shook his head.

"Rodney Somerfest. He kept coming back," Fred said.

"He threatened us," Morgan Flower started, and stopped again. Liz Harmony should have driven her Mercedes over this flower, not given him a place in her bed.

"Another small recital," Fred said. "I have been waiting so long for the opportune moment. You may listen while you are thinking about that drink. Flowers—well, if anybody / Can the ecstasy define, / Half a transport, half a trouble, / With which flowers humble men, / Anybody find the fountain / From which floods so contra flow, / I will give him all the daisies / Which upon the hillside blow. Thank you, Mrs. Fortuney.

"Let's have that drink. We'll drink to Mrs. Fortuney, shall we? She was right after all. You won't need clothes. It's warm. Where do we go, downstairs? Or do you have a little something tucked away here?"

"It's finished," Flower grumbled.

Fred let him lead the way downstairs. "Two years of my life," Flower complained as he descended. "Two blessed years."

"And all so perfectly conceived," Fred said. "The marina. The lap pools, the restaurants and crematorium. But how were you going to handle the golf?"

"Helipad, with links on the mainland. Memberships automatic in exclusive clubs, twenty minutes away. What's not to love?"

A dresser in the dining room supported decanters filled with liquids.

"I brew liquor never tasted," Fred remarked. "Well, almost never. Poetic license."

Flower disregarded the decanters, opened a cabinet door, and took out vodka, pouring himself a significant helping in a glass that looked to have been designed for sherbet. Glass in hand, he led the way into one of the parlors and sat below a particularly dyspeptic female ancestor the extent of whose disapproval became apparent as soon as Fred turned on lights.

"OK. We can still pull this off," Flower began. "It was already complicated. And it's more complicated now. All the publicity and the accidents. I've got nothing to do here but think. Which I do and I've done. And I can tell you, it's still do-able.

"The hard thing is, Fred—may I call you Fred?—The hard thing is, Fred, Liz can't get a line, or at least she can't explain it to me, on what it is exactly that you want. So make it simple. Man to man. Nobody listening here except us monkeys. What do you want?"

"Nothing," Fred said.

"You're fucking joking. Or, no—don't play cute. There's times for cute, and there's times where cute is just a pain in the ass. Nothing?" Morgan Flower's mouth hung open. The only way he could think to close it was to fill it with vodka and let the muscles recall that the liquid would leak out again unless the lips were sealed.

"Correction," Fred said. "I do want something. I want a phone." He went to an odd little table that had been designed for a telephone long before the phone was invented, picked the phone up and dialed.

"Your principal," Flower concluded. "Makes sense. Who you with?"

"Silent partner," Fred said. He let the ring persist until it produced the sleepy and angry voice of Detective Seymour. "Sorry," Fred told him. "I didn't notice your first name. Fred Taylor here."

"Where the devil are you?"

"I have Morgan Flower," Fred said, and gave the address. Flower, standing suddenly enough to slosh vodka, seemed prepared to run. Fred moved closer to him, giving the address. "If you can, get someone over here to scrape him up. That would be good. He's drinking, and I don't have the patience to get between him and it."

"You can hold him?"

Fred looked across the room. Morgan Flower, with his bottle and in his skivvies, was exploring the enormous, vague territory that lies between astonishment, hope, and despair. "Sure," Fred said.

"He broke in here," Flower shouted.

"It's OK," Fred said. "Someone's coming along to arrest me." He hung up and Flower made a lunge for it.

"Better we talk while we can," Fred said. "Between us. Just man to man."

It was an hour before a group of local uniforms marched Morgan Flower away "for questioning." Twenty minutes of that time had been involved in countering Flower's claim that Fred had broken in. The word of a man in hiding who is wanted for questioning in a matter of murder is not much better, in fact, than the unspoken word of a dead man. Worthless, even if true.

"I'll be back in Stillton by breakfast time," Fred promised. "I'll lock up."

But they watched him leave the house, and locked it behind him, before they drove away.

Fred left the Lexus in Clayton's space, next to his own car, and entered the Mountjoy Street basement. He'd use the phone there. Then, if there was time, he could take an hour or two on the couch or—even better—have a look at Clay's Bierstadt research. He was rusty on Bierstadt. Likely as not Gordon Hendricks' big *Albert Bierstadt, Painter of the American West,* was at this moment sitting on Fred's desk, bristling with Clayton's Post-it notes.

He'd telephone, then decide if sleep was necessary.

Chapter Sixty-three

Meg Harrison responded to Fred's knock, but slowly. It wasn't quite six in the morning. "What the fuck!" she declared from her side of the closed door.

"It's Friday. Big day. Big crit," Fred called.

"Who is that?" If Meg was impaired by sleep it didn't sound like it. She woke up running.

"It's Friday. It's Fred."

The door faced Fred blankly. On the far side of it, silence.

"I brought coffee," Fred said. "It may be cold by now." No fear. He'd bought it two hours ago, on Charles Street, in Boston. "They have Morgan Flower," he added.

Meg Harrison opened the door. "Three cups?" she said.

"I get started ordering coffee, I just keep on," Fred explained. He wandered past Meg into the galley kitchen. "Good. A microwave. I got black, on the theory that it's easier to add sugar and cream than to take it out. When it comes to the kitchen arts, that's about what I know."

The front room was pretty much as he recalled it from the night he had entered, Monday night, his first night in Stillton. The chairs, the three closed doors; though what should be the bedroom door was closed on a trail of red plaid blanket.

"Hasty exit," Fred said.

The long green robe Meg was wearing did not close, unless she was holding it closed. Underneath was one of those flimsy garments there must surely be an appropriate name for, at least in catalogues.

The closet door with the full-length mirror propped against it.

"Can you do the microwave?" Fred asked. "They all work differently."

"Morgan Flower," Meg said dangerously.

"Three cups," Fred said. "Thinking Missy might want one. It's early, but it's a big day, what with the crit. We don't want her to miss it."

Meg said, over the microwave's roar, "Missy's not…" at the same time as the bedroom door opened on a young woman wrapped in the rest of the red plaid blanket. Her black hair was short and tousled. She stood about five foot six. Her face, pink and pudgy, was hard to make out clearly this early in the morning.

"Hi, Missy. I'm Fred," Fred said. "The substitute teacher."

Behind her in the dim bedroom, a navy blue sleeping bag, shoved into the room with haste in response to Fred's knock.

"I can't shake your hand," Missy said. "Let me put on something."

"Just don't go out the window," Fred said. "OK?"

"It's raining," Missy said. It was indeed raining—more heavily than when he had come in the front door. The outside in the rainy dark of a dismal morning was not an attractive option anyway. "Besides, I don't have a car."

"Just—before you get dressed—so you know. I didn't want you to miss the big crit. You can participate. I'll explain after you're dressed," Fred said.

The door closed hastily on the falling blanket.

Meg said angrily, "You don't have a clue. You've been in town three days? Here's your coffee. Sugar? Milk?"

Fred shook his head. "I get pretty good mileage from guesses," he said. He took his coffee over to one of the chairs and sat looking at the dark window streaked with rain that was lit from this side by the light of the room. Behind him, the sounds of movement could be explained by those of a woman exchanging a blanket for clothing more suitable for daytime wear in a cold wet climate with a foghorn you wanted to strangle.

"What I think," Fred said, "when we take a look at the drawing Missy's been working on, later this morning, in the crit; we're going to see the work of a good potential sculptor. If I'm lucky, Meg, maybe you'll explain what that means."

The microwave roared until it rang. Meg took out her coffee and added sugar, taking her time stirring.

"Because—and here I'm still guessing," Fred said. "You are a serious teacher. Therefore you want the best for your student. Therefore…"

"It's not like you think," Missy said, bursting in from the bedroom. She was barefoot, with jeans and a big pink sweatshirt that matched her finger- and toenails. Her hair had become slightly more tousled.

"Fred brought coffee for everyone," Meg said.

"I like tea," Missy said. She went into the galley kitchen and clattered water into a kettle, and unwrapped a teabag to drop into a mug.

"Most everything's not like I think," Fred agreed. "But it turns out it's always like something."

"She is already a good sculptor," Meg said.

"Plus I'm doing your assignment," Missy said, without turning around. "Which I don't understand it. And Meg can't explain it either. This kettle takes forever."

"You had the assignment from Susan Muller," Fred said.

Silence. The back of Missy's neck tensed, then relaxed.

"It's OK," Fred said. "Susan's a very good liar. She's also a loyal friend. Loyal, and subtle and, I'd say, completely reliable. She didn't tell me where you were. And she hasn't told anyone else. I'm sure of it."

"My father," Missy said, turning, with accusation.

"He's in the dark," Fred said. "As far as I know, anyway. But my guesses are only so good so far. I'll fill you in. Then, if there's time, to save time, maybe the two of you will agree to give me some facts."

The kettle screamed.

Chapter Sixty-four

Missy sat on the floor in a corner, with tea so doctored with sugar and milk that it would satisfy the minimum daily requirements for everything but tea. Fred said, "First, I'll tell you what I think is none of my business. The question, is a first-year student having an affair with her so-called Lit teacher? That's not my business. If it's anyone's business at all, it's not mine.

"Now…"

"There's nothing to eat," Meg said. "There'll be donuts later, at the crit. The academy's too cheap to pay for them. I do. Randy'll have them ready. There's never enough, people think—but there are always some left over. So, if you can wait…"

"Thanks," Fred said. "Now. In addition to everything else that can go wrong, and *should* go wrong, between a father and a daughter—and this is a subject I know nothing about at all since I have never been either of these things, a father or a daughter…

"Let me back up. Missy, speaking just as your teacher, tell me, did it make sense to you, that theory about the people who made the pyramids getting their plans from folks who came down from the stars?"

Missy chewed her plump lower lip. "I like the theory. And they made it sound good. But it's crazy."

Fred told Meg, "Just so you know, the TV was on too much for an empty apartment. Even if you don't pay your own electric…"

"I do," Meg said.

"The TV stayed on, back there in the bedroom, when I first came and we talked here in this room. Then that night, when you weren't here and I happened to pass and the TV was on, back of the blind, last Tuesday. That program was on at the time. Everyone in town was watching."

"I was drawing. In here," Missy denied it. "I was *listening* to the program is all. You can't draw and watch TV both at the same time."

"So," Fred said, "I reckoned the apartment had more than one person in it. And remembering how you bought more burgers and fries than you needed, Meg—also, more important, how fast you raced upstairs when you thought Morgan Flower had come back…"

"I gave her refuge," Meg said. "It has to happen sometimes. We take risks for our students. All the time."

"I'd taken some papers and stuff," Missy said.

"Missy…" Meg interrupted sharply.

Fred agreed. "Meg is right. It's prudent to breast your cards. Make the other guy show his hand before you show yours, if you can. If I were going to hunt for those papers, and I'm not, I'd look to see if they might be in a plastic bag concealed inside the wet clay of a figure that's been wrapped to keep it moist. Since that's where I'd look, someone else might also think of it."

Silence.

"Point noted," Meg said.

Fred went on, "My speculation was, or is, Missy—don't answer this—your loyalties got knocked sideways. Your loyalty to the academy…"

"He made me come. My father," Missy said. "An accountant was my dream. Can you believe it? An accountant with a great car." She laughed. "What did I know from accountants? I saw a show…"

Fred continued, "Missy, you learned, or you understood, that your father's interest, his financial interest, his bank, rather than being helpful as it seemed, giving mortgages, might lead to the collapse of the academy. In fact, that was the plan."

"Meg explained it," Missy said.

"And Morgan Flower was working against the academy, and with your father."

"To blow the whole thing apart and build this foolish resort," Missy said. "It's a good place. They believe in me."

"You had some people worried," Fred said. "But not worried enough. When you disappeared."

"She sent him a note," Meg said. "I insisted."

"'I'm OK, don't try to find me,' like that," Missy explained. "Just enough."

"And there wasn't much sign of your mother in the mix," Fred said.

"My mother lets him do it," Missy said. "As long as she thinks I'm not dead."

"Well," Fred said. "Here's *my* cards on the table. I was minding my own business, in Boston, when these two guys walked in. Abe Baum, the lawyer for the board, and Parker Stillton, who represents himself as a friend of the academy. They say that Missy and Flower have run off together. Maybe that's a crime. And/ or they're worried it was a suicide pact. Because of a note on Missy's desk."

"It worked!" Missy exclaimed. "Susan thought of it. 'I died for beauty.' I said, 'No way would anyone take a poem seriously.'"

"But in any case," Fred pushed on, "No way was your father worried about your life. He knew you and Morgan Flower were not together. And he also knew that you had whatever it was you had, which is also not my business though I would be interested. He wanted me to find you, because he wanted whatever you had. And he sent that Abe Baum to get me. Not the best move he ever made."

"I have to get dressed," Meg said. "We've got twenty-five drawings to put up before eight o'clock."

"Twenty-*six*," Missy said, getting up from the floor in a single fluid motion so quick you'd have to play it in stop-frame in order to understand the release and interactions of the various stresses and supports of muscle and bone.

Meg Harrison, shedding her robe, strode into the bedroom saying over her shoulder, "It's better you stay out of sight, Missy. If Fred can be trusted. Fred, am I right? No one else knows?"

"It's a small town," Fred said. "All I can tell you is, I haven't talked."

"I'm not missing Basil Houel," Missy said.

Meg came out of the bedroom belting her jeans. She was otherwise dressed in scuffed work boots and a quilted poncho of patchwork fabric. "Wait a minute," she said. "I thought you were lying, Fred. To get in the door. Is it true, what you said? You said, 'They have Morgan Flower. What do you mean, they *found* him?"

"He has family in San Diego," Missy said.

"So he *said.* Everyone lies," Meg said.

"They wanted to talk to Flower about Rodney Somerfest. What I heard, last night, they picked him up for questioning. I wouldn't mention it outside this room, maybe. If you don't mind?"

"Trouble shooter," Meg said. She drank the end of her coffee. "Don't you two talk while I'm in the bathroom."

She went in and turned on the fan. Fred and Missy stared at the rain.

Chapter Sixty-five

It was letting up, the rain. "It's like this in the morning," Missy said. "In Stillton. Water all around, there might as well be water everywhere else. It, like, saves time."

She and Meg were gathering themselves together, Meg being resigned to Missy's decision to come out of hiding. Fred had told them, "The plan they had, that Morgan Flower was part of—I can tell you right now, that plan is coming apart."

"Is he all right?" Missy asked.

"I didn't hear," Fred said. "Those papers you have, you'll make sure they are in a safe place."

Meg nodded grimly.

"Oh. The homework," Missy said. She put her rolled drawing under her arm and moved the mirror so as to open the closet door. She pulled out a brown envelope, sealed, and addressed to *Professor Fred*. "Susan didn't catch your last name," Missy said. "This is the best I could do. I didn't have the book, and all."

Fred said, "I appreciate it. I'll look forward to this. We'll walk over together?" The women had raincoats. Fred had picked up his own jacket, which Clayton had left on the back of his desk chair, with a courteous note. Bill Wamp's jacket was in the back seat of his car. "Or we can drive," Fred offered.

He let them off at Stillton Hall. "Just drop in if you have nothing better to do," Meg said. "It can be interesting. You know the students a little bit now. Also, there's going to be Basil Houel."

Fred pulled up in front of the admissions / administration building just as Phil Oumaloff arrived, on foot, in the company of a narrow male of indeterminate age, dressed in a blue greatcoat and one of those Greek fisherman's caps. Phil was on parade in the guise of Aristide Bruant, in that broad-brimmed hat of wet leather and a cape that almost screamed, "Who do you think you are, for God's sake?"

Keeping ahead of Fred, and disregarding him, Phil herded his companion past the rented lady of yesterday, whose early morning disapproval searched beyond the room and into the darkest corners of the universe.

"We are expected for coffee," Oumaloff announced. The woman's questioning look forced him to add, "With President Harmony."

"I'll ring her again," the lady said. She took a badge from her purse and managed to pin it to her gray cotton blouse with one hand while she worked the switchboard. *Mrs. Druse.*

"She should be here," Oumaloff said. "This was arranged."

"President Harmony doesn't answer her line. It's all I can tell you. In the manse. She's not in the office either. It's locked."

Dampness dripped from the men's outer garments. Mrs. Druse regarded the falling drops with disfavor.

"Never mind," Phil said. "I misunderstood. Since we are expected, it will be at her home. Mr. Houel is our guest today. Should anyone need us, we shall be at the manse."

Basil Houel, having been introduced to the temporary secretarial staff, allowed his cap to tilt forward far enough for drops of water to fall from its visor onto the papers on her desk.

"It isn't far, Basil," Phil said, sweeping the cape, and the artist, toward the entrance. "Far more appropriate. More private in the manse."

"The fat man makes paintings of boats," Fred told Mrs. Druse as the door closed. "The thin man does trash."

Mrs. Druse gave a long sigh. "May I help you?"

"I'm Fred Taylor," Fred said. "We met yesterday. I'm new here too. I think—don't we have faculty mailboxes?"

"If you're expecting a message, I have to line them up. I'm just getting settled. There's messages on the main line, and then I've got blinking lights on her private machine, her line to the desk. I was just trying to reach her. She doesn't answer. I told you. It'll take me a half hour to sort them out. Can you come back?"

"I'll wait," Fred said. He found a chair and pulled it across the vestibule until it stood near the desk, but not so near as to be intimidating. "I expected to see President Harmony," Fred reminded her.

Liz Harmony's voice spoke aloud into the room from the machine, "Doris, please telephone…" until Mrs. Druse deftly switched the machine to silence as she fitted an earpiece. She listened, taking notes that she fielded from Fred's eyes. She listened and took notes for twelve minutes until the tape ran out.

"That's *Professor* Taylor?" Mrs. Druse asked, folding the pages of notes away briskly.

"Fair enough," Fred admitted.

"President Harmony has scheduled your report for the executive committee of the board, meeting in executive session, this evening at six-thirty. Please be prompt."

"Got it," Fred said.

Mrs. Druse said severely, "In a second message she adds, 'Be sure Professor Taylor understands that this meeting is limited to himself and the executive committee of the board.'"

"Got it," Fred said. "Would you help me get oriented? You must have a list of who's on the board, and who's who, and who the executive committee might be?"

"I might have that," Mrs. Druse said. If she did, however, she had no intention of sharing it. Fred stood. Mrs. Druse added, "If you need anything typed, for the meeting, I can't help you."

"Got it," Fred said.

The phone rang. "Good morning. Stillton Academy of Art," Mrs. Druse said. She listened, said, "He's right here….No…. Yes…. Oh, I'm sorry, Detective. All right. But please, don't tie up the line."

She held her receiver toward Fred. "Don't tie up the line," she instructed.

Seymour's voice. "So. At least you're in town. It's no damned use to me you're in town if I don't know where you are."

"That makes sense," Fred said. His gesture to Mrs. Druse might translate, "This'll just be a moment." The line clicked. Another call trying and failing.

"We'll talk in the cruiser," Seymour said. "Come on outside."

Chapter Sixty-six

Fred climbed into the car. Rain beat down on the roof.

"Two hours last night with Meeker's parents. I got nothing. Any uniform these days, they think, Good, I can get grief counseling. Shit, can't they let a man do his job? I get a week off at Easter. St. Thomas. With the wife. I'll sleep then, I guess," Seymour grumbled, putting the car into slow motion. "Fat chance. She'll want to go dancing. Then up in the morning early to look for shells. It's a vacation, she'll say. Not a rest cure."

Seymour pulled into a lane that seemed quiet, and mostly vacant, down near the working edge of the water where boats were upended and lobster traps moldered in side yards.

"You picked Harmony up," Fred said finally, after they had spent enough time looking at the slow action at sea.

"Where you think you get off I do not have a clue," Seymour said. "It's not the wild west. It's not the flaming movies, Buddy. Nobody appointed you a special deputy, running around like you are, making arrests. Who the fuck do you think you are? How did you know where Flower was? How long did you know it, and why didn't you tell me? I can put you away, you know. Material witness."

"I visited with the guy until you people arrested him," Fred countered. "I put together where he had to be, and checked it out. As for the deputy thing—I could never keep track of a hat."

"And you're just trying to help. Trouble-shooter. Concerned citizen."

"Still, I notice you did pick him up," Fred said. "Despite what seems a certain impatience with me. And as I say, I also notice you picked her up. Not my business, obviously, but did she…?"

"I have seen pointless outrage in my time," Seymour said. "But she just about beats all. We're keeping it very quiet. Not because you suggested it, Fred. Because that's what we do. We'll have to let her call her attorney. In due course. But on occasion the red tape develops an unfortunate snarl that turns into a tangle that turns into a knot.

"Don't mind me. I'm stalling, shooting the breeze until you feel you have something relevant to say."

"I'm comfortable," Fred said. "Hell, sitting in here, I'm even dry."

"Just coincidence, you figuring out where Morgan Flower was holed up?"

"I couldn't get Harmony to say anything about the guy, so I figured she was hiding something. Amateurs," Fred said. "They don't like leaving anything to chance. Amateurs working together, they don't like either one to be out of sight very long. So he had to be where she could keep track of him. That was my guess, and it panned out.

"Neither one knows you've picked up the other, I imagine."

"Why tell them anything?" Seymour said. "You're right about Flower. I owe you this much. Put a bottle where he can see it, and not touch it, he talks. He lies, sure. His lies are more coherent than hers are but still, when you get enough lies, they start falling together and making a pattern. Match her lies against his, you start getting a story. Plus there's what's going to be his prints on the tarp in the trunk of his car they thought they'd washed all the blood off. Assholes. Amateurs, yes, you got that right.

"My techs can move fast. Meanwhile we're telling the lawyers, the press, the rest of them—these things take time. And you know and I know the blood is going to be from this former director, this Rodney Somerfest. *Why* I don't know. *Why*, I don't care either. That's for the folks in the DA's office to figure out. We get the facts. They make up the stories. They love stories.

"All we do, we tell them what we found. Flower was in Harmony's bed in Boston. Fact. Tarp was in his car, where we found what are going to be Flower's prints, and I think Harmony's, and blood from that place in Somerfest's head where one of them hit him. Fact. Fact. Fact. What he was hit with we may find out, but I doubt it. It'll be in the drink, where they put *him,* like a couple of morons, before they checked the tide tables and Flower crouched down in the back seat of her car while she drove him back to her place in Boston. That's all speculation, but we'll get there.

"Moving on. I like you, but that won't stop me locking you the fuck up. Whether you knew where he was or guessed where he was, you should have told me, not gone in like your own SWAT team. Do me a favor. Maybe I'll cool down. What he said to you, which you may have to stand up in court and swear to it, and I want a signed statement, also on tape…" Seymour took a little black gadget out of his suit coat pocket, flicked a switch, and told it, "Fred Taylor, witness," ran through the date and time and circumstances and place, "when you confronted Morgan Flower with the fact of Rodney Somerfest's death, what did he say?"

Fred's answer was clean and clear. "Morgan Flower said, 'He threatened us.'"

Seymour flicked off the switch, put the box back in his pocket and said, "There. OK. Fact." He grinned. "Thanks. The prosecution might not be able to use it. But when the other side objects that it's hearsay or some damned thing, and the judge throws it out, the jury is gonna remember it anyway."

Fred said, "I think hearsay…"

"I don't give a shit about hearsay," Seymour said. The rain was letting up. Seagulls flew at the edge of the water but had no effect on its action. "Hearsay today and gone tomorrow. Harmony wants to lay Somerfest off on this student, Peter Quarrier."

"I bet," Fred said. "I could use one of those boxes."

"Nice gadget. It broadcasts too. In case you want to over-power me, take the box and toss it out to the nearest of those goddamned seagulls which are going to follow us all the way to St. Thomas. There's a simultaneous record at headquarters."

"That could be trouble if you forget the off switch," Fred said.

"Also," Seymour said, "say there's a couple of you working the same project, but on opposite ends of the block, your partner can pick it up, like a walkie talkie."

"And it texts?"

"Too complicated. Too expensive. Anyway, why you're here, in addition to this…" Seymour patted the pocket with its black box, "you're a wild card, and I can't see what you want. Don't tell me again what you want or what you're doing. I've got enough lies from Flower and that wind-up random shit-storm Harmony, who is as much fun as seven mothers-in-law locked into one burlap sack. But whatever you're up to, so far, you're helping. Maybe you just lucked out, like you say. I don't believe it. But, hey, we've got Morgan Flower and enough *out* of Morgan Flower to hold President Royal Highness Harmony for a while.

"To answer your question, we picked her up early and quiet. Nobody knows."

"Did you happen to locate Somerfest's clothes?" Fred asked.

"Amateurs manufacturing evidence," Seymour said. "You never know. Don't tell me my business, do you mind? I will forget these positive feelings. Listen, we've been on this five hours. We'll find Somerfest's clothes or we won't. If we do, the prosecution makes it part of the story that convicts these ass-holes. If we don't, the prosecution makes *that* part of the story that convicts these assholes.

"We do facts. That's as far as we go. It's the stories that get the convictions."

"So, all the academy knows is, Liz Harmony has disappeared," Fred confirmed.

"Right."

"I should probably let you know. Now you've got Harmony where *she* won't hear it. I might have started the rumor that Morgan Flower was picked up."

"Might have," Seymour grumbled.

"Couldn't be helped," Fred said. "Means to an end."

"What end?"

"I'll keep in touch," Fred promised. He opened the cruiser's door.

"There's an empty bunk in the cell where we've got Harmony. Don't rock the fucking boat," Seymour warned.

Chapter Sixty-seven

Outside Stillton Hall the yellow crime scene tape had been rolled away. In a more urban art school, it would already be incorporated into one of those amalgams of found objects that strive to make easy comment on the day by suggesting irony. Wrap it around a hamburger. Wrap it around the first communion photo. Or it might otherwise serve for a prank.

Nine o'clock. Fred's classroom, Stillton B, was empty. The action was in Stillton A, or in the corridor outside the classrooms where students conferred as they messed with their lockers.

"Morning," Fred told those who might catch his eye—but he was not familiar enough to have earned conversation.

"No signatures!" Meg's raised voice came from Stillton A. "I told you no signatures. If I see even the ghost of a signature, the drawing comes down. Cut it off if it's there."

She came into the corridor through the swinging doors at the moment Fred reached them. "Give 'em a minute," she said. "The idea is, today, we look at the work independently of knowing who made it. That way, though everyone knows, everyone says what they want to without being responsible for hurting anyone's feelings. It works, to a degree."

"Basil Houel's arrived?"

"He'll make an entrance in half an hour or so."

"Entrance, hell! I saw him with Phil Oumaloff a while ago. If they come in together, it's already a whole grand opera."

"Phil has him this afternoon," Meg said. "Touring the studios.

Phil's a blowhard, and I wouldn't hang his work in my motel if I had a motel, but a lot of what he says is useful for students. No, our deal is, Phil stays out of the crit of the first-year drawings. He'll get his chance later, at the end-of-the-year review."

She yelled out, "We're coming in. Don't be standing next to your own drawings. Who made them is irrelevant. That's what we're pretending."

She whispered, "Like shit!" and led the way through the swinging doors.

Enough wall space had been found and cleared for all twenty-six life-sized drawings. The figure modeling works in progress had all been jammed together at one side. The students had gathered in the center of the room, where the model's platform gave many of them a place to sit. Marci sat there, in a green jumpsuit, looking across the room at a drawing of a naked young woman holding a push broom, the brush upraised, as if saluting the author of the work-study program. The idea was a good one if she had found a more competent draughtsman to execute it.

"Fred's not going to say anything," Meg told the room.

Fred looked past the students at the collected drawings. It was a touching display, if a little unnerving. There was Randy—was that Randy? He was drawn on brown wrapping paper, with charcoal and white chalk for the highlights. Emphatically circumcised.

Meg's own work—those symmetrical figures looking stunned—had these been inspired in part by the yearly experience of seeing her own students confronting themselves in the buff, and seeing how little romance is really involved in the facts of the human body, without the cooperation of miles and miles of interlocking stories, hopes and dismays?

Susan Muller had managed some advanced shading on one knee. The other had been wiped away.

Students drank coffee, or Coke, or whatever else they were drinking.

"Here he is," someone said, and Randy himself, in the flesh, came in with a high pile of pastry boxes. These went to the model's platform, and the students got busy.

Susan Muller, the three-dimensional one, was conferring with Missy Tutunjian in a corner near where the stands had been placed with their draped figures—the works Fred had seen in progress last Tuesday, between his own classes. Fred's eyes swept the room, looking either for a recognizable rendition of Missy Tutunjian, or for the drawing that loudly proclaimed, "I am a sculptor."

"That's Arthur Geekas," Fred remarked. The surprise came not from his recognition of his student's face and posture in the drawing, but from the fact that he recalled the student's name. Arthur Geekas. *Intro to Lit.*

"I'll be back," Fred told Meg. "It's interesting."

Fred sidled along the empty corridor and looked through the glass panels of the swing doors and into his classroom, Stillton B. The man in the blue greatcoat and fisherman's cap was in there, standing under the high trap door, and looking upwards.

"Upstaged by donuts," Fred remarked as he entered the room.

Basil Houel stared at him dumbly. Fred eased closer. "You came back," he said. "But you're too late. I have it." Basil Houel kept staring but edged sideways.

"No quick moves," Fred instructed. "Whatever else you are, you're a damned blamed fool to stay in town."

"What are you?" Houel started. "Get out of my way." His outrage was severely marred by indecision.

"The issue is more what you are," Fred said. "And whether they can make a case it was premeditated. You stopped in the other night to check your stash."

"What do you mean, you have it?" Houel said.

"The thing was too big to move by yourself and you wouldn't share. Someday, you figured, you'd get hold of it. All for yourself. Meanwhile it's masked by one of your careful renditions of trash."

"We can't talk here, or now. You have a deal in mind, obviously," Houel sneered. "Like you might wonder—and I know—what is this thing?"

"Fred said, "There's nothing you might say that I want to hear. Listen to me. You are boxed in, Houel. The scalpel came in handy, yes? You thought you needed it to get through the dried paint on the trap? Stay where you are."

The man's features, skinny and sallow under the cap, had winced in a signal of contemplated quick emergency action. His spindly shoulders tensed. Fred grabbed the painter's right arm, hauled it behind his back and up.

"I have nothing to say," Houel mumbled, changing tacks, as if he had been practicing the line but missed his cue until the prompter shouted.

"What did you do, stop in once or twice a year to make sure it's safe, until you could figure a way to smuggle it out?" Fred said. "Skinny guy like yourself, it wouldn't be easy. Might as well try to shift five or six dead men on your own. Or is Phil Oumaloff in this with you?

"Not that I care. How did you get up there?

"Then the next plan—it was all going to be yours some-how once you became Basil Houel, the director of this two-bit academy."

"Nobody had a clue," Basil Houel whispered. "It could be worth a million dollars. We'll go partners. Let go." His plunge forward was half-hearted.

"It was my student you killed," Fred said. "You've known that mural was up there since fat Phil Oumaloff, your mentor, sent you up to the garret and you reported back whatever you did report. You were dumb enough then, but you've had time since, years, to figure it out."

"It's not true," Basil Houel tried. "Listen, I've got a buyer…"

Fred nodded. "Of course. Not interested. Not relevant. You're out of it now. You want to concentrate not on financial gain, which is no longer an option, but on getting prepared to be put away for life. Either you surprised Tom Meeker or he surprised you. However the conversation went, you should start rehearsing. Because you were spotted in town that night. By Oumaloff? By Meg? Wait a minute. Phil's in it with you? Or he isn't. I don't care. However it happened, and so you're here this morning, the honored guest. You spent the night with him."

"Phil Oumaloff will be my alibi," Houel said. The fight had gone out of him, to be replaced by inept guile, insufficiently rehearsed.

"Your prints are on that scalpel. Be thinking about that," Fred said. "Don't talk any more. Your alibis or your excuses or your claims of justified self-defense. I just don't want to hear it. I don't have the time or the patience. There's a studio full of students excited that a slick son of a bitch like yourself makes time to review their work. I'm staying beside you while you do it. That's an obligation you have undertaken, and since it will prolong your illusion of freedom, let's go do it. You've got till noon to be the distinguished guest. After that, I'm busy, so I'll turn you over to the boys in blue. They'll love the uniform coat you prance around in. I'll be watching your hands all the time, Basil. The room's full of knives. You know that.

"Also—let's go—your paintings are as cruel as they are trivial and cynical. If a jury could understand paintings, you'd be screwed, buddy."

Chapter Sixty-eight

He'd been obliged to borrow a cell phone from one of the students, during the break, and telephone Seymour with the unsatisfying message, "Can't talk. Meet me at Stillton Hall at noon."

"It's deputy fucking Fred. What do you have, more instructions?" Seymour growled.

Basil Houel, five feet away, was engaged with Meg in a precise analysis of the differences between a drawing by Degas (not present) and one of the student exercises.

But he was listening. "Someone you'll want to talk to," Fred said. "About the dead student. Could be another coincidence. I don't want to get in your way."

"Like shit! I'll be right there. And you be there."

The handover had taken a good deal of time, in fact, most of the afternoon.

Seymour had had the sense to get Houel away from the crowd, and settled behind the steel mesh in the back of the cruiser, as soon as Fred made the introduction, "This is Basil Houel, a distinguished alumnus. He wants to talk with you about the death of Tom Meeker."

Students on either side, who had been trailing the guest, stared in an almost menacing way. Meg Harrison, coming out of the building at a run, had something to say.

"You, Fred. In front," Seymour demanded. "Let's move." He slipped into gear and peeled away as soon as Fred's door slammed.

"Talk," Seymour demanded, heading out of town. Fred explained with a brief summary: the hidden treasure; the prospect of theft and gain. The unhappy meeting between Meeker, who was looking to prove his manhood on an absent Morgan Flower, and this accidentally armed and surprisingly dangerous alumnus. Basil Houel rested mute in the back seat until, "He hates my work," Houel said, as if that fact alone had led Fred to commit this outrage.

"It's true," Fred told Seymour. "I do hate his work."

Seymour said, "I wouldn't know. When it comes to art, I've had it up to here, around here. Kiss me goodbye. All I need—we'll take this gentleman to somewhere more comfortable, and less crowded, on the mainland, and ask him questions. Starting, 'What were you doing in Stillton on the night and early morning of Thursday last?'"

"I am an artist," Basil Houel said from the back seat.

"Save it. We'll start like we always do. Name. Place and date of birth. Place of residence. Then we'll get to the nitty gritty. Fred, you're staying with me. There's too much here I can't follow, and I've taken the back seat passenger mainly on faith. Faith is not a commodity I have in fat supply."

Fred folded his arms. "More fun for you, maybe, if you take his story separately from mine. What I'll do, in the car, while we ride, I'll fill you in on the treasure this guy wanted to steal. It belongs to the academy and I'm going to make goddamned sure they keep it safe. At least for the moment, that's my mission."

"A man with a mission," Seymour said.

"Just passing the time while we ride," Fred said, "Let me start by filling you in about Aubrey Bierstadt."

"*Albert*, asshole!" Basil Houel chimed in from behind the mesh.

The rain had stopped as soon as they were out of Stillton.

During the course of the afternoon, at Fred's suggestion, Seymour had made a telephone call to Phil Oumaloff, putting him on speaker. Oumaloff confirmed that he had run into Basil

Houel in town, in the small hours of Thursday morning. "I don't sleep well," Oumaloff had bragged. "I stroll and philosophize. And there was Basil. He comes back to Stillton on occasion, to recharge his batteries, and to obtain my counsel."

They were in what Fred, in his former life, would have called a safe house—a nondescript three-decker in the outskirts of Rockport whose interior showed signs of significant security. Basil Houel, having failed the opening stages of the conference Seymour initiated with him, had been taken elsewhere in the building "to collect his thoughts."

Seymour, sitting back of a battered desk, glared balefully at his partner. "Take as long as you need," he said. "I am all ears. Unless you prefer to collect your own thoughts in a room we have downstairs?"

"I'm going to need your help with some loose ends," Fred said, "getting them tied up out of the way. We're leaving it kind of late. If we hurry, we can still…"

Seymour said, "This better be good. But don't waste my time trying to get loose. I trust you as far as I can throw you. I am your asshole buddy until further notice. Go ahead. Whatever you have in mind, convince me."

◇◇◇

Mrs. Halper caught Fred on the fly, moving quickly to get to his room. "She'll see you," Mrs. Halper said. Fred came back to the desk from the stairs.

"Who'll see me? I didn't think I was hiding."

"Lillian Krasic," Mrs. Halper said. She handed over the envelope, with the return address *Stillton Inn*.

"Can't stop," Fred said. It was getting on six. He tossed the envelope onto his bureau for later, showered and changed to clothes that, if not clean, were at least not wet.

◇◇◇

"Everyone is here, Professor Taylor," Doris Druse said accusingly as Fred entered the building. "And two other gentlemen who insisted they would be welcome. But the problem is, I have not been able to speak to President Harmony. I begin to be worried."

Fred said, "She may have been detained. I'll get started."

"It's an hour of overtime already," Mrs. Druse said. "Does she want me to stay?"

"Wouldn't hurt, somebody smart at the switchboard," Fred said. "I'll go on in."

The door of the board room opened on what Fred might have called a small group of well-heeled faces. Parker Stillton and Abe Baum he knew. The rest were faces—six of them, two female, four male.

"Please don't get up," Fred started. "President Harmony has been delayed. I'm Fred Taylor. I know two of you. The rest, I don't care. Unless—wait a minute—let me guess—is one of you Aram Tutunjian?"

A bulky man, almost orange with unreasonable tan, against hair too black, and a suit to match, stood. "Your daughter's OK," Fred said.

"Where...?" the man started.

Fred held up the black box he'd borrowed from Seymour. "I don't care who you are, and I care even less what you have to say. Someone will care. To be fair, and to save time, I'll tell you, this thing records every word we say, so you probably want to say nothing. You lawyers agree?"

Baum and Parker Stillton crammed their lips together and shook their heads, letting the others see them do it.

"Good. Notice these lawyers. They won't even allow themselves to be recorded agreeing with me that you should say nothing. That's good. Efficient. Because I'll be glad to get finished with this. I'm picking up family at Logan in a few hours. I'll fill you in with what I know and what I want. Then I'll leave you to your meeting. No, don't say anything..." A woman had opened her mouth. Bright lipstick. Nice, honest face. Who knows?

"The board of Stillton Academy of Art purged itself of oddballs and non-conformers until you were all of one mind. You'd kill the academy and deliver its assets into the hands of a second entity, the Stillton Realty Trust, that you all belong to. Not Aram Tutunjian. That might be a conflict of interest. No, he just guides the mortgages on the academy properties you were prepared to buy back after the bank foreclosed.

"Liz Harmony brought in a ringer, this real estate development planner, to case the joint, work with it, and design the cash cow resort you all were dreaming of, Stillton Sound Resorts, a privately held luxury whatever the hell you would be pleased to call it and sell once you had complete control.

"Hold on. Don't talk."

"Don't talk," Abe Baum confirmed.

Fred went on, "Whether or not it would hold up in court, as you all know, once Stillton Academy closed, according to the will of Josephus Stillton, whatever might remain of its assets would devolve to Parker Stillton. And any other Massachusetts Stilltons, but I sure as hell can't find any. Not with that double L.

"You made a mistake when you brought Rodney Somerfest in. Thought you had a patsy with business sense. Business sense he had, patsy he wasn't. Of all the properties you bought or tried to buy, or took options on, the only big holdout—how many years was this brewing?—was Lillian Krasic and her Stillton Inn.

"Rodney Somerfest tried to buy it on his own. The board got wind of his move and fired him. He demanded a big cash payment to keep his silence. And all of you poneyed up—the realty trust did. The academy was already stripped clean.

"You'd been trying to buy from Lillian Krasic yourselves, but she wouldn't sell. You got fed up and fired her.

"Two wild cards. A student, a woman, got close to Morgan Flower. Got close and caught on, and looked like she might make trouble. That's one.

"Second, Rodney Somerfest kept coming back. He wanted more money and / or he threatened to blow the whole thing sky high. Whatever. Between them, somewhere, somehow, Morgan Flower and Liz Harmony killed him and did a damn fool job of ditching his body. You all knew him, I guess. That's a whole human being, a life. A life destroyed. On behalf of the glittering promise of development."

Chapter Sixty-nine

"How deeply the rest of you might be implicated in the murder, that's a question. But at the minimum you're all involved in conspiracy and fraud," Fred said.

"This is actionable," Parker Stillton said, in such exact concert with Abe Baum and one of the female suits, it seemed like a Greek chorus in one of those ill-advised attempts at a modern rendition of an old tragedy.

"There are two men dead." The voice came from the woman with the friendly honest face and the bright lipstick. Did she show the good grace to be alarmed—even dismayed? Might it have struck her, at least, that the student might have a mother?

"The second death, we can say, is not your problem," Fred replied. "Except in the larger sense you've forgotten, that you are all responsible for the welfare of this institution you are strangling to death. The first murder is a problem for you since it can be seen as part of the conspiracy. In my opinion Parker Stillton and Abe Baum may have known nothing of the killing of Rodney Somerfest at the time they recruited me. Nevertheless, they were working for the conspiracy. Because they wanted me to find that girl, Tutunjian's daughter. And whatever documents she had taken with her.

"As I see it, the least you were hoping for was to reduce the academy to an entity so tiny and pitiful that, if you had to keep it running, you could convert it into a gallery operation, something like that, not-for-profit still, that was surrounded by your lovely resort and might give watercolor classes on Wednesday mornings.

"But that's over. Because you all probably don't want to be part of a conspiracy that includes murder, is my thinking."

"Those murders were accidents," somebody blurted.

"Not my business. When greed gets going with enough steam, it doesn't care much about human life. You're responsible for the greed. Here's what I want," Fred pressed on. "Don't talk. Each one of you, or the Stillton Realty Trust, acting for you, is going to realize this evening that you have unwittingly and inadvertently entered into what amounts to a conflict of interest.

"Each of you, or the Realty Trust acting for its members, will give to the Stillton Academy of Art the charitable contribution of—let's say—two million dollars. Per head. In cash or in kind. That includes your bank, Mr. Tutunjian—or you yourself, I don't care. The resulting fund will be held in escrow until a new board is appointed. Because you are all resigning.

"How you arrive at a truly disinterested board, I don't know. You haven't had much practice. I'll make one suggestion—a candidate—Parker Stillton knows him—Clayton Reed of Boston. He knows the art world and he knows a lot of the people board members ought to know, and he even has patience with them.

"So. The academy is in trouble, and it's your fault, and you can fix it. As far as the financial part of the trouble is concerned, the fund you set up in escrow will help—and might help the Attorney General, when that office wakes up, to look on you more kindly after you relinquish your plans. Clay Reed, the man I mentioned, happens to be friendly with the Attorney General—not that I am suggesting—as others of you might be as well.

"The academy will be in a position to start paying back its mortgages; and the Realty Trust will inevitably continue as owner of much of the town of Stillton. You will still be in a position to wreck a sleepy, silly town, if you want to. But you'll do it not over the dead body of, but in consultation with, a revised and strong academy.

"That's all. No. Not all. You may wonder, Does Stillton Academy, given all you have done to destroy it, have the power to fight you if you don't like my idea, and decide not to become heroes.

"By great good luck, the academy owns a treasure. You none of you know. A good thing. Because you would undoubtedly have sold it to each other, cheap. Here you were, making this complicated grab for land, and all the while an easy treasure was just lying around where anyone could pick it up. Don't get ideas. That treasure is under guard. It will stay under guard until the new board finds a way to turn it to the best advantage of the academy. Here again, and it is not my business, the man I mentioned before, Clayton Reed, might be helpful."

Clay would be disappointed, because he wanted it for himself. And he might not be entirely happy with Fred for a while. Still, he was an honorable man, and he would also enjoy strutting around as a trustee, should that eventuate. It wasn't a bad idea.

"With the finances secured, the academy can continue to go after accreditation with a straight face. The faculty looks OK. The students are strong enough. The buildings look solid. You need ventilation, insulation, a new roof here and there—but none of that needs to concern you. It's all for the new board.

"Any questions?" Fred waited, enjoying the grim silence of the group, until Abe Baum asked, "Where is she being held? President Harmony?"

"I fear I am not at liberty to divulge your client's whereabouts," Fred said. "Mr. Tutunjian, let your daughter alone for six months, is my advice. By then she'll see that you are not adversaries after all.

"Incidentally, there are uniformed cops at the exits. I brought them with me. I'll leave you all to your meeting. No applause, please."

◇◇◇

But applause did greet him in Stillton B. Meg had gathered a group, and the group had apparently phoned others who had nothing better to do than to assemble in the life room to hear Fred's speech.

Fred handed the black box to Seymour, who was dabbing disgustedly at the brilliant orange oil paint that decorated the left elbow of his light tweed jacket. "We can get that out with turps if we act fast, maybe," Meg said. Fred handed Bill Wamp the borrowed red plaid jacket. Students hovered and jostled, among them Emma, and that lover of Peter's—what was his name? Yes, Aldo. And Peter Quarrier, restored to his colleagues. Fred had pushed hard for that, but Seymour hadn't seemed interested. Houel must have caved.

"This fictional treasure you mention," Bill Wamp said. "Wouldn't that be nice? It's a great threat if they bought it, but that gang…"

"It's real," Fred said. "It's why Basil Houel kept coming back. To check. To make sure it was there until he could find a way to smuggle it out. It's over our heads. A Bierstadt mural, rolled up. As big as a ballroom; and it's a beauty."

"Holy shit!" Bill Wamp said.

"I thought you were talking trash and hot air," Meg said.

"No. Don't mention it. In terms of value, I'm thinking it's enough for a solid new endowment. If it's played right. Now that the word is out, you might want to keep the place under some kind of guard," Fred suggested. "Given that anyone can get in at any time. You artist types. You don't seem to know what locks are for."

"Which one is the girl, Tutunjian?" Seymour asked, running his finger down a page of scribbled notes. Missy held up her hand hesitantly. "Whatever you have, we're going to want it," he said.

He was rewarded by Missy with a smile of brilliant non-committal.

"And you," Seymour said to Fred. "Do I lock you up after all, or may I expect you to come when I call?"

"Option B is better for me," Fred said. "I'm supposed to get to Logan to pick up the woman I live with—I mentioned her to you, Molly—and her kids. They couldn't hack all the fun in West Palm Beach, had to get an early flight home."

"I'll call your escort off," Seymour said. "Don't leave the state. And get a cell phone some day, would you?"

It was raining when Fred left the building.

Phil Oumaloff was just puffing up, wet leather hat, cape, and the rest of it.

"What's going on?" he asked. "What's going on?"

Chapter Seventy

Fred told Mrs. Halper, "The sneakers were a godsend. Do you mind? Will you trust me? I'll FedEx them back."

He'd brought the box of papers, including the Bierstadt butterfly card, for Mrs. Halper to hold at the desk until Meg Harrison called for it. He'd have to call Meg and explain.

"Overnight," Mrs. Halper said. "Have you seen Susan Muller? She's supposed to be at the desk. Listen…"

She did not wait for an answer. Good thing. Susan Muller was drinking beer in the life room, where Seymour was manfully avoiding the issue of wisps of illegal smoke.

"Listen," Mrs. Halper said. "Lillian Krasic really wanted to see you. And it looks like you're heading out now, though you'll have to pay for tonight. Twelve hour notice. That's the policy."

"You'll get it. Where is she?" Fred asked her. "Tell you the truth, I have a phone call to make, to my employer, that I'll be really glad to put off."

"Third floor. She's in back. Where you can see the lighthouse and if the weather is good…"

"I'll drop in now if it's not too late," Fred said.

"I'll phone her you're coming."

Lillian Krasic opened the door into 1950, everything plastic and chrome and Herculon covered with clear vinyl and couches and carpets and herself in a housecoat and a spectacular painting by

Albert Bierstadt hanging directly opposite the door: *Storm in the Rocky Mountains*; no possible doubt. Big picture, ballsy and dirty, about two foot by three, turbulent, even under all that dirt, with rock and cloud.

"Please come in, Mr. Taylor," Lillian Krasic said. The housecoat was poppies on a field of broad woman—maybe seventy years' worth of woman.

"Thank you," Fred said. According to Molly it was not polite to enter a person's living space and look only at the walls. Here were no books, but magazines. Aside from the Bierstadt, the pictures were only clowns, and flowers in vases, and student versions of the lighthouse, or boats, or a female portrait of a tender girl who had a lot of blonde curls.

"The thing was, why I wanted to see you," Fred said.

"Everyone else in the world. Every stranger," Lillian Krasic said. "Sit. Everyone comes saying one thing but what they want, really, is to buy my house out from under me. So I don't let them in. No one gets in.

"I loved that school. I love it. The people. The work. Everything going on. Never mind. I just wanted to lay eyes on you. Because you gave good advice."

"Don't sell, you mean?" Fred prompted. He'd followed her directions and sat in a plastic chair from which he could enjoy the incongruous magnificence of the unframed Bierstadt while Lillian Krasic said whatever she wanted to say.

"So I figured out, if you weren't trying to buy the Stillton Inn and leave me in an old folks home, like Mrs. Harmony wanted to do, and all the rest of them, what *were* you here for? I'd offer a cup of tea, but you won't be here that long.

"So I asked around," Lillian Krasic said. "Fred Taylor. Boston. Nobody knew."

Knickknacks everywhere. Cats, especially. China cats. A strong smell of cat in the room. And that of the cat box. Everything in the place was clean, except for the painting. Underneath all that dirt, a chorus that was all the color and speed of light.

Lillian Krasic continued, "Until I found someone who knew. Never mind who. You work with a man in Boston. Very private. Very all to himself. A collector. Yes? Named Reed. Mr. Reed?"

"Yes," Fred said.

"Because the thing is, this painting," Lillian Krasic said, "On the wall there. The one you keep trying not to look at, out of politeness. It's by Albert Bierstadt."

"I see that," Fred said.

"There were three. Mr. Stillton wanted my grandfather to have them. So he did. Now this one is mine. One's with my sister in Denver. The other one, I don't know. It was smaller. My parents…anyway it doesn't fit."

"I like it a lot," Fred said.

"And sure, I won't sell the Inn. But I still can use money. I'd like to travel the world. So I asked them from Skinner's."

Boston's must successful auction house for art, as well as a hundred kinds of other things: instruments, jewelry.

"Two nice people came out. This was two years ago. Because I wanted to know. I knew it was worth good money, but how much? And these things can change."

"It's true," Fred said.

Wind against rain against cloud against light; as life itself defies light, and feeds on it. A showman, Bierstadt. A showman with a decent soul.

"They said four to six million dollars if they sold it for me," Lillian Krasic said. "And they'd put it on the cover, there'd be a newspaper article, people from the museums would bid against each other…"

"It's true," Fred said. "They can do a good show, these auction houses. And everyone applauds when the bill runs up to where it should choke a horse. It's as good as the circus."

"But I don't want that," Lillian Krasic said.

"So you'll keep it," Fred said. "I would. Maybe get it cleaned if you can afford that."

"No," Lillian Krasic said. She had sat down on the couch, denting the vinyl covering, so that Fred could enjoy the painting behind her without seeming to look away. "I want to travel first class. And I don't want anyone to know how I came into money. It would ruin my friends. What I want to know—this Mr. Reed. Since Skinner's said four to six million dollars, might he be interested for seven million? I know that's an extra million, but to me it seems…"

"I'll ask him," Fred said.

If Clay wanted to dicker, he could dicker.

It wouldn't be like him not to.

There wasn't much left to gather together. Some books—the Emily Dickinson, Craven's *Famous Artists and their Models*, a couple more, belonged to Morgan Flower. Along with his key to Morgan Flower's apartment, Fred left the books with a note on his bedside table, *Property of Morgan Flower*.

Not that Morgan would want them back.

As Fred drove out of town, a lone seagull gave an ambiguous cry.

To receive a free catalog of Poisoned Pen Press titles, please contact us in one of the following ways:

Phone: 1-800-421-3976
Facsimile: 1-480-949-1707
Email: info@poisonedpenpress.com
Website: www.poisonedpenpress.com

Poisoned Pen Press
6962 E. First Ave. Ste. 103
Scottsdale, AZ 85251